P9-BBP-125

RECKONING

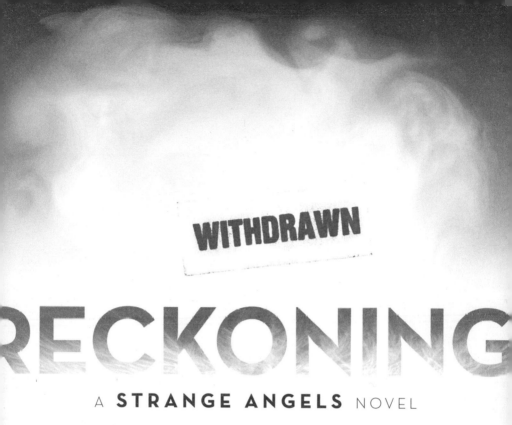

WITHDRAWN

RECKONING

A **STRANGE ANGELS** NOVEL

LILI ST. CROW

razOr
bill

Fitchburg Public Library
5530 Lacy Road
Fitchburg, WI 53711

Reckoning

RAZORBILL

Published by the Penguin Group
Penguin Young Readers Group
345 Hudson Street, New York, New York 10014, U.S.A.
Penguin Group (USA) Inc., 375 Hudson Street, New York, New York 10014, U.S.A.
Penguin Group (Canada), 90 Eglinton Avenue East, Suite 700, Toronto, Ontario, Canada M4P 2Y3
     (a division of Pearson Penguin Canada Inc.)
Penguin Books Ltd, 80 Strand, London WC2R 0RL, England
Penguin Ireland, 25 St Stephen's Green, Dublin 2, Ireland (a division of Penguin Books Ltd)
Penguin Group (Australia), 250 Camberwell Road, Camberwell, Victoria 3124, Australia (a division
     of Pearson Australia Group Pty Ltd)
Penguin Books India Pvt Ltd, 11 Community Centre, Panchsheel Park, New Delhi – 110 017, India
Penguin Group (NZ), 67 Apollo Drive, Mairangi Bay, Auckland 1311, New Zealand (a division of
     Pearson New Zealand Ltd)
Penguin Books (South Africa) (Pty) Ltd, 24 Sturdee Avenue, Rosebank, Johannesburg 2196,
     South Africa

Penguin Books Ltd, Registered Offices: 80 Strand, London WC2R 0RL, England

10 9 8 7 6 5 4 3 2 1

Copyright © 2011 Lili St. Crow
All rights reserved

ISBN 978-1-59514-395-2

Library of Congress Cataloging-in-Publication Data is available

Printed in the United States of America

The scanning, uploading and distribution of this book via the Internet or via any other means without
     the permission of the publisher is illegal and punishable by law. Please purchase only authorized
     electronic editions, and do not participate in or encourage electronic piracy of copyrighted
     materials. Your support of the author's rights is appreciated.

The publisher does not have any control over and does not assume any responsibility for author or
     third-party websites or their content.

For Christa Hickey, true blue.

Acknowledgments

Thanks again to Mel Sanders, Christa Hickey, Miriam Kriss, and Jessica Rothenberg. Special mention must go to Lea Day, Bookweasel and Research Helper extraordinaire as well as Hutch and Bogna. (Any errors are mine alone.) Last but not least: You, dear Reader. Let me, once again, thank you in the way we both like best.

Let me tell you a story…

People like us don't give up.
—Sixten Zeiss

CHAPTER ONE

Stealing a car was easy. The hard part was putting up with the whining.

"I can't believe we're doing this," Graves muttered for the fiftieth time. I kept the speed steady, an even fifty-five. It was an older red Subaru sedan, and I'd checked for insurance papers before we'd taken it. Someone would be inconvenienced, but not completely out of luck.

When you're running from the king of the vampires, you can't afford to be *too* choosy. But I was glad I'd been able to avoid being a complete douche.

"Well, if you'd like to hike out there on foot, be my guest." I didn't reach for the volume knob to drown him out, but it was close. Little Richard wailed softly from the speakers, robbed of all his sass. The all-wheel drive would be nice when we started to hit the hills. "Or if you want to be caught without wheels when the vampires find us."

When. Not if. Because they're going to. After all, I'd stabbed the closest thing they had to a king through the heart and escaped. You don't have to be a genius to figure out that will piss a monster off.

It was a partly sunny late-spring midafternoon and we were on the freeway. I actually missed the food back at the Schola Prima. At least it had been pretty fresh, and there'd been plenty of it, brought up on a tray each evening as the Schola woke and the *djamphir* started getting ready for another night of fun and games learning to hunt suckers.

I would groan at having to get up, blue-eyed Nathalie would laugh, and the night would start with breakfast and a hot shower while she set my mother's room to rights. And I would secretly feel glad not to be alone.

Now I just felt empty and nauseated. Plus my head hurt, and even though I was exhausted, I hadn't been able to sleep for more than a few broken hours. I'd been too busy jerking into wakefulness every time the cheap hotel room creaked, or a car backfired, or the boys' breathing changed. It didn't help that the motel'd had paper-thin walls, either.

But options are sometimes limited when you're running for your life.

Ash lay curled up in the backseat. He'd been asleep since we hit the city limits, snuggled up like he didn't have a care in the world. I'd managed to get him mostly cleaned up, but he was still barefoot and greasy-haired. He'd put away even more food than Graves this morning, and that was saying something. We'd spent seventy bucks at a Denny's off the freeway for breakfast, then stopped at a McDonald's and loaded up. Cheap food, but both of them needed the calories. A werwulf and a *loup-garou* would heal up in a matter of hours, but only if they had enough food to fuel the metabolic burn. So both of them chowed down, and they were looking pretty pink by now.

The greasy paper and wrappings went in an already-full rest-stop trash bin four hours ago, and I hoped we couldn't be tracked from them.

Neither Graves nor Ash knew how to drive, so it was all on me. Driving wears on a body, Dad always said. It was why he taught me to spell him as soon as my feet could reach the pedals.

Silence, broken only by Little Richard going to town like he wanted to reach through the speakers and shake me for keeping him turned down. My hands ached, white-knuckled, on the steering wheel.

"I didn't mean that." Graves hunched in the passenger seat, as far away from me as he could possibly get. He was pale under his half-Asian coloring. The dark brown roots of his hair showed as he ran a hand back through it, wincing as he hit tangles. "I just meant, shit. I can't believe I'm out."

I can't believe you got kidnapped in the first place. I sighed, easing off the gas to drift behind a red semi creeping in the right-hand lane. Big fluffy white clouds sailed across the sky, but the spring sunshine was enough to make it hot under the dome of the car. My window was half-open, and the roar of the slipstream sent me bullets of concentrated scent. Fresh-cut grass, car exhaust, blossoming things, tree pollen—you name it, I smelled it.

It was distracting. Especially with the car full of the reek of wulf and *loup-garou*, neither of them too fresh and one of them, at least, nervous as hell. Next hotel we used would *have* to have a decent shower. I reeked of *nosferat*, fear, and cinnamon buns, not to mention old dried rusty blood.

The fear and the blood, well, I could deal with that. But the spice scent was just a reminder of how much things had changed. I'd changed. I'd finally "bloomed" and become toxic to suckers.

Not that anyone was noticing.

I rolled my window down a little more. Suddenly remembered something. "You need smokes?"

"Nah. Not yet." Graves stared out his window, running his coppery fingers over the armrest like he was searching for a way out. "Come on, Dru. We can talk about it, right?"

Talk about what? Where would I even begin? *Hey, dude, sorry I didn't come rescue you sooner. Sorry you got bit by the boy in the backseat when he was still a slavering wulfen broken to Sergej's will and trying to kill me, back in the Dakotas when you were living in a mall and I had to shoot my dad because he was a zombie. Sorry I dragged you into this. Sorry I didn't tell you what had happened in the gym with the Queen Bitch of the Schola; maybe if I had you might not have run off and got kidnapped. Oh, and while you were being tortured, I was kissing the guy who hates you most.*

Yeah. Where to begin?

And I totally felt like an idiot for hoping he'd notice that I'd bloomed. I looked different now. Wider in the hips and a little bigger in the chest, and my face was heart-shaped like my mother's instead of long like my father's. My hair had streaked itself with blonde like I'd gotten a salon highlighting job, sleek curls instead of frizz—and the shape of my mouth had changed too.

Seeing a stranger's face in a mirror is like vanishing. For a moment you're not sure who or what or where you really are. Maybe Graves just didn't notice.

How could you not notice, though? And if he did, he could've said something. Even *hey, gee, nice hair*.

But me expecting him to pay attention to a little thing like that right after he'd escaped a hole where he was being tortured by vampires wasn't exactly fair, was it.

Yeah. Fair. Nothing about this is fair.

No. There really wasn't anything to talk about right now. Nothing I felt like saying, or things I felt like saying that wouldn't be kosher.

So I settled for prevarication. "I dunno." I checked my blind spot, hit the blinker, and gave it some gas. We slid by the limping candy-red semi like we were on rails. The sun came out for a moment just as we crested a hill, and the scenery was breathtaking. Pleated green hills rolled away, Pennsylvania opening up with late-spring color. It was probably gorgeous around here in the fall, too. I eased the accelerator down another tick.

Unfortunately, there was also a highway patrolman in front of the semi. We breezed by him; I swung back into the right lane and kept an eye on the rearview. *Don't act nervous. Not any more nervous than anyone else around a cop. You've got ID; you memorized the address on the paperwork.* The *touch* throbbed inside my head, bruised and overworked, echoing like it was in a cathedral instead of a bedroom. The little tickle that warned me of danger was working overtime, and I couldn't tell if it was because I was exhausted and hungry no matter how much fast food I took down, because I'd bloomed, or because we'd fought off Sergej and were still alive.

The world just seemed so much bigger today. And to top it all off, my jeans weren't fitting right. Because the shape of my hips had changed. If I crouched down, I'd have a plumber's crack, dammit. I hoped my T-shirt was long enough to cover it until I could figure out what size I was now.

My right hand played with my mother's silver locket, picking it up and dropping it against my breastbone. The metal was only skin-warm. Not throbbing with heat or icy cold, thank God. Not warning me.

Graves shifted restlessly. "Cop." Oddly breathless. "If he—"

"He's not gonna." I tried to sound sure. "We're a touch under the speed limit; he's got no reason to run our plate; we probably haven't even been reported yet. Chillax."

"I can't believe this." He moved again, and I wanted to tell him to sit still. He was broadcasting "guilty" and "nervous."

But we pulled away from the fuzz; they weren't interested in us. The patrolman seemed to be pacing the semi for some reason, and I forgot him as soon as he dropped out of sight behind us on the highway's curves.

I checked our gas. We had a full tank and no reason to stop until it was time to stuff more calories into the boys. Graves looked fine, if dark-eyed and a bit gaunt—the welts and cuts and bruises had vanished once he'd gotten some sleep. Ash, of course, was dead white, greasy-haired, barefoot, and completely feral. It was like having Tarzan on a leash. Between the two of them and my own dishevelment, we were going to cause comment unless I stuck to the bigger towns for stopping today. "We'll stop in a few hours for clothes and more food. If you can hold out that long."

Another shrug. "Little hungry. But still. We need distance, right? And you know where we're going."

"I do." Of all the places I knew, this was the one I'd held like a secret, just in case. "Somewhere safe." *Nobody will think to look for us there. And if they do, it's home ground. Gran's folk could fight a guerrilla war up there. Done it before.*

That wasn't comforting. We had no supplies to fight with yet. And digging in your heels against the damnyankees wasn't like fighting off suckers. *Nosferatu* were an entirely different ball of wax.

Just maybe I could figure out a better plan once I got there and could *think*. Right now I was running on nerves, a latte from McDonald's, and a steady lump of odd warmth right behind my breastbone that made me sick to even think about because of what it contained. Blood. Anna's blood.

My lips, smashed against Anna's cold neck, opened, and the fangs slipped free.

I tried to rip myself away. Her fingers closed on my nape, iron hard. "God damn you," she whispered. "Drink. Drink so you can save them."

I wasn't listening. It was like someone holding a kitten's nose in a dish of milk. A hungry kitten.

No. Not hungry.

A thirsty kitten.

My fangs slid into her skin so easily, and a gush of hot perfume filled my mouth. Anna was saying something, whispering in some foreign language, and the touch *turned it into words inside my head.*

"Hate you," she was saying. "Hate you, Reynard, and you deserve it . . ."

Her whispering in my head had gone down, but I could feel it—something in me had been pulled around. Twisted, or just turned, torn open and strained. Either Anna's blood or the blooming had done it, and if I moved the wrong way I might sprain myself.

"You care to share, or you want to keep me in suspense?" A sarcastic bite to the words. So Goth Boy was feeling better.

Hurrah.

I grabbed my temper with both hands. Gran would've been proud of me. "We're heading to the hills. Once we're there, I'll figure out what to do next. When I've got a plan, you'll be the first one to know."

"The hills? Like, banjos and toothless dudes? Yeah. We'll blend there."

I almost snapped. "What's *your* idea, Goth Boy? Whatever it is, it better be good and it better involve money. My stash isn't going to last forever, and getting more isn't a huge trick, but it takes planning. I know what I'm doing, I've done this before, stop *riding* me!"

I didn't realize how sharp my tone was until Ash's head poked up in back. He stared at me, warily, little orange sparks threading through his irises. I let out a long sharp breath.

Calming down was not going so well.

"Sorry." I continued. My voice was very small. "Go back to sleep, Ash. I'm just tired."

Ash tilted his head and settled back down. I could tell just from the staticky silence that he was awake, and watchful.

"We could stop and rest." Graves actually relaxed a little, settling into the seat. "Wish I could drive. I just . . . I wanna help, Dru. I wanna *do* something."

I nodded. My jaw hurt, because I was clenching my teeth. *Yeah. I wish you could help me too. There's no help for this, Graves. I'm all we've got right now, and I got to start thinking. But I'm so goddamn tired.* I unfroze my jaw. "There's a map in the glove box. Open it up and find where we are, then I'll ask questions."

I didn't really need to; I'd planned out our route at the rest stop while Graves took Ash into the little boys'. Now *there* was something I could be grateful that I didn't have to do.

"You got it." He looked happy to be given a task, the green glow coming back into his eyes, and when he had the map out he dug in the pocket of his long black coat and fished out a pack of Winstons. I glanced at him, my eyebrows raised.

He actually smiled. It was a thin bitter grimace, but better than nothing. "Swiped 'em from the rest-stop vending machine. You mind?"

It was my turn to shrug. "Knock yourself out."

"Goddamn. It'll be my first since they . . . you know. Can't wait." His eyes lit up, and for the first time he actually looked . . . well, like himself. Instead of a thin wounded shadow of the boy I . . . liked? Loved? Didn't know what the hell to do with?

Yeah. Graves was full of surprises. I don't know why I always felt it right under my ribs, high up on the left side, every damn time he pulled one out.

But my shoulders went down, I took a deep breath, and by the time the cigarette lighter popped out I could actually lighten up on the wheel a bit. My fingers were no longer white-knuckled, and after another ten miles Ash actually started to wheeze-snore a little. I tacked our speed on up to seventy and settled in.

PART ONE

Chapter Two

We didn't make the sort of time I hoped, but we got there. By late evening on the third day we were all sick of each other. Graves lit another cigarette, and the brief flare from the lighter he'd found somewhere made me blink.

I slowed down even more, squinting through the film of road grime on the windshield. The car bumped over washboard, and Ash made a small puppy sound from the backseat.

I hoped he wasn't trying to tell me he needed to pee. "We're almost there," I said for the hundredth time. "Just hold on."

"Where the fuck are we?" Graves clutched at the dash. "There's no light."

I knew what he meant. When night falls in deep Appalachia, it falls *hard*. There's precious little orange citylight or townglow out here where the trees press close and the land pleats up like Gran's face when she tasted something disagreeable. Up on the ridge roads sometimes you have star and moon to go by, when you can see them through the trees. But down in the hollers the dark is a living thing, and our little cone of headlight shine didn't show much except the rutted-out road between dust-bleached, choke-close trees. A few places even had creepers coming across the road, a sure sign that nobody had been up this way by car in a while. We'd left town behind at dusk, and I was feeling my way.

The last turn—a sharp, almost axle-breaking right—and I could *feel* the trees drawing away. The road disappeared in a sea of high grass, and our headlights swam through it.

"Jesus," Graves almost moaned. "There's no road. Does this place have plumbing?"

"Will you quit bitching?" I'll admit it. I snarled. My ponytail was a mess, and curls hung in my face. "There's a well, and an outhouse. It's better than being killed by vampires."

"Bang," Ash piped up, but softly. He was scooting between windows, looking on one side, then sliding across the seat to look out the other way. The car rocked slightly every time he did it, and I'd given up trying to buckle him in. The grocery bags in the backseat—enough to get us through a couple days, at least—rustled, and I groped for the window crank. My window rolled down, and the smell of spring, thin earth, rock, trees, creepers, the familiar metal tang of the crick down the way—it all about rocked me back on my heels.

It smelled like home.

The boys were quiet for a little while.

"You're smiling." Graves said it like he was surprised. He could probably see me just fine in the glow from the dash.

I found out I was. It wasn't a big wide stupid grin, but it felt close. "Smells like home, that's all. I lived here for a long time."

"That must be the drawl you've got. Southern honey, anyone?" Lightly teasing, and amused.

I perked up a little. He sounded more and more like himself, the farther we drove. Bitchy and annoying, but still *himself.* "I don't *drawl.* Yanks just talk weird. Bite off all their words like they're personally offended by each one."

He rolled down his own window and sniffed, cautiously. How he could smell anything with all the smoking he was doing was beyond me. "I'm Midwest, babe. That don't make me a Yank."

The longer I grinned, the more natural it felt. "You're above the Mason-Dixon, boy. That makes you Yank automatically."

"Great. And I suppose you're Johnny Reb."

It stung, but I knew he had no idea. "Don't say that kind of thing around here, okay? As a matter of fact, someone comes around, let me do the talking."

"Yeah." He held up a hand, examining it like he'd never seen it before. Took a drag, let the smoke curl out through his nostrils. "Do I have the wrong skin tone for this red neck of the woods, Dru?"

Are you trying to call me a racist, or just my folk? "Jesus." I tried not to roll my eyes. "I'm more worried about the vampires finding out we're here. You stick out, I don't. Much, I guess."

"Have you looked in the mirror lately? You don't blend, kid."

Perversely, I felt warmed. "So you noticed. I look like my mom a bit."

I should've known it was too good to be true. "Some mom," he muttered. "You look . . ."

I waited, but he didn't finish the sentence.

All the good feeling drained away. He'd seen me drinking someone's blood. He'd also seen me kick vampire ass. And he'd looked completely disgusted. Now this. Great. Just *great.* "What? Unwashed? Redneck? Uneducated? Toothless? Like my mama and daddy were cousins? Shut *up,* Graves. Until we get to the house, shut your goddamn Yankee-ass mouth and let me drive."

He subsided, sucking on his cancer stick like it held the secret to world peace or something. Ash's back and forth sped up a little. "*Ash!*" I barked. "Pick a side, sit down, and sit still!"

He did. Right behind Graves, cowering up against the window like he wasn't sure if I was going to reach back and smack him. The silvery stripe in his hair gleamed in the uncertain dimness.

Great. Perfect. Just *wonderful.*

The house hove into view across the meadow. I was finding the driveway more by instinct than anything else; the meadow had reclaimed the ruts in a big way. Dad and I had only been back here once to close everything up. If we were lucky, the house would still be sound. If it wasn't, well, it was only temporary. There are a lot of things you can just live with in summer.

Winter would be a completely different story. But by then we would be on the road to somewhere else. If we survived.

I didn't want to think about it. Here was Gran's, and Gran's was safe, and for the time being that was enough. I'd kept this place like a card in my back pocket; it was my last best draw.

"You grew up way out *here?*" Graves sounded horrified.

"I told you to shut up." But there was no heat to it. Of *course* he'd be horrified by the sight of Gran's high narrow shotgun house, weathered boards festooned with creepers and kudzu, the pump out front still wrapped securely. There was another pump in the kitchen, and there was the crick if the well was low. Looked like nobody'd been at the cordwood, which should be nice and seasoned now. The chicken coop listed, its front door open and the fence around it pulled half-down. There'd probably been a few storms, and the fencing around the coop was one of Gran's Perpetual Endeavors. Like baking biscuits or trying to civilize me into wearing a skirt.

The Packard slumped under a mound of creeping green in

the carport; I could still remember driving down off the ridges with Gran's terrible labored breathing in the passenger seat, bumping and swerving toward the hospital down the valley.

I blew out between pursed lips. The *touch* flexed inside my skull, and a tingle ran through every tooth I had. But especially the sharp upper canines.

Fangs. I ran my tongue over them carefully. They were just sensitive, not warning me. I hadn't tasted the rotten wax-orange that would tell me danger was close. Instead I was just jumpy as hell, tetchy, and exhausted. Not to mention feeling a queer pain in my chest. Like my heart was deciding all this was too much hassle and it would just crack in half. Save the king of the vampires and everyone else the trouble of killing me by taking care of business at home, so to speak.

I squinted as we rolled to a stop, sliding the car into park. Yes, there were fine thin blue lines slipping through the physical fabric of the walls, knotting together and twisting in complex Celtic designs. The walls remembered Gran's wards. She'd redone them every night and made me do them too, with her rowan wand and without, with candle and salt or just plain will. I could almost see the trembling of a candle flame behind the shuttered windows, a faint star of light.

My knuckles were white on the steering wheel, again.

All that warding, all those floor washes with yarrow and lavender, all those little tricks like doubling back and spitting to break a trail. All the times she questioned me—did I see anything or feel anything wrong? Was there anyone in town asking questions? All the care she took to scrub me down and keep me scented like something else.

It hit me all at once. She'd known what I was. Or she'd known something. She'd been protecting and training me as best she could.

Of course she knew. She'd take one look at Mom and figure

something was up, and you just knew Mom was here at least once. Gran also had those fights with Dad, about me. *"Whatchu gonna do wit dat chile, Dwight?"*

My arms shook. The steering column groaned, and Ash made a little whining sound in the back of his throat.

"Hey." Graves reached over. His fingers were warm. He pried my right hand off the wheel, one finger at a time, and didn't seem to notice or care that my fingernails were lengthening. Sharp and deadly, a hell of a new manicure, the changed structures in my wrist aching as the claws slid free. "Hey. Dru. Dru-girl, come on. Breathe."

"I think my grandmother knew what I was." I managed to get the words out through the obstruction in my throat, but only barely. "But I never did. I had no clue."

"Was it bad for you?" He slid his fingers between mine. Holding my hand, as if he'd never looked at me like I was some slimy thing from under a rock. As if he hadn't spent the last three days getting on pretty much every nerve I had left, and me returning the favor. "Here, I mean?"

Tears pricked hot at my eyes. "Not here. Everywhere else, but not here. She, um, she died. I was twelve. I drove her to the hospital in the valley, and . . ." The words wouldn't come. How can you tell someone what it's like to have the whole world whacked away from underneath you?

You can't. It just doesn't happen. Sometimes people understand because they've been there.

And then I felt like an idiot, because Graves . . . well. He'd been living in the *mall*, for Chrissake. You don't do that when your family life is highly satisfying and safe.

And even that had been taken away from him the instant Ash's teeth had closed in his flesh. It was my fault in the first place, too.

Because Ash had been after me.

Graves leaned over, transferring my fingers to his right hand and awkwardly sliding his left arm around me. I was still in my seat belt, and he somehow wasn't. He tightened up, and I leaned over into him. Took a deep breath, smelling cheap hotel soap and the last thing we'd stopped for—fried chicken in a supermarket deli, where I'd pushed the cart through the aisles and got everything we could afford that I thought we would need for the night. The bags in the back were still rustling a little as the breeze fingered its way through the car, a secretive sound.

Underneath the food, he smelled like wulfen and strawberry incense, male with moonlight mixed in. The tears were pushing out past every wall I had, hot and slicking my cheeks. My nose filled up, and I snuffled like a five-year-old.

"It's okay," he whispered. "It's okay. I promise. Everything's gonna be all right."

I knew he was lying. Everything was not all right, and things were getting more fucked-up all the time.

But at least he said it. I was grateful for that, and it helped.

Besides, they were both depending on me. Ash could probably get away if the vampires found us, but Graves? Not likely. Not in the shape he was in.

I was the responsible one, and just because I'd been utterly sucking so far at *everything* didn't mean the pressure was off.

It just meant I had to do better. We were safe for the moment, so I had to get my head together and start doing right.

Still, I stayed there for a couple minutes while the Subaru idled and the headlights glared at Gran's house, my face turned awkwardly so I could bury my nose in Graves's neck. I was all torqued around like a pretzel, but I didn't care. He smelled safe and he held me, and he kept repeating it.

"It's okay, Dru. It's gonna be okay. I promise. I'm sorry, everything's gonna be fine. You'll see."

He said it like he was thinking *he* was the responsible one. And it felt so good I just let him do it. For a little while.

CHAPTER THREE

The key was still under the north side of that granite boulder, the one Gran poured milk over every new moon. The walls were still solid, thank God. The place smelled mildewy, and Gran would've got on me to clean every damn corner before turning in.

First things first, though. I hiked out to the corner of the meadow with a flashlight and found the connection box; when I flipped the switch, the tiny light came on, a sweet green flash. I could've sobbed with relief. Gran didn't believe in "payin' for the fool 'lectricity," and this tapline had been here for decades. It was a pure miracle it was still working. If it hadn't been, well, I'd brought a can or two of gas for the genny, but that wouldn't take us far.

I hiked back to the house and found Graves and Ash taking the dustcovers off of stuff. They were shaking them off the front porch, too, which meant Graves was thinking. "Nice place," he said over his shoulder as he passed me with an armful of canvas sheeting, his torn coat flapping around his knees. His eyes gleamed green in the dimness; the Coleman lamp I'd set on the kitchen table was feeble to say the least. "Good vibes."

"Bang!" Ash nodded enthusiastically, bounding after him, pale bare feet slapping the polished floorboards. I found the moldering wooden-and-cardboard box of lightbulbs on its familiar shelf, right where Dad'd left it. Screwed the first one into the hanging cord over the kitchen table, and *voila!* The pleased exclamations from the boys made me feel like Edison himself.

The next step was priming the pump in the kitchen with a bottle of distilled water. When I worked the handle it made a gawdawful screeching, but I'd thought to bring some WD-40 and that made it just groan and shower rust flakes. After a few more pumps, though, things eased out. I worked it until a gush of rust-colored water came out, kept on until it turned clear and cold. Mineral-smelling well water, and plenty of it.

"Thank you, sonny Jesus," I muttered. It was just what Gran would've said. "God willing and the well ain't dry."

Next thing—a fire in the potbellied iron stove. I worked the damper, hoped the chimney wasn't blocked—fortunately there was a bit of a breeze, and I could feel the air moving past my fingertips. The stove was cleaned out, a neat fire laid among spiderwebs, so I just had to grab the matches and light her up. The draw was fine, and in a little bit I had a merry crackling blaze. Night would get cold around here even in spring, and all we had were sleeping bags. I wasn't sure if moths would've gotten into Gran's quilts too.

I'd solve that problem when I hit it, but even moth-eaten quilts would be better than none.

The boys had finished carrying everything in from the Subaru by then, and Ash let out a little cry of joy and wandered up to the stove, stretching his hands out like the fire was his personal friend.

The plates and skillets were dusty, but I just rinsed them off. Gran would've had my hide, but by this time I was yawning and working through mental mud. I locked the front door, told the boys to arrange the sleeping bags upstairs, and put together something easy—bacon, pancakes from mix, eggs. I could've made this in my sleep, and I pretty much did. When the boys tromped downstairs I was already coaxing the balky old electric stovetop and thanking God that I didn't have to cook on the potbelly. I can do it, sure, but it's no fun.

"More food?" Graves stretched, yawning hugely. Ash galumphed over to the stove and crouched, staring in through the grate at the fire's orange and yellow crackle. His eyes ran with orange sparks, and his expression was such serene contentment it was hard to believe he was the same creature who'd been almost-eight feet of unstoppable Broken werwulf.

Now there was a thought I didn't want. Could he change into his wulf form now? And once he did, could he come back?

Don't borrow trouble, Dru.

"I'm not complaining," Graves added hurriedly. "Can I help?"

"You can check the icebox." I pointed with one of Gran's old wooden turners. "If it's working, load the stuff from the cooler in there and put the cooler on the porch. And don't bitch if you don't like scrambled eggs; that's all I'm making."

"Won't bitch. Scout's honor." He gave me a fey grin, green eyes lighting up. "Well, I was never a scout. Couldn't afford it. But still."

Well, ain't we cozy. I was beginning to get whiplash, he was going back and forth so fast between hating me and actually seeming to think I was okay. "I kind of wanted to be one too, but they don't take girls."

"What about Girl Scouts?" He opened up the ancient, tiny fridge and stuck his hand in. "Looks like it's working. This is really cool."

"Girl Scouts have great cookies. But too many girls. I don't get along with girls." *Except Nat, and she probably hates me now.* I poured pancake batter, heard a satisfying sizzle, and poked at the bacon. Considered cracking some eggs, decided to leave them for last. "I guess I never will."

"There's time. I don't get along with chicks either. Well, except you. You're, like, the only girl I've ever met who isn't . . ."

Maddeningly, he stopped. I was too tired to even wonder what I wasn't. There was a long list of things I wasn't, starting with *cute* and probably finishing up somewhere near *lovable*.

I brushed my hair back, wishing my ponytail would hold. Tomorrow I'd find some string and braid it up.

Braiding made me think of Nathalie at the Schola Prima again. I'd gotten along with her just fine, until I'd been a total bitch. Granted, I'd been getting ready to go rescue Graves . . . but still.

The longing to see Nat, her sleek head tilted to the side and her wide cat-tilted blue eyes considering an outfit or the mess my hair had become, shook me right down to my bones. I sniffed, wiped at my nose with the back of my hand, and turned the pancakes. Graves busied himself loading up the fridge. Ash rocked back and forth in front of the stove, humming tunelessly. Graves carried the cooler out on the front porch, and when he didn't come back, I figured he was lighting another cigarette.

The way things were going, I might almost take up smoking myself. Dad would've killed me for even thinking about it.

But he was dead. He'd never take me up about anything ever again. My throat was sore, something stuck in it, but I just cleared it a few times and concentrated on cooking.

The ancient Folgers can for coffee grounds, eggshells, and vegetable scraps to go in the compost heap was rusted but still sound.

I tossed the eggshells in and had a plate together in a trice. "Ash! Come on. Take this to the table. Graves, get him a plastic fork, and one for you too." I felt like Gran, hollering from the kitchen.

"You gonna eat?" Graves ambled back in, his chin set stubbornly and his eyes dark. Almost black.

I looked back down at the skillets, the pop and fizzle of bacon filling my head for a moment.

"Yeah," I lied. "But there's work to be done first. Come on, you two. Tuck in."

* * *

The wide loft held Gran's big four-poster and my smaller corn crib, and the mattresses reeked of mildew even though we'd wrapped them in plastic. But the quilts, packed in mothballs and plastic, were still good. The moths hadn't gotten at them at all.

I meant to carry my brand-new sleeping bag downstairs after a while. I thought if I sent the boys up to get settled and gave them enough time, they'd be out cold and I'd be able to sneak my bag downstairs and stretch it in front of the door.

Plus, there were things to do to close the house up for the night. I finished by warding the walls again, watching the faint blue lines running through the wood take on fresh life. They didn't need to be redone so much as refreshed, and it was amazingly easy. I just had to remember to think *up* high enough to get the second story involved. I could almost hear Gran muttering to herself while she followed me around the open room that was the entire first floor, checking my work.

I was hungry, but my stomach had closed up tighter than a fist. The effort of warding made my head swim, and every bone in my body ached down deep. I sat down on the loveseat to rest, just for a second. It was an old horsehair thing, meant for company—Gran always sat in her rocking chair and I used the old hassock, or I sat at her feet while she knitted. The bare bulb in the kitchen gave off a mellow glow, and if I shut my eyes and inhaled, I could almost smell her.

Tobacco juice, a faint astringent old-lady smell, baby powder, and the musky yeasty scent of cooking good things and working hard all day. Her spinning wheel sat under a drop cloth I'd told the boys not to touch, but I could almost hear its hissthumpwhirr and her occasional soft mutters as she spoke to God or told me things.

I loved to listen to Gran talk. She was always rambling, said it was a product of living alone. Dad was never the chatty type, but days with Gran were a constant stream of information, admonition, attention. *Do it this way, hold that end up, good girl . . . I could tell him, now what's the price of cotton, but he wouldn't listen . . . Yes, you look like your daddy, that's a look like a mule, fetch me my scissors and go check the coop for eggs. My, you're good at findin' eggs, it's a true talent, Dru-baby. Come now, no use wastin' sunshine.*

She taught by example, but the talking was something else. A lifeline, maybe.

I folded over and pulled my feet up, lying on the dusty loveseat. It felt good, even if the thing was harder than the floor and slippery too. The fire glowed through the stove's grate, and the good scent of seasoned wood burning—I'd banked it just before I warded everything—was like a warm blanket.

Blanket. I didn't have one; I'd left them all upstairs. I was going to get cold if I settled here for long.

I didn't care.

My eyes drifted shut. I was so, so tired. The wards in the walls hummed to themselves, and that was something new, too. I'd never *heard* wards before, singing in high crystal voices that turned into harmonies where the knots laid over doors and windows twisted.

Well, Dru. You got here, and you got both of them here. Tomorrow you start figuring out a longer-term plan. But you did what you set out to do, and there hasn't been a vampire attack. Yet.

I told myself not to borrow trouble. Curled up even tighter on the love seat. It just felt so damn good to stop moving, to stop concentrating so fiercely on the next thing, and the next, and the next . . .

That was the first night I slept, really slept, since rescuing Graves. Every muscle in my body eased its useless tension, relaxing all at once. I went down into darkness, and there were no dreams.

Except one.

INTERMEZZO

He crouched, easily, *on the edge of the rooftop, blue eyes burning and his sharply handsome face haggard. Lines etched themselves onto teenage flesh, and for a moment you could see just how old Christophe really was.*

The city spread out below him, jewels of light and concrete canyons, the exhaust-laden wind ruffling his slicked-back, darkened hair. The aspect flickered through him, his fangs sliding free and retreating as dull hopeless rage flitted over his features.

He'd never looked like this before.

"We need you," someone said behind him. Bruce moved in the shadow of an HVAC vent, restlessly. The crisp British accent made every word a precise little bullet. "Don't throw your life away, Reynard. It's no way to honor her memory."

Christophe actually flinched. Something I'd never seen him do before, something that seemed utterly alien to the maddeningly calm djamphir I knew. "She's alive."

"How could she have survived that? We found traces—you saw the

blood. She wasn't even half-trained, despite our best efforts. Sergej"—
The name sent a glass spike of pain through my dreaming head, and
both of them tensed—"took her because Leon betrayed her, and Anna
probably helped."

"So now you're willing to impute blame to Milady." Christophe's
shoulders straightened. He lifted his right hand. Something gleamed
slightly in his palm, and my dreaming self's gaze was riveted to
it. "Really, ibn Allas. You never used to be this quick to call Anna's
behavior what it is."

"Anna is a spoiled child. She's never grown up." Amazingly, Bruce
almost snarled, his lip lifting and white fangs flashing for just a moment,
the aspect curling through his hair. "But speaking of that doesn't help
this situation. We didn't find her body, or Anna's, but we're still looking. The whole place is a mess." He took a deep breath, shoving the
aspect down. "If he had both of them, we would know. He would be
walking in daylight and we would be under siege." Bruce's dark eyes
glittered. He looked like a wreck, too—his clothes were singed and torn,
one half of his face deeply bruised, and he slumped wearily. "Please,
Reynard. The Order needs you."

"My little bird needs me more. I told you, keep her safe and you
have my allegiance. This? This is not safe." Christophe straightened,
and now I could see his clothes were in rags too. Vampire blood smoked
on him, the steam rising hard to see because of the fume of rage covering him.

"We don't even know—" Bruce began, helplessly, his hands spread.
Trying to smooth the waters, like he always did.

Christophe rose with slow, dangerous grace, balanced on the very
edge of the roof. "I know. If she was dead, ibn Allas, I would be, too.
I would kill them all until they dragged me down. My heart is still
beating, therefore, she is still alive." The lines on his face smoothed

out. The gleam closed itself up in his fist, fingers clenching, his face settling into chill certainty.

If he'd ever looked at me this way, I would've never let him touch me. I would have been too busy backpedaling and getting out of his way.

"Give us time. We'll help, we'll bargain with the Maharaj—"

"Don't mention the djinni-children to me; they don't care for our troubles." Christophe laughed, a bitter little chuckle. "And your help gave Leontus the chance to betray her. I took you at your word, Bruce. I believed you when you said he would guard her all the more carefully because of Eleanor's death. I believed him."

"I believed him too!" Bruce yelled, but it was too late. Christophe had already leapt, straight off the ledge, plummeting into the screaming wind—

CHAPTER FOUR

I **sat straight up** on the loveseat, my fingers clawing at empty air like I was going to grab Christophe's sweater and pull him back. One of Gran's quilts slid to the floor in a heap. I did actually throw myself backward, hitting the high hard back of the loveseat and giving myself a good jolt.

Graves tore out of the sleeping bag and leapt to his feet. Sometime during the night he must've crept downstairs, because he was on the floor next to the loveseat. My heart hammered, pounding in my throat, and my fangs tingled. For one nightmarish moment I didn't know where I was, and the scream caught in my throat.

The deep thrumming rattling everything not nailed down was a growl. It came from Graves's chest, and his eyes were wide, green, and blank. The Other—the thing wulfen use to change and *loup-garou* use for mental dominance—rippled under his skin, his shoulders bulking up as he hunched them, ready for attack.

I clapped my hand over my mouth. The *touch* throbbed inside my head, little invisible fingers soaking in the anger radiating from him in red-violet waves. Beyond that, the glow of the wards sparked, bright blue. Out in the meadow, nothing. Just static, the formless buzz of the country before your ears adjust and start hearing the wind and the crick and the animals again. It's like they have to shift between city and country tuning.

Morning sunlight filtered through the shutters, bars of gold with dust dancing in them. Graves's growl petered out. He half-turned, glanced at me with that empty green-glowing gaze, and for the first time since I'd met him, Goth Boy looked completely dangerous.

I swallowed, hard. "I'm okay," I managed through my clenching fingers. "I just . . . I had a dream." *About Christophe.* The words stuck in my throat. "Jesus. What are you *doing?*"

He just stood there. The anger leaked away, bit by bit. Sense stole back into his mad green eyes, and for a moment I wondered why I wasn't scared of him, especially since he looked ready to rumble.

I mean, I was *apprehensive*, yeah. But he hadn't been fixing to hurt me. No, he'd been focused on the door.

In case something was coming *through* it.

Something like that makes you think. It really does. Unfortunately, I couldn't figure out what I was supposed to think about it.

Graves eyed me sidelong for a long while. Finally, the last of the anger died down. I saw it creep back into him, sinking under his caramel skin. You couldn't see the marks of torture on him anymore, and the anger was something new.

Not anger. Rage. He didn't have that before. I was the one who had that before.

I guess being tortured by vampires will do that to you. Guilt bit me hard, deep inside my chest, again. "Graves?" It was hard to talk, because my fangs were out and my hand was clapped so tight over my mouth I could barely move my lips.

I didn't want him to see. To remember that he'd seen me with my face in Anna's throat, drinking her blood.

He crouched, suddenly, and his hands moved. I almost flinched before I realized he was smoothing out the sleeping bag. "Nothing. Not doing nothing."

A high dull flag of red stood up on each sculpted cheek under a screen of dark stubble. The stubble was pretty new; he'd been a smooth-cheeked boy when I'd met him. He still needed a few meals to replace muscle mass; wulfen metabolism burns pretty hot to fuel the change. It would burn in him to give him their strength and speed, even though he wouldn't get hairy.

Not much, anyway. No more than any regular boy.

The tingling through my fangs receded. I finally peeled my hand away as he started rolling the bag up. My hair was probably sticking up all over, but I felt loads better. Not even stiff, but as if I'd taken a deep, refreshing nap. And there was the quilt—he must've brought it downstairs and covered me up. I searched for something to say. "You didn't, um, want to sleep upstairs?"

Way to go, Dru. State the obvious.

"No." The rage flushed through him again, retreated. "I didn't."

The *touch* was stronger now, and if it wasn't for Gran's training I probably would've been seriously disturbed by how strongly his anger rang in my skull. "Graves—"

Now why did I sound breathless?

"Look." He finished rolling up the sleeping bag, snapped the elastic loops over it, and glared up at me. "I know I'm just a *loup-garou*, all right? I *know*. I'm just the deadweight holding you down. You dragged me along and I'm glad about that. I'm even glad I got bit by that thing up there. I handled everything they threw at me, and told *him* to go fuck himself more than once. *Sergej.*" He all but spat the name, and his face twisted up, bitterly. "So quit treating me like a little kid, Dru. I ain't been a little kid for years. I'm not as Billy Badass as some of those stuck-up *djamphir*, but I'm learning and I'll be hell on wheels when I'm done. You won't ever have to worry again."

Where did that come from? My jaw had dropped. I stared at him. *What the hell?*

"You don't think I can hack it." He leapt to his feet, carrying the sleeping bag with him. He'd slept in his coat, too, and it flapped as he moved. I'd stitched it up, clumsily, and now I was wishing I'd done a better job. "Well, I've got news for you. I already have. Whatever it takes to make you see, I'm gonna *do* it. You get me?"

Silence stretched between us. "Um." I searched for something to say. I settled for the absolute truth. "What? No. I don't get you. What the hell are you on about?"

I got one long, very green look, his eyebrows—eyebrow, actually, since nobody had held him down and plucked him up yet—drawn together and his mouth a bitter scowl. I was struck once again by how cute he'd gotten. Those cheekbones, and those eyes.

How had I ever thought, even back in the Dakotas, that he was dull? Or gawky?

I had the weird sinking feeling I was missing something important. What a thing to wake up to. And the dream was still filling my skull like cobwebs, something important glimmering in its depths.

He filled his lungs, his chest swelling as if he was growling again. When he opened his mouth, though, the only thing that came out was a yell. "*I love you!*" he shouted, his eyes glowing laser green. "I *love* you, okay? I'm not some hopeless retard you pull along behind you because you feel sorry for him! *I love you and I'm going to prove it!*"

I had the exquisitely weird sensation of being transported to a parallel universe. Or of waking up in a movie where everyone knew the script but me.

A different kind of silence, now. It was the kind where something you can't take back is still vibrating in the air, all around you. We looked at each other for what felt like the first time, Graves and me, and in that moment the last bits of the kid he'd been completely fled inside my head.

This was a new animal. And he was looking at me like he expected me to say something.

"I never thought you were a hopeless retard." I sounded very small, and very young. I found out I was hugging myself, too, scooted back on the loveseat like it was a raft and the water around it was full of sharks. "You just . . . I . . ." Every word I'd never been able to say to him backed up, crowding around me and squeezing all the air out of my chest. "I thought I disgusted you," I said finally. It was hopelessly inadequate. As usual. But Jesus. Waking up from a dream about one guy and having another one yell something like that, it's confusing.

To say the least.

He actually cocked his head and stared at me like I was speaking in Swahili. "What?" As if all the air had been punched out of him.

"The, um. Sucking blood thing. And . . . I can't . . . sometimes I just can't *explain* things to you. I can't tell you. It all gets balled up and you get mad and stomp away and—" I was actually working up a good head of steam here.

"I'm sorry." The words jumped out. He hugged the sleeping bag, hard, tendons standing out on the backs of his hands. The flush on his cheeks had died away, so that under his caramel coloring he was ashen. "I was angry. Didn't want to hurt you."

Well, thank you sonny Jesus, we're getting somewhere. Finally. "If it wasn't for me you wouldn't be in this."

Bitterness, then. His shoulders hunched and his face turned old. A shadow passed through his eyes, turning them mossy instead of emerald. "Yeah. I'd still be cowering. Hiding in the fucking *mall.* I'm *glad* I got bit, Dru. If I coulda done it earlier, I would've."

Jesus *Christ.* He'd *seen* the Real World by now. It wasn't anything anyone sane wanted to be involved in. There's a *reason* people run away from it. There's a reason cops and governments sweep weird shit under the table. It's because *nobody wants to know.* They don't even have to work that hard; nobody goes looking for this sort of thing—the kind of weird where you can seriously die. They all go looking for the Saturday-trip, New Age, crystalgazing weird you can come back from.

Except Graves and me, we'd been stranded out in the black. Out in the place you can't get back from and you just have to deal with. "You can't mean that," I whispered. My arms were around my knees. I was curling up into myself like a fern, or like he was shouting at me. My heart was triphammering. *Wait. Let's go back a couple seconds here. Did he really say what I thought he just said?* "Graves—"

He flung out one hand, like he was blocking a dodgeball. "Bullshit. I *do* mean it. Best thing that ever happened to me, Dru. What was I gonna do—try to go to college with no money? Work my way through and hope someone would throw me a bone or two?" A swift snarl passed over his features, and his hair stood up in vital springing curls. "No way. This is my chance to be good enough. I'm taking it. You'll see. You'll just *see.*"

He dropped the sleeping bag. It hit the floor and keeled over, and he turned on his heel. Bare feet smacked the worn floorboards, and it took him less than a half second to undo the lock on the door. He plunged out into the morning, and the door slammed shut behind him. Shivers rolled through me, first hot, then cold.

What. The hell. Just happened?

A soft sound alerted me. I looked up, and there was Ash, crouched easily on the pulldown steps that led to the loft. He cocked his head, and greasy hair fell in his face. He was barefoot too, and he'd somehow lost his shirt. His narrow chest was dead pale, and muscle flickered under his skin.

Wait a second. Just hold on one goddamn second. Graves said he . . . did he actually say that? *Did he say what I think he just said?*

We looked at each other for a long time, the Broken and me. It occurred to me that he was waiting for something. For me to make the world settle down.

Except everything was still spinning around me, and if I didn't hold on, I'd be flung off. I hate that feeling.

I'd been spinning since Dad died, in one way or another.

But Ash was counting on me. Examining me solemnly, his face like a child's. Wide open, and scared, and utterly trusting all at the same time. *You're going to make the bad stop, right?* That's what was painted all over him, from the way he crouched to the wide eyes and his mouth just a little bit agape.

"It's okay." I tried to sound steady. "Everything's all right."

"Awwight." His mouth worked loosely over the word. I'd shot him in the jaw with Dad's silvergrain bullets, and some of the silver was probably still in there, buried in the bone and preventing everything from changing back and forth right. Or, even scarier, the silver had worked its way out and now I had the thought that he was free of Sergej's hold but somehow still Broken, and I didn't know enough about how to fix him.

Every single problem I'd forgotten about while sleeping came crowding back. First on the list was breakfast.

I felt like falling asleep on the loveseat had twisted the world off course again, just a fraction. I wasn't complaining, but I wished Graves would've waited until I'd had some coffee and I could *think* before he laid that on me.

Did he just say what I think he just said?

Ash slid down a few more stairs, slinking bonelessly on his hands and feet like a cat. "*Hongwee.*" He nodded vigorously. "*Hongwy.*"

Great. He'll have a three-year-old's vocabulary by the end of the week. Stellar. "Yeah. I was just thinking about breakfast."

It hit me sideways.

Graves. He'd really said that.

I love you. That was good, right? Good, hell. It was outright *great.*

Except every time things got better with him, I ended up even more hopelessly confused. I groaned, gingerly got up from the love seat in case I'd stiffened up overnight, and found out I hadn't. "Outhouse first," I amended. "Then breakfast."

Ash actually let out a crow of delight. Then he was out the door too, quick as a flash. Which would leave me to make breakfast alone.

Did he really say he . . . loved me? Maybe it wasn't hopeless. Maybe I could learn to say the right thing the next time he laid something like that on me. Maybe I had a chance.

Wouldn't you know, I found out I was grinning. Ear to ear, despite every single problem crowding in around me.

Grinning. Like a total fool.

CHAPTER FIVE

brought the ax down cleanly, with a terrific *thwack*. The log split. I didn't even need a wedge; it was child's play to get the freshly sharpened ax blade going fast enough. The wood was well seasoned, but it was the *aspect* flickering through me that did most of the work.

I was getting used to this new body. Hips a little bit wider, chest-works definitely a little bigger—the two sports bras I had were not going to cut it after a while; I had overflowing cleavage you could lose a quarter in. I'd managed to buy two pairs of jeans in a new size yesterday, T-shirts in medium instead of small, and every piece of clothing I'd ever owned before was *so* not going to fit me now.

But all that was kind of made up for by the fact that my hair was behaving, silky curls lying down—and the fact that I was now strong as any of the boy *djamphir*. Reliably strong, the *aspect* simply stepping in like clockwork instead of needing rage or bloodhunger to fuel it.

Hallelujah. I didn't have to get mad or suck someone's blood to use superstrength. It was a frigging miracle.

The only mirror in the house was a polished piece of metal

hanging near the kitchen window, where Gran would check her hat before she went to town. It was enough to show me that I didn't have anything huge stuck on my face, but the changes I'd seen in hotel bathrooms, thankfully, didn't show up much.

Graves didn't say anything else, but I caught him looking at me every once in a while. When he thought I didn't notice.

Ash, of course, was oblivious. I don't think how I looked mattered to him in the slightest. He darted in, scooped up one half of the log I'd just split, and balanced it on the ancient chopping block. Then he hightailed it back to the woodpile and watched.

I drew the ax up, smoothly, inhaling, and let out a sharp *huff!* as I brought it down. *Got to do it with the breath, Dru. Ain't no other way.*

Gran's voice was a thorny pleasure. Any moment I expected to see her striding into the meadow, clicking her tongue at the long grass she'd take a machete to every once in a while. She'd descend on all three of us and put everything to rights, toot-sweet, with not a second to spare or a long gray hair out of place.

Ash darted in again, put the unchopped half of the log up, and leapt back with an armful of stovewood. I brought the ax up and down again. Like riding a bike.

Bright mellow sunlight poured over the meadow, showing a sheen of sweat on Ash's arms. He was bulking up a bit, the steady calories doing him a lot of good. Gran always said fresh air was good for anyone, too.

After we had enough wood to last a week, I set Ash to stacking it and stamped inside.

"You're handy with an ax." Graves was up to his elbows in soap-suds, scrubbing the dishes. *I'll clean,* he'd said. *You go out and get some sun.*

I'd bit back the acid comment about Gran revolving in her grave to have a boy wulf cleaning her house, and just gone and done it. Right now, though, I was kind of wishing I'd stayed inside. Pumping bathwater was going to be a bitch.

"Got to be, in these parts." I grabbed a bottle of distilled water and cracked it, took a long pull. "I'm going into town in a bit, now that we know the house is still sound and we can stay here a couple days. We need more supplies." I waited for some sign that he was willing to talk about something else. Something a little more personal.

I know enough about boys to know that they get uncomfortable with that sort of thing. So I figured I'd just . . . let it rest. For a little while, at least.

And, well, discretion's the better part of valor, right? Except I was pretty sure the word for waiting until he said something else wasn't discretion or politeness. It was flat-out cowardice.

He hunched his shoulders. Worked at the cast-iron skillet like he wanted to scrub it into a wafer. I was going to have to season it again before I could use it.

"This is pretty cool." He glanced out the window. "You could hide up here for a while."

That's the idea. "I guess." I stalked over to Gran's hassock, grabbed my black messenger bag. It still smelled like vampire blood, and I was damn lucky to have it. I'd hung the long slightly curving wooden swords—*malaika*—safe in their leather harness, on a peg by the front door. The funny thing was, that peg was just right.

The *malaika* had been my mother's. They looked like they belonged there. I couldn't remember what might've hung there before, and that bothered me. I thought I'd remember everything about Gran's.

I settled down at the kitchen table with a fresh legal pad, the atlas I'd picked up, and Dad's little black address book. All his contacts were in it. One of them at least had been *djamphir*. The rest, who knew?

I had Dad's billfold, too. Mom's picture was missing, but given recent events, I was lucky to have this much left from him. It made me wonder where the truck was. Christophe had told me it was in storage somewhere; I'd always figured I'd pick it up later, somehow. If I needed it.

I set the address book down precisely, looked at the legal pad, and uncapped a blue Bic.

"What are you up to?" Graves glanced back over his shoulder. I'd managed to get all of us some jeans and T-shirts, nothing fancy but serviceable. The dark blue shirt strained at his shoulders. Boy was no longer a medium, that was for damn sure.

We'd both changed so much.

"Planning. This is short-term. Anyone who goes digging through paper will find out Gran's property's in trust for me, with a couple investments paying the taxes. Someone will eventually track us, or figure out I've gone here to lick my wounds. We can't stay here past fall, and that's if they don't find us first."

"They. The vampires, and . . ."

And the Order. Staying with them is about as safe as a sack of snakes for you, and I'm not sure I like it much either. "And anyone else. So I need short, medium, long-range, and contingency plans. You think this stuff over before you have to." I stared at the blank paper. "Dad used to say that."

"Your accent's getting thicker." He rinsed the skillet, working the pump like he was born to it. "It's cute."

Did that count as being willing to talk about something emotional? A reluctant smile pulled at my lips. I ducked my head, letting my hair fall down. Awkward silence reigned in the kitchen. He kept washing, the white bar of a dish towel over one shoulder.

I flipped idly through the book. Dad's crabbed, neat handwriting, in different pen colors. I found Augustine's name and address and numbers, with the inked cross Dad used to mark a safe contact.

There were other hunters. How many of them were *djamphir*—or something else? Could I still trust them? Would they know what I was now that I'd bloomed? Would any of Dad's friends or contacts sell me to Sergej if Dad wasn't around?

It was a horrible thing to think.

There were a handful of people I could trust. Less than that, because the only ones among the living were up here with me. Christophe . . . maybe I could trust him, since Leon had been lying about him selling Graves to Sergej. But still, Christophe and Graves'd "had words," Graves said.

Words about me.

I glanced up at Graves's broad back as he finished rinsing a plate. Looked down again just as quickly, stared at the blank legal pad. "Can I ask you something?"

His shoulders stiffened. But he sounded easy, relaxed. "You bet."

Chill, dude. I'm not going to ask you to repeat the L *word. I know boys hate that.* "Outside the gym. The night you disappeared. You and Christophe. What exactly did he say to you?" I had the Cliffs-Notes version, so to speak, but I wanted . . . more. "I mean, if you don't mind telling me."

"He had a group of *djamphir* buddies with him." Graves set the plate in the rack, gently. Put his hands down on the lip of the utility sink, dropped his head forward. His hair curled over his nape, but you could still see the vulnerable-looking spot there. "He asked me if I thought I was any good for you. I said I knew I wasn't, but I was all you got and I was stepping up. He laughed at that, and we got into it. Kind of . . . well, a shoving match. Guy stuff." He let out a long, harsh sigh. "It ended up with things getting serious. He said I wasn't doing you any good. That you deserved better."

Oh, Jesus. I tasted burnt metal, swallowed hard. My fingers tightened on the blue Bic. "Graves—"

"I told him that you deserved better than a creepy little fuck like him, too. That was about it. I went for a run to cool off and the vampires nabbed me." He pulled the plug on the sink; on either side, framing the window, were shelves holding the sum total of Gran's china. There was a gleam on the windowsill, a random reflection of sunlight.

We'd have to keep washing like mad to make sure we had clean plates. All the pots and pans were hung around the stove, and Graves straightened. He started hanging things up, each in the correct place. Which meant he'd been watching me.

Soapy water slipped down the mouth of the drain. The gurgling was loud in the silence between us.

"You shouldn't trust me," he said finally, grabbing the edge of the sink again and holding on for dear life. Muscle stood out under his T-shirt. "*He* broke Ash. *He* could've broken me. I could be even more dangerous than that Anna chick. You shouldn't have come to rescue me."

He meant Sergej, and I could see Graves's point. But still. All the breath rushed out of me; I had a hard time finding enough to talk with. "I couldn't leave you there." If I let my head hang any further I'd snap my own neck. My mother's locket was a cool weight against my breastbone. "You wouldn't break, either."

Why did that make his shoulders hunch even further? He balled up the towel and slung it in the sink. "Doesn't matter. Christophe's a bastard, but he's right. I'm no good for you, not like this. And now you're going to have to worry about whether or not I'm a traitor. Smart, isolating us all up here like this."

Could this go any worse? "We're *safe*, not isolated. And what the hell? Are you smoking crack? One minute you say you . . . I mean, one minute you're fine, the next you're telling me you're a liability and not to trust you. Will you just pick hating me or being my boyfriend and get it over with? One or the other, *jeez*." I couldn't put all my aggravation into the last syllable, but I tried. My throat was dry and my palms were damp, and the Bic made a little screeching sound as my fist tightened and the plastic flexed.

He shrugged. Let go of the sink and turned on one heel, but didn't look at me. His profile was sharp, the bones standing out under the skin, and for a moment he looked too exotic to be real. "Who's on crack now? I don't hate you, Dru. Jesus. That's the *problem*."

"Wait, we've gone from using the L word to me being a *problem*?" I'll admit it. It was pretty much an undignified screech at the end. "Well, I'm sorrrrrr-ry!"

Yeah. When all else fails, take refuge in sarcasm. I could've slapped myself.

He just gave me a bright green glance and stamped away, out through the front door and into the sunlight. At least this time he was wearing shoes.

I sat there, breathing like I'd just run a four-minute mile, the pen making weird little sounds as I tried to get my fist to loosen up.

Serves me right for asking him, really. First he kissed me, then it was weeks with nothing but a peck on the cheek every evening, and then he loves me, then I should suspect him. I closed my eyes. Just when I thought everything had gotten just about as complex as it could, something new came along. I never knew where I was with Graves, in the friend zone or . . . somewhere else, somewhere I'd like better if he didn't keep shoving me away.

At least with Christophe, I was only uncertain in the sparring room.

The dream rose up in front of me, Technicolor vivid. I could almost taste the night wind and smell the decaying vampire blood on them both. Bruce, the head of the Council, always trying to smooth everything over. And Christophe, certain I was still breathing.

My *heart is still beating, therefore,* she *is still alive.*

Funny, but I never even considered that he might've been talking about someone else.

Why was I even thinking about that? All the time Christophe had been hanging around, I'd felt like I was betraying Graves by even considering him as . . . well, as a serious prospect.

He's old. He knew my mom, *for Chrissake. And he's . . . he's . . .*

I couldn't find a word for what he was. A hot flush raced up from my throat, and my mother's locket warmed. Something brushed my cheek when I lifted my head, and I found out I'd reached up, my fingertips following the familiar curves of Graves's skull-and-crossbones earring.

I popped the back off, pulled the post out, and laid the earring on the table. I still had a diamond stud in my other ear, one of the ones Christophe had given me before I went into that rave and played bait for suckers. My first vampire kill that night, and Ash had been there too.

It felt like a million years ago, like another lifetime. How many times would I get that feeling, like I'd started out on a whole new life? How many times would I get comfortable just to have everything I depended on whacked away underneath me?

This sucks. It was weaksauce, sure. But I couldn't come up with a better term.

I popped the back off the diamond too, laid it down. There. The two of them, side by side. Both gleaming in different ways.

To hell with them both. I should get a pair of earrings that said *boys are stupid.* Nat would've approved.

I angrily wiped at my face and stood up. I had to move, the itching in my bones *demanded* I move. I paced over to the sink and stood where he'd been, grabbed right where he'd grabbed. There were little indents in the utility sink's sheet metal where his fingers had dug in.

Boy don't know his own strength, Shanks had remarked once. *Does anyone, really?* Christophe had replied.

The window over the sink was dusty, a spring heat-haze making the tree shadows at the edge of the clearing run like ink on greased plastic. I shuddered, like a horse run too hard and stopped too quickly, and something brushed my hair. A warm, forgiving touch, like familiar work-worn fingers.

It's all right, babygirl. Like I was five years old again, scared in the middle of the night, or seven and crying at the table because some kid at the valley school called me a bad word because my daddy was gone.

I whirled. The locket bounced against my chest, warm metal. The fingers patted the top of my head, a quiet, soothing movement.

There there, chile, babygirl. It's all right. A breath of tobacco and baby powder, spice and stiff old-lady skirts.

"Gran?" I whispered.

There was no reply but the sough of wind against the roof and the grass, trees sighing, the burble of the creek down-away. I heard a high excited yip—Ash, delighted by something else.

I edged away from the sink like it had grown horns. Gooseflesh stood out all over me, hard little bumps, and the *aspect* smoothed down over me in waves of comforting, drenching heat.

If Gran was here, she'd set everything to rights. Some part of me had probably thought she would just appear, or that something would be here to save my bacon. I was always more comfortable with someone telling me what to do, so I could just follow the numbers and my training and . . .

But there was nobody and nothing *left*. Nothing to trust, nothing to depend on, and I couldn't keep us here forever. Someone would find out about this house, probably sooner rather than later, and they would come riding in to yank it all away from me.

This ain't gettin' you nowhere, honeychile, Gran's voice piped up, faraway and faint. I retreated to the table, turning to keep the windowsill in view like I expected something to move over there.

I grabbed the atlas. I needed to plan, not sit around whining or scaring myself. Thinking I heard her was like a dash of cold water, slapping me into functioning again.

If Graves couldn't figure out if he loved me or hated me, maybe it was time for me to start fishing in a different pond. Except I didn't have a different pond, since I'd pretty much accused Christophe of selling Graves out and told him I hated him.

Dadblastit, Dru girl, you're woolgathering. Chop some wood, chase them chickens, or draw some water. Quit your mooning. Gran's voice, sharp and clear, like she'd caught me hiding behind the coop. I flinched guiltily, because for a second I could've sworn she'd just waltzed in through the front door and took me to task.

God, I wish. I miss you so much. The dry rock in my throat wouldn't budge.

Hell, I should have been worrying about hearing voices. That was the problem with the *touch*—you could go off the deep end and mistake shit for Shinola, as Dad would say. And maybe I should be worrying more about little things like keeping us alive and less about my seriously messed-up dating situation.

I hunched down in the rickety split-bottom chair, opened the atlas and propped up Dad's contact book, and tried to do just that.

CHAPTER SIX

"**I'll be back** in a couple hours," I said an hour later, desperate, but Ash shook his head. He held onto the door handle, grimly, and there would be no way of getting into the car unless I crawled in through the other side. Then, if I tried to pull out, he'd either break the door handle, the door itself, or run after me. And he was wulfen. He could definitely keep up with the car unless we were on a straight shot of freeway, and he could find me in town if he really took a mind to. "Jesus, Ash, I'm just going into town! I won't be gone long."

Ash shook his head even more vigorously, greasy hair flying. Bits of leaves and twigs threaded through the dark matted strands, I still hadn't found wherever he'd flung his shirt, and he was barefoot. Mud striped his chest. He'd seemed pretty happy, until I put my *malaika* in the back of the Subaru and my bag in the passenger seat. He'd let out a howl and bounded off the steps, nearly colliding with me, and grabbed the handle on the driver's side.

Perfect. I wanted a hot shower, not just a sponge bath. Not to mention a club sandwich and some coffee that didn't come from a percolator. I was pretty sure I could just be an object of gossip if I went into the diner in town, but Ash? He'd make me an object of outright speculation, no matter if I behaved correctly or not.

He inhaled, opened his mouth. "*Noooooooo.*" A long, drawn-out syllable. Then he changed it up. "Nonononono! Wif! Go wif!"

"For the *love* of *Pete.*" I put my hands on my hips, and for once I sounded like Dad when he was exasperated past bearing with a malfunctioning engine. Too exasperated even to swear, and that's saying something. "You do *not* have to go with me. It's just down to the two-bit town in the valley. I'll be back in a couple hours, max. You stay here with Graves." At least, I was thinking Graves was still around here. If he went wandering off in the woods and got lost, that would just put a capper on the whole day. I'd left his lunch under Saran wrap on the table, and the *touch* throbbed like a bad tooth inside my head, a feedback squeal from my own frustration.

The *malaika* were bulky, but I didn't have a holster for either gun we had, and I didn't have the patience to jury-rig something. Besides, during the day around here, I didn't want a telltale bulge under my shirt. Country people understand guns, sure. But I wasn't one of the locals anymore.

If I ever had been.

Ash dug his bare heels into the dirt and glared at me. Orange sparked in his irises. He set his chin and took a firmer grip on the door handle.

When he'd been almost-eight feet tall and all hairy, at least he'd been less trouble.

I tried for patience. "Look, you're not even cleaned up. You've got dirt all over you. People will stare." *That's a bad thing, in case you're wondering.*

His ruined chin thrust out further. Here in the sunlight, you could see the scars clearly. They were a reminder I could've done without. I remembered him trying to change back into a human shape, and the sobbing when he finally had a human throat again was the kind that will stick in your dreams. If I didn't have so many other nightmares, it would've been a starring attraction.

Of course, I was dreaming other things nowadays. Things that might or might not have been happening. *True-seeins*, Gran called them, and I hadn't been wrong yet.

If she was dead, ibn Allas, I would be, too. There was something in that scene I wasn't getting, and I didn't have time or energy for enough heavy brooding to figure it out. At the very least, Christophe suspected I wasn't dead, and he wasn't stupid. He'd found me before.

He would do it again. He'd probably also try to drag me back to the Order, where I was "safer." No way, no day. I didn't like the idea that someone in the Order could sell me—or, God forbid, sell Graves out—again.

And here I was wasting time arguing with a half-Broken werwulf who couldn't even *talk.*

"Oh, what the hell." I threw up my hands. "Get in, then. But don't make any trouble, or I'll . . ." I decided to leave the threat hanging. What could I do to him? A big fat pile of nothing, that's what. At least when he was all tall and hairy, I didn't feel so bad about locking him up somewhere safe and going about my business.

He didn't waste any time. He was in the backseat in a trice, bouncing up and down so hard the springs groaned. "Settle down," I told him. "We need this car."

I opened the driver's side door, did a sweep of the sun-drenched meadow. No sign of Graves, and the clouds stacking up to the west told me there would be rain before long. A spring storm, maybe. That would be all sorts of fun and mud. I could even smell it on the wind, grass and trees sensing a long drink coming and releasing their little perfumed cries of joy.

The *touch* throbbed uneasily inside my head. I tasted citrus, but only faintly, and it wasn't wax-rotten. Trouble coming, but nothing specific enough for me to take any precautions. Best thing was to just get everything done as soon as possible, so we could leave in a hurry if we had to.

I'd left Graves a note under his plate. *Went to town, be back in a bit. Keep the fire going.* I thought of adding *I'm sorry,* but I didn't. What did I have to be sorry for?

Other than getting him bit and dragged into this whole ungodly mess, that is. Still, he said he didn't mind. Did that mean I only had to be sorry for liking him, or for getting him kidnapped and tortured by vampires, or what?

He *liked* being a part of the Real World. I don't know if I exactly enjoyed it, but I knew I'd never want to be one of the oblivious. Did that make me an asshole?

I couldn't even figure it out anymore, and it wasn't the kind of problem I could do anything about. I sparked the car, the engine roused, and Ash made a little squeal of glee.

"You sit yourself down and put your seat belt on," I barked, and he did. He rolled the window down, though, and spent the entire bumpy ride down the ridge and down the county highway with his face in the slipstream. Don't ask me, I don't know.

* * *

We would have been okay, except for the Charleston Chew. I didn't realize Ash had kiped it until we were outside the big wide Sav 'n' Shop grocery store that used to be a Winn-Dixie when I was young, and I heard the man shout *"Hey! Hey, you!"*

I turned incuriously, and he was bearing down on us—the manager, a big potbellied good ol' boy with furious little piggy blue eyes behind thick horn-rim glasses, pasty cheek flab under a greased dark comb-over. His polyester tie flapped and the wide yellow sweat stains under his armpits married the fussy shine on his wing tips to make the picture of what Gran would call "a bitty-ass man too big for his britches already."

It wasn't her most damning epithet, but it was close.

I looked at Ash. Who tore the wrapper open and made a small *hmm* of contentment. That was when it occurred to me. *I didn't pay for that. He must've just grabbed it.*

"Oh Lord." *Give me strength. Jeez.* I yanked the balky cart to a stop. It had a screechy wheel and wobbled alarmingly, but it was the best on offer. The clouds were coming up fast and the smell of rain was an overpowering, sweet green haze. Stormlight gathered, yellow–bruised in all the corners, making every edge stand out sharp. The shadows had turned to deep fuzzy wells. "Ash. Where the hell did that—"

"Stop right there!" Piggy Eyes was really worked up. He almost plowed into us. "You gonna pay for that? Huh?"

"I paid for everything else, sir," I drawled, and Ash took a huge bite. He chewed sloppily, observing the scene with bright-eyed interest. I cursed inwardly. "I didn't see he had that, sorry. Here." I was already digging in my pockets for the change.

An ugly flush spread up Piggy Eye's cheeks. He was obviously unmollified. "That yourn? He retarded or somethin'?"

Gran would've fixed him with a glare, so I did. "That's my kin, sir." It was like channeling her, and I had to try hard not to smile as I offered him two crumpled dollar bills. "He's *special*. Here."

I should've been aiming for a submissive tone, I guess. Or at least something conciliatory. Instead, I sounded like I was brushing him off, and—here's the bad part—there were a couple of wide women in print shorts, locals by the look of them, passing by to head into the store's air conditioning.

One of them laughed, her flip-flops making regular little smacking sounds against cracked pavement. Her shoulders were permanently sunburned, and her blouse had a tropical print way too bright green to do any good for her complexion in this lighting. "Lyle's about to do a citizen's arrest right there again." She spat tobacco juice, a pungent brown streak, and the other woman chimed in with a cackle that would have done Witch Hazel proud. They swept on into the store, the automatic door wheezing tiredly shut behind them.

Petty tyrants don't like being laughed at. Piggy Eyes Lyle flushed an even darker brick red, and his meaty paw shot out. The *touch* snapped inside my head like a wet sheet shaken before you put it on the line, and I realized he'd been following us through the store, watching us.

Watching me, in particular. And the things he was thinking squirmed inside my head like maggots. I actually flinched as his fingers closed around my upper arm.

"You're comin' with me." He squeezed, hard. He had only human strength, but the *aspect* woke with a jolt, smoothing over my skin with oil-soft heat. My fangs tingled, and I clapped my lips shut over them. The thirst tingled in the back of my throat, bloodhunger waking up. It was weird—it was taking over that other place on the back of my tongue, the one that warned me of danger. It didn't feel right, but I didn't have time to think about it.

The sun dimmed. The clouds had found us.

Ash growled. The sound rumbled free, a warning I was used to from hanging out with wulfen. It deepened at the end, and anyone with any sense would've backed up in a hurry.

Lyle, however, had no common sense. He actually shook me, and tried to drag me off my feet. I planted myself, the grocery cart giving a screech, and was thinking furiously about how to defuse the situation when three things happened.

One, the sky darkening in the west rumbled. It was a long menacing roll of thunder, and it scraped along my nerve endings like a wire brush. Every hair on me tingled like the lightning was going to strike right at me. The second thing was pure bad luck—a county sheriff's car bounced into the parking lot, its springs groaning. The man behind the wheel saw us just as Ash dropped his half-gone Charleston Chew and—this was the third thing—launched himself at Piggy Eyes Lyle so fast the pale streak in his hair seemed to stretch like taffy.

Ohshi—I dropped down, knees loosening and my free hand flashing out. I hit harder than I intended to, a flat-palm strike with almost every ounce of the *aspect* behind it. It sank into Lyle's middle with a meaty crunch lost under the roll of thunder, and the fat man flew back. His fingers ripped my T-shirt as they tore free. Then I was airborne, springing like a jack-in-the-box and colliding with Ash just at the top of his leap. We hit the ground hard, pavement cracking as quarter-sized spatters of rain hit the dusty earth.

I found out I had my right hand clamped at Ash's nape. He was growling and struggling, but I had a good grip, just like with a disobedient puppy.

"No," I said sharply. "No. NO!" I braced my foot, my other knee grinding into a hollow in the pavement. No—not a hollow. It was the dent I'd made while landing. The *aspect* flooded me, smoothing down my skin in a wave of sweet heat. My fangs tingled, and the bloodhunger woke in a sheet of red. It pulled against every vein in my body, turned the entire back of my throat to a desert, and the anger woke up.

I didn't need rage to trigger the *aspect* now. But it was kind of a habit, and besides, it felt so *good*. Like I was in control of the whole stupid, tangled situation.

Like I finally had a clear-cut problem with an easy solution in front of me.

Ash struggled. I was grinding him into the concrete, and I didn't much care at the moment so long as he stayed still. I glanced up. The county sheriff's car had jounced to a stop, and the man inside was staring so hard his eyes bugged out, visible even through the windshield and the gloom under his ten-gallon hat.

Uh-oh. Think fast, Dru.

Luckily, the Sav 'n' Shop was our first stop. We could easily leave the two bags of groceries if we had to. I'd paid with cash; there was no trouble there. How to get out of here without John Law following in his car or calling in a plate number that wouldn't match the Subaru because I'd switched them out . . . Christ.

The biggest problem, and the one I had to solve right now, was the werwulf growling and scrabbling, his bones crackling as the change tore through him.

If he goes into changeform, will he be able to come back? I didn't know. Clear plastic goop started hardening over the world, which meant I was using superspeed even while standing still. Raindrops flashed, caught in stasis, and the sheriff's car door made a groaning sound as it was slowly, slowly levered open. He'd grabbed a frigging shotgun, I could see the shape through the windshield, and things were about to go critical.

Think, Dru. What would Dad do?

Every muscle tensed. I dug into the pavement and pushed myself aside, whipping my right arm back. The *aspect* flared, my mother's locket a spot of molten heat. Ash went flying, fur running up over his flesh in liquid black streams. The silvery stripe on his head flashed once before the darker clouds swallowed the sun completely. Thunder boomed again, distorted because I was already moving, flashing through space to slam into the cop car's door. Pulled the force back at the last second, but I still heard snapping bone.

Gonna hurt someone if you're not careful, Dru-girl. Dad's voice, calm and clinical. *Get that gun away from him. Make sure he's down. Then get the hell out of here, and take your damn groceries with you.*

The car door came off like peeling a strip of birch bark, hinges squealing, a fountain of sparks as the wiring for the windows and locks tore. I brought it up and spun, drove it through the windshield. Safety glass imploded. The cop was down—an older man with a high hard gut, his hat blown free and skipping across the parking lot in slow graceful arcs, his eyes bugging and his mouth wetly open. His left leg bent at a funny angle inside his regulation-issue pants. He was older than Dad, and the look on his face was pure terror.

He was afraid. Of *me*.

I bent and grabbed the shotgun, a flicker of my hand. It was so easy to bring it to my shoulder, brace it, and—

What am I DOING?

He was scrabbling away, too weak and slow to be a real threat. My head snapped up, scanning the parking lot. Not a soul to be seen. Ash lay on top of an old Buick, the hood dented and windshield cracked. I'd flung him pretty hard. He shook his head, melting back into boyform, and I pursed my lips, let out a high piercing whistle.

It was Gran's "call the hounds" sound; it was instinct, and it worked. Ash's chin came up, and he looked at me. His eyes glowed orange.

We need to get the hell out of here. Now. I jerked my head, the *touch* an invisible rope pulling at the meat inside my skull. He clambered down off the car in weird, stuttering fast-forward and bounded across the parking lot on all fours even though he was boy-shaped again. Toward the Subaru, thank God.

I hope they don't have security cameras here. I glanced at the cop. The shotgun whirled in my grasp; he was raising his hands like he was going to plead with me not to hurt him. I socked him, once, with the shotgun's butt, a nice clean hit gauged on the soft side. His head snapped back and he slumped, eyes fluttering closed. For a moment, standing outside myself, I was horrified.

The world jolted back up to normal speed, achingly slow. Ash skidded to a stop in front of the Subaru, looking at me. His irises were still orange, still glowing, and his gaze was utterly blank.

Waiting for the next command. *My* next command. Nausea rose deep and hot inside me. Had he looked at Sergej that way?

I am so not ready for this.

I snapped a glance at Piggy Eyes Lyle. He lay, head cocked at a weird angle, up against two dented, broken newspaper boxes. Bile rose in my throat. I'd hit him too hard.

Was he still alive?

Yes. I heard his pulse, faint and weak. A thin thread of blood slid down his chin, and as the wind veered, I could *smell* it.

It smelled good. The bloodhunger woke up, the dry spot at the back of my throat opening like a flower.

Walk across the pavement, step by step, bend down. Grab him, push his arm up to lock the joint so he can't struggle, and tilt the head back. There will be a nice big throat, with a nice big jugular. Bury your fangs. And the moment his heart stops, you know he'll never watch a teenage girl walk through the supermarket again. It's yours.

Your *power. The blood will slide down your throat, it will be sweet and smoky, and—*

I knew that tinkling, sweet, girlish voice. It was Anna. A warm place dilated behind my breastbone, and I heard her laugh. Whispering, taunting, cajoling.

I thought I'd gotten her out of my head, that I'd burned through the blood I'd taken from her.

I was wrong. And what would Graves think of this, if he could see it?

What would Dad think, if he was still alive and not just zombie dust? Or Gran?

Time snapped, stinging, like a hard elastic band against flinching skin. I had the two plastic-and-paper grocery bags in my free hand. Threw them in the backseat as Ash cowered.

Like he was afraid of me. Hunched down, his entire body the picture of submission.

"Get in!" I yelled, the shotgun held loosely. Nobody in the parking lot. The rain began to slant down in earnest, dark drops on the dusty ground merging. It didn't cut the smell of blood. My entire body shook, jitters racing through me.

Ash scrambled into the car. I swept the parking lot again, shotgun held ready. Lightning sizzled overhead, photoflash-searing the entire scene into my head. I dropped into the driver's seat, braced the shotgun. Sparked the car and laid rubber out of the parking lot.

Some shopping trip.

CHAPTER SEVEN

The windows were all down, rain lashing through and thunder booming. Water smacked the side of my face, a welcome coolness. I kept us on the road, trying not to bend the steering wheel. Ash had slithered over into the front passenger seat and whimpered, crouching in the bucket seat and staring at me.

I didn't have the heart to tell him to sit down and shut up. He shook and shivered every time thunder boomed. Spring storms are like that—they sneak up on a body. Gran said they hid on the ridges, and the only way to tell one was coming was to have a war wound or an old broken bone.

Gran would have been horrified at what I'd just done. Not so much the busting up a couple of grown men, though that was plenty bad.

No, it was the bloodhunger. If she was still alive to see me sucking blood, or even just *wanting* to suck blood, what would she think? She'd be disgusted, just like Graves. And angry.

I didn't do it, though. I didn't!

My conscience wasn't having any of it. *You wanted to. You know you did.* I blinked furiously, the water in my eyes was making everything blur.

Ash let out a yelp. I jerked the wheel, and we drifted out of the oncoming lane. There wasn't another car on the road for miles, and my entire body was shaking with the hunger's aftermath. Like little armored rabbits were running around under my skin. My veins throbbed dryly, and my eyes were smarting. A hot trickle slid down my left cheek.

I wished I could stop to roll all the windows up. Ash twitched. He had his arms wrapped around himself, and the next glare of lightning made him flinch again.

"It's all right." I had to work to make myself heard above the rain-noise. "It's okay. It's not your fault."

Except it kind of is. What the hell, stealing a two-bit piece of candy? But I couldn't be too mad at him. He wasn't even in his right mind. And I've dealt with guys like Piggy Eyes Lyle all over the country. It was a point of pride with me, knowing just how to slide out of Situations. Except I hadn't slid out of this one. I'd acted just like a punk kid, and—

But I am a punk kid, something inside me whined. *I never asked for this!*

I kept checking the rearview mirror. No headlights, no sign of pursuit. If they had cameras at the supermarket we were probably hosed. We'd have to run anyway, ditch this car in the first city and grab another one. I'd done the planning, especially to get us liquid resources. But all that wood I'd chopped was going to be useless.

Don't worry about the firewood, for fuck's sake. Worry about something useful.

Like, how was I going to explain this to Graves? That was going to be all sorts of fun in a handbasket. I heaved in a breath, two, and more hot trickles slid out of my eyes.

Cold rain smacking my face through my still-open window did a sucky-ass job of covering up the fact that I was sobbing. Great gulping heaves, tearing through me like a crowd of hobnailed boots against a street, beating out cadence.

Did I kill him? Lyle's head had been twisted so strangely. But I'd heard his pulse, faint and thready. Maybe he'd be okay. Someone would come out any moment and find him and the cop there, the sheriff's car busted up and the shotgun gone. At least we had another gun, and a shotgun was far from the worst thing to have out in the hills or on the run.

I hope I didn't kill him. It wasn't like my first vampire kill. I'd felt sick over that, but in the end it was like cutting off the head of a poisonous snake with a shovel. It just had to be done, and thank God I wasn't the snake.

Or was I?

Lyle had just been a garden-variety human jerkwad, not a blood-sucking fiend looking to kill me as messily as possible. Lyle didn't even know *nosferat* existed, or *djamphir* or *svetocha* or werwulfen —

Ash whined again. He reached out, tentatively, and his pale slim fingers brushed my shoulder. He patted, again and again, like I was a dog that needed soothing. My shaking sobs were oddly unconnected, like my body didn't even belong to me. The *aspect* was hot oil over my skin, smoothing down and getting rid of any hurt, filling me with a buzzing. My fangs poked at my lower lip, and the twin sharp pressures sent a fresh bolt of nausea through my growling stomach.

I was *hungry*. Not just hungry, ravenous. And thirsty, too. The bloodhunger taunted me, the entire inside of my throat on fire. Water wouldn't help it. The only thing that would help was calming down and forcing myself to eat something human.

That's the problem, Dru. You ain't human anymore. You're one of those things Dad would've hunted. You suck blood.

Human *blood*.

No wonder Graves is so disgusted all the time. Even if he says he ain't.

That was the wrong thought. I let out another sob. I couldn't seem to stop. It got darker, and thunder rumbled again. I realized we were coming up on our turn and hit the brakes hard. We slewed through standing water, bumped onto the indifferent paving, and kept going. The way everything was coming down, we were looking at a washed-out road damn soon, and a slog through the mud to get back up to the cabin to collect Graves and pack up if that happened. It was just too dangerous to stick around here now, and I had nobody to blame but myself.

I just kept driving. The all-wheel drive handled the transition to rutted washboard beautifully, and we were halfway up the side of the ridge before I realized it. Trees thrashed, lightning going off in waves and the thunder closer and closer.

This ain't natural. Gran's voice sounded worried inside my head, and that faint ghost of citrus on my tongue taunted me. I sniffed, wiped at my cheek with the back of one wet wrist. It didn't do much, and the rain flooding in through my window didn't help. I didn't want to close it, though. I needed the air.

Another sob dry-barked out of me. I ignored it. The crying was just another storm. I could just hunker down until it passed, couldn't I?

Ash whined again, the sound coming from way back in his throat. He kept frantically patting my shoulder, and when I snapped a glance at him I found he was visibly shaking and even whiter than usual. Bedraggled, covered in mud, and wet clear through, his eyes ran with orange light and fastened on me. He tilted his head, the silvery stripe in his hair gleaming with its own weird light. I snapped my nose back forward and stared at the road.

A flash of white drifted across my vision. It resolved with quick charcoal lines, as if someone was motion-capture sketching it on the air itself. It was an owl, and it slid through the heavy rain in merry defiance of normal owl behavior. The *aspect* spiked under my skin.

Turn left, Dru. Now.

I didn't argue. Whenever Gran's owl showed up, it was always best just to follow.

Only it wasn't Gran's owl. It was my *aspect* in animal form, and one more reminder of why I'd never be normal. Or strictly human.

I twisted the wheel. We jounced off the road just in time, avoiding a pretty bad deep-foaming washout. There was an alternate route, though, for just such an occasion. The turnoff was conveniently close, but immediately the Subaru started juddering and fighting. We had to slow down to a crawl, and I finally gathered myself enough to roll my window up and turn the defroster on max. Ash grabbed at the dashboard, riding the car's shuddering like a surfer. He still whined, but instead of patting me he kept his hand on my shoulder, fingers tensing. Not driving in, thank God. He had wulfen claws, and I didn't like the idea of having my shoulder ground up like meatloaf.

"We'll be okay," I said, shakily. Another sob came along; I bit it in half and swallowed it. Rain poured in through the other three windows. This was not going to do the upholstery any good at all. "We'll take this route. It'll—"

The car slid sideways. I turned into it, cursing a blue streak— Dad would've yelled at me for using That Language, and I never would've dared around Gran. But neither of them was here so it was just me, the *touch* filling my head and pouring out through my arms as I wrenched the steering wheel and goosed the accelerator instead of the brake. You never want to hit the brakes in a situation like that.

The tires bit; we made it through and bumped up into a pair of overgrown ruts that was the alternate path. It would take us longer, but on this part of the ridge there was less chance of washouts. The trees glowered, leaves falling like the monsoon rain, and I judged we were about a mile from the house. We'd have to cover three miles of rutted track to get there, though.

Good thing there's moonshine runners in my family tree, right? Along with vampires.

Oh, God. I grabbed the steering wheel with both hands, exhaled hard, and saw Gran's owl again, flickering through falling water in a soft blur. It was *dark*, especially under the trees, and my head hurt. Whether it was from the crying or something else, I couldn't tell. Glass spikes pressed in through my temples, and my nose was running so hard I had to root around for some damp fast-food napkins to wipe my top lip. I shivered, the trembling communicating itself to Ash.

"Bad," he whispered, under the straining engine and the drumming of rain. Thunder drowned out most of what he said next. "—sowwy. Osh *sowwy.*"

My heart squeezed down on itself, hard. "It isn't your fault." I heaved a sigh, kept a sharp eye on the ruts ahead. The ghost of oranges on my tongue taunted me. "I could've just paid for it without getting mouthy. I screwed up, not you. It's not your fault."

I mean, what else could I say? It's not like he did it on purpose. I was the responsible one. I'd just failed. Again.

He shut up, but he kept hold of me. Crouching on the seat like that probably wasn't comfortable, but I had enough to worry about. The sobs juddered to a stop, and it took forever, but when we bumped out into the meadow I heaved a sigh of relief. Gran's house stood on the far end, lit by garish flashes of lightning, and it took me halfway across the meadow to realize something was wrong.

The flickering orange light from inside wasn't right. It was open flame, shining out through the windows and sending gushes of billowing black smoke up into the drenching blanket of water falling from the sky.

Gran's house was burning. And my mother's locket was a chip of ice against my chest. The owl turned in a tight, distressed circle in front of the car, veering sharply away just before it hit the windshield, and I began to get a very bad feeling.

Just then, slim black shapes boiled out of the undergrowth, and I reached for the shift lever as if in a slow terrible nightmare. The lightning showed their slicked-down hair and ivory-gleam teeth, the eerie quickness of their movements, and the hatred blurring around them made the *touch* ache like a sore tooth inside my head.

Vampires. They'd found us. But I didn't taste the wax-orange foulness that usually warned me of them. Just that ghost of citrus, like orange juice you've forgotten you drank an hour ago.

There was no time. I couldn't hope to get us down the ridge before they hit the car. I couldn't even make the tree line.

Ash howled and pitched himself aside, fur rippling up over his dirty skin. The passenger window, only partly rolled up, shattered. Thank God he hit the ground outside before changing, because otherwise he'd've gotten stuck halfway through. Fur boiled up over him, his bones crackling as he swelled, his boy voice deepening and swelling into a wulfen's roar.

I sat there, one hand numb on the wheel and the other in midair, and the only thing I could think of were the *malaika* in the cargo compartment. I popped my seat belt, grabbed the lever that would put my seat all the way back, and started scrambling for my life.

CHAPTER EIGHT

The rear hatch opened; I hopped out and my sneakers sank into mud. The rain was an immediate battering against every inch of me, and the *malaika* were heavy in my hands. The *aspect* poured over me in a wave of smooth-oil heat, fangs prickling my lower lip. I jerked the wooden swords free of the leather harness and pelted around the corner of the car.

Ash hunkered down in the rain, almost-eight feet of werwulf with huge shoulders under a mat of wiry fur. The streak on his head gleamed, rain slicking everything down and outlining muscle under his pelt. His claws dug into mud with tiny splorching sounds lost under a roll of thunder, and the vampires skidded to a stop, throwing up sheets of mud-laced water. The grass exploded like jackstraws, and they snarled.

Eight of them. All male, all burning with visible hatred under the lash of rain, hourglass-shaped pupils sending black threads out into their irises as the hunting-aura took them. It's like the *aspect*, that aura, but it's made of pure revulsion. They just loathe everything around them so much.

Or maybe it's just the living they detest, even as they feed on them. Even though they're, technically, living too. They're the part of life that hates itself.

Why didn't I sense them? The faint citrus taste sharpened, as if I was sucking on a piece of orange candy.

Danger candy, I'd called it, my warning taste. Why was it failing me now?

It didn't matter. Eight against me and Ash were bad odds. But I'd bloomed, right? Not so bad now. Especially if my *aspect* held, spreading out in invisible lethal waves.

Where's Graves? In the house? "Ash. Ash!" I had to shout over a long rattling roll of thunder. "Go find Graves! Find him *now!*"

Ash growled, his claws digging into mud, and I was afraid he wouldn't listen. Time to think fast, only what could I do? If he decided not to do what I told him—

Silly, Anna's voice whispered inside my head. *Keep the Broken with you; he's good cannon fodder. But if you really want him to obey, do this.* And her ghostly, manicured fingers drummed against my skull.

The *touch* flexed inside my head, my will grinding down as the bloodhunger dilated in my throat. My mother's locket burned with fierce cold, the silver stinging me.

I pulled the *touch* back, hurriedly, shaking my head. Water flew.

Ash let out a yelp and skipped sideways as if stung. I felt as if I'd just swallowed Anna's blood again, and her training opened up inside me, ghostly silk-hung corridors stretching in every direction. Eight vampires, a storm that was certainly the work of a very old and powerful sucker, and the werwulf who'd saved my ass time and again whirled and pelted away with spooky blurring grace.

How did I do that?

Anna. Somehow, in drinking her blood, I'd taken more. Whether she'd intended it or it just happened because we were both *svetocha* was a question I'd worry about later.

If I survived this.

My grasp on the *malaika* firmed, became natural. The curved wooden swords whirled in circles, rain dripping down the back of my neck as my hair finished plastering itself to my head, my braid a heavy sopping rope. I should have been shivering and terrified out of my tiny little mind.

Instead, I dropped into first-guard, bent my knees, and had to control the urge to fling myself at them. They spread out, fangs bared, and the hiss-growl of pissed-off vampires turned the rain to trembling, flashing needles of ice. *Which one's the leader? Pick off the leader first. But they all feel the same age, which means—*

I realized my mistake just as the rest of the vampires showed up. These eight weren't the only ones. They were just the quickest on the scene, so to speak.

More deadly black shapes knifed out of the dark between the trees, lightning crackling as the sky overhead tore itself apart, and I braced myself. The *malaika* spun, and there was no more time for thinking.

I *moved*.

The first vampire fell, choking and clawing at his throat. The happy stuff in my blood that makes me *svetocha* also made me toxic to suckers now that I'd bloomed. The *aspect* flared, almost visible as it battered at the ice pellets now raining down on me. Stinging hail lashed and my right-hand *malaika* sheared half the sucker's face off. Black blood exploded, hanging in a freezing arc before the hail scattered through it.

He didn't look more than sixteen. None of them did, but the

way their faces twisted into plum-colored evil was ageless. Their eyes were black from lid to lid now, and their cold hunting-auras hit the wall of heat that was my *aspect*. Traceries of steam exploded as I leapt, *malaika* whirling with a whistling sound over the crack of thunder. Landing, *splorch* of mud under my sneakers, skidding but that was all right, on my knees and tearing a long furrow across the meadow's face as I slid, bending back under claw strikes as they tried to get through the shell of toxicity and tear my throat out. Vampire blood sprayed, acid-smoking as it hit chill-wet air. Steam twisted into sharptooth shapes and I gained my feet again with a lurch. Mud splattered and grass flew as I twisted aside, my foot flashing out and kicking another sucker with a crunch.

The world was slow, and I moved through it with whispering, eerie speed. It didn't even feel abnormal to be sidestepping through time and space this way. It wasn't the plastic goop slowing everything down—no, this was just me tearing through the snarled fabric of the normal. Bloodhunger flamed all the way down my throat, exploded in my stomach.

The malaika are meant for circles. This circle, here, is where you move. These circles are how the blades move to defend you. And this circle is how you attack against many opponents. Focus, now!

So long ago, Christophe teaching a *svetocha* how to fight. I couldn't tell, now, if the memory was Anna's or mine. Lightning crawled inside my head, bloodhunger turning the wide wet lake of the meadow into shutter-click images. Whirling, my left-hand blade a propeller, smoking vampire blood flung like a gauntlet, splashing the rest of them. They circled, and I didn't have to worry about which direction to strike out. I'd hit a *nosferat* wherever I swung, and they were going to tighten the ring. I was toxic, yeah, but there were so *many* of them, and weight of numbers would tell on me.

"*DRU!*" he screamed, and lightning struck the top of the ridge. The blast of thunder hit at almost the same moment; I swear to God I felt the wall of air molecules cracking against each other press along my entire body as I leapt, spinning in midair and striking out with feet and blades. My heart hammered, because I knew who it was.

He'd come for me. Of course he had.

He *always* did.

He tore through the vampires, blue eyes alight with terrible fire and the rags of his black sweater melded to his body, his own *malaika* blurring as I landed and struck out again. They choked, their faces flushing as my *aspect* burned. It used to be that only terror or fury would make that oil-soft heat lay itself against my skin, and I still felt the rage, wine-red and perfume-sweet, curling through me. Nobody was bleeding here, yet. Nobody except the vampires, and the thought of sinking my fangs in them wasn't appealing.

But if someone had been here, someone human and helpless, like Tyle—

It hit me from the side, a thunderbolt of force. I flew, oddly weightless, holding onto the *malaika* as if they'd somehow break my fall. The sucker died in midair, choking on his own blood, but I hit the ground *hard*, all my chimes ringing and my head full of a flash of brief starry nothingness. The vampire's body rolled to the side, convulsing as it shredded itself, toxic dust runneling through its flesh.

My name, yelled hoarsely. Screaming, the glassy cries of furious *nosferatu*. Roaring, a werwulfen in full battlemode. It was a good thing there was so much thunder, I thought weakly, because otherwise we were making enough noise to be heard in the next county.

Bloodhunger pulsed against my palate, wiping away the trace of oranges. Consciousness returned in a rush. I struggled up, vampire blood smoking on my clothes, and heard someone else screaming.

There was no pain in that cry. It was a long howl of absolute rage, and when I shook the daze out of my head and made it to my feet, shoving aside a heavy weight of swiftly decaying sucker bodies, I saw him.

Christophe bent back, his booted foot flashing up to strike the sucker on the chin. This was a female, her long hair matted with ice, hail suddenly pounding all the way across the violent shipwrecked mass of the torn-up meadow.

Gran's house was still burning fiercely, and a lean dark shape bulleted across the clearing, the silvery streak on its low narrow head actually smearing on the air. Ash hit the girl vampire from behind, and I realized this was the sucker who had birthed the storm. She *felt* old, a terrible weight of hatred and cold spreading out from her in concentric waves. Not as ancient or as powerful as Sergej, but enough.

Ash's hit jolted the girl vampire forward, but she half-turned with impossible quickness and one white hand flashed out. He tumbled away, hair melting and his boyshape rising for the surface, a supple white snake under curling darkness.

Christophe! I shook my head, trying to *think*. The entire meadow was littered with broken bodies. They twisted and jerked as decay claimed them—suckers rot fast when they're bled out, especially when hawthorn wood or a *svetocha*'s nearness has poisoned them.

He drove her back, making a noise that was pure inhuman rage. It managed to drown out the thunder, and a draft of warm apple-pie scent hit me in the face. It had an undertone of copper, which meant he was bleeding, and oh God the smell of it stroked right across the bloodhunger with a cat's-tongue rasp. It reached all the way down to the floor of me, jerking against my control and pulling on every vein in my body.

A hand closed around my arm. I let out a cry and recoiled, but it was Graves. Bruising crawled up his face, his lip was split, and his clothes were grimed with mud and more blood. The smell of him, strawberry incense and silvermoon wildness, the blood a bright copper-satin thread holding it all together, smashed into me. My fangs ached, a sweet tingle of pain. For a hideous half second I quivered, everything in me tensing, ready to knock him down and bury my teeth in him.

Graves was shouting something I couldn't hear over the thunder. His mouth worked, and he tried to pull me toward the car. I dug in my heels, *malaika* dangling from my nerveless hands. Not just because he was bleeding, or because the bloodhunger was snarling all through me, but because I couldn't look away from the fight in front of me.

Christophe closed with the girl vamp again. Ash flowed upward, melding back into changeform, his eyes alight with mad orange. Thunder roiled, and the remaining vampires were massing behind Ash. Not so many of them—a dozen at most. Still, enough to do some harm.

Ash and Christophe needed me. At least I wasn't useless here, as long as my *aspect* held.

And now that I'd bloomed, it would.

Christophe blurred, striking at the girl vamp with inhuman speed and precision. But she was too fast, and he was flagging. I didn't know how I knew, unless it was the *touch* tolling inside my head like a bell. I felt the sweat on his skin under the pouring icy water, felt the burning of his own *aspect* as if it was mine.

I tore away from Graves. My sneakers almost drowned in the mud; hail stung as it peppered down. My *aspect* turned scorch-hot, steam rising directly from my skin as I screamed, a falcon's cry.

Gran's owl appeared out of nowhere, filling itself in with swift strokes, and hit the girl vampire with a crunch I felt like my own bones breaking. A wingsnap, and it veered away, claws dripping. Her young-old face was a black-streaked mess now, her eyes black from lid to lid and spreading fine thin threads of gray out like crow's-feet wrinkles.

Thunder shattered the sky overhead, four separate bolts of lightning slamming down at once, and the girl vampire choked. She was so *fast*, backpedaling as I drove onward, my *malaika* whirring. Ash let out a howl, leaping for her, but it was Christophe who flew past me, the *aspect* slicking down his hair and filling the air around him with crystalline crackling fury. He hit her like a freight train, and the tearing ripping sound of the *malaika* in vampire flesh cut the thunder short.

Black, acidic blood sprayed. Ash hunched even further, his warning growl taking the place of the storm. The hail turned to rain, a regular spring downer. The remaining vampires fell back, their unlined faces twisting with confusion as well as hatred now.

Christophe didn't stop. The blades kept tearing at the body, and the hiss-growl that came from him was a *djamphir*'s scariest warning. His chest seemed too small to make such a sound.

Oh, God. I kept going past him, heading for the group of suckers clumping and backing away from Ash. Thunder receded, lightning striking other hills. The eerie storm-lit darkness began to seem less, well, dark. My *malaika* blurred in twin circles, vampire blood spattering away from the hawthorn, a preparatory move. Graves was suddenly beside me, his eyes burning green and his boots landing in the mud with sucking splashes that would have been funny if he hadn't been making the same sound as Ash—a low thrumming that raises every hair on the body, because it reaches right into your bones and reminds you of a time when human beings huddled in dark caves and the things that ran by night had teeth and claws even fire wouldn't scare away.

Even worse, it sinks its fingers into the low crouching thing in every human, the thing that lurks under civilization and socialization.

The thing that *hunts*.

The vampires broke and scattered. Ash twitched, his hide rippling in vital waves. The silver streak on his head glowed eerily.

"*Get them!*" Christophe screamed. Ash leapt forward, and so did Graves. I would have too, but something hit me from behind. I went down *hard*, mud splattering everywhere and pea-sized hail embedded in the meadow's surface abrading my bare arms like the world's biggest sandpaper belt.

Christophe had my wrists, holding the *malaika* down and pressing me into cold mud. "Stay here!" he yelled, over a last retreating peal of thunder. "*Stay!*" Then he was up and off me, scooping up his *malaika* and vanishing. Little whispering sounds chattered as he moved too quickly to be seen, streaking past the other two and plunging into the woods.

Oh, hell no. No way. But I just lay there for a moment, my ribs heaving with huge shuddering breaths. The rain poured down, but the whole house was blazing. Black smoke billowed. Why was it burning like that?

I managed to make it mostly upright. Cold mud closed around my knees with sucking fingers. I stared at Gran's house, now an inferno. Orange flames, full of evil little yellow chuckling faces with leering mouths. All our supplies, gone. Gran's spinning wheel, her pots and pans, *everything*. My only safe place, my last best card.

Gone.

My heart cracked. I hunched there on my knees, my mouth ajar, stunned.

I hadn't been smart enough or fast enough. How had the vampires found me? How had *Christophe* found me?

And where had Graves been all this time?

I found out I was crying again. The bloodhunger curdled inside me, and thick, hot tears mixed with cold rain. I was covered in mud, and I'd just managed to lead the vampires to the only thing I had left.

Was there anything I wouldn't destroy just by breathing near it?

I bent over, hugging myself, and sobbed while the storm retreated.

CHAPTER NINE

Christophe drove like he'd been born in the hills, blue eyes narrowed and the mud drying on him as the storm retreated. He worked the wheel, hit the brake as we bounced through a rill of runoff, the light now regular rainy-day gray filtering through the mud-spattered windshield. Graves lit a cigarette and coughed in the backseat. Ash hunched behind me, making a little whining noise every once in a while. At least he was having no trouble shifting back and forth between wulf and boy.

Hurrah for him.

Christophe swore passionlessly as the car skidded, twisted the wheel again. Pale skin showed beneath the rents in his jeans and sweater. I wiped at my cheeks with the flat of my muddy hand. The broken window let in a steady stream of cold wet air, and the rain was slowing. Soon it would stop altogether, the sun would come out, and steam would rise in white tendrils from every surface. The roads would look like streams of heavy fog. Juicy green pressed close against the car, no longer pale and leprous under queer yellowgreen stormlight.

"They broke right in," Graves said again, exhaling hard. "Right in, and the place was burning. Jesus." Cigarette smoke mixed with the reek of decaying vampire blood, the fresh copper of other blood, the gritty dark scent of mud. And thin threads of spice, both from Christophe and me.

I was smelling like that place in the mall with the big gooey cinnamon buns. The ones your blood sugar spikes just walking past. Christophe, as usual, smelled like pie filling. I suppose it might've been okay, because it calmed the bloodhunger down. How I could smell anything after so much wet and crying, I don't even know.

But there was also the reek of unwashed werwulf and the thin colorless odor of rage seeping into every surface. The mixture was enough to give you a headache, and my temples throbbed.

Christophe stared through the windshield. A muscle in his cheek ticked steadily. I kept looking at him in little sips, stealing his face. Even covered in mud and blood and rotting black, he was beautiful. Not girl-pretty, or the type of boy-pretty that means a guy's too busy checking his hair in the mirror to pay attention to anyone else. No, Christophe just . . . worked, the planes of his face coming together in a harmony that made him complex and wonderful all at once.

Like that old saying, a sight for sore eyes. My eyes *were* sore, from crying. Glancing at him made it better.

Right now he looked *dangerous*, too. He was pale, and his jaw was set so hard it wasn't too big a stretch to imagine his teeth shattering.

He'd only said two things. *Are you hurt?*

And, when I'd stammered that I wasn't, he'd looked right through me, his jaw working and his eyes cold. *Get in the car.*

Just as I thought about it, Christophe spoke. "*Loup-garou.*"

Graves exhaled hard, again. Another puff of cigarette smell. It made my nose and eyes water uselessly. "Yeah?"

"If you *must* smoke, hand me one."

"Sure thing, man." Graves's hand came over my shoulder; Christophe took the cigarette without looking. He stuck one end in his mouth, cupped his palm around the other. A flick of something in his hand, and he inhaled smoothly. Exhaled a stream of smoke.

He'd just lit it without a lighter. Dad's old friend Augie used to do something pretty much like that. It was a great trick. Maybe someday they'd teach it to me.

Ash whined deep in his throat.

"I know," Christophe said. "Peace, Silverhead. All is well in hand."

I swallowed. My dry throat clicked. "Christophe."

He tilted his head, slightly. Under the mud and water, blond highlights slipped through his hair. His fangs had retreated. "Milady." Quietly. He took another drag, twisted the wheel savagely as we bumped through a shallow stream. He looked like he knew where we were going.

I was glad someone did.

How did you find me? What's going on? Where's the rest of the Order? Are you still mad at me? First things first. "I'm sorry."

He gave me one very blue, almost-startled glance. "For what, *milna?*"

Oh, Jesus Christ. "For . . . for telling you I hated you. For accusing you. For—"

"It is—" He swore again, breathlessly, and hit the gas. We bumped through a screen of underbrush and hit what looked like another overgrown rumrunner's road, and immediately the car settled down. I had a deathgrip on the door, though, and didn't loosen up. Tears still leaked down my cheeks. Wiping them did no good. My head ached, pounding dully, and my eyes burned. The *aspect* had settled into soothing warmth, spreading over my skin and working in layer by layer.

He paused, continued. "It is of no consequence." He relaxed slightly. "You don't smell like blood. Are you hurt?"

I told you I wasn't. But I took stock, looked down at myself. I was covered in filth. The upholstery in here was never going to recover. Safety glass jolted free from my window, tinkling, as we hit a series of washboard ruts. "I'm okay. How did you find—"

"You can hide from the Order, *moj maly ptaszku*. You can even hide from my father, God willing. But me? No. Not from me." Amazingly, he grinned. It was a fey expression, eyes glittering and lips pulled back; it was like he was sparring again. And enjoying himself. "Just glad I reached you in time."

I tried loosening up on the door. No dice, my fingers didn't want to let go. "The Order—"

"Would you like to call in? They will be overjoyed to hear from you." Why did he sound so goddamn amused?

Everything I wanted to say rose up inside me, got tangled up, and settled in my throat like an acid-coated rock. Christophe gave me another glance. With the cigarette, he looked a little older, nineteen-twenty instead of a youngish eighteen. *Djamphir* are mostly too graceful and pretty to be believable. Even smeared with mud and guck, his clothes torn up and the rage burning in him, he looked great. He looked completely in control of the situation.

Thank God. Relief made every tight-strung nerve in me go loose, all at once. "What, so someone there can hand one of us over to the vampires again? No thanks."

On the other hand, the Order was good protection. Mostly.

He shrugged, mud crackling as it dried on him. His hair dripped on his shoulders, the blond highlights slipping back through it as his *aspect* slowly retreated. "I shouldn't have trusted Leontus. The fault is mine."

Well, I wasn't about to start throwing stones. "I trusted him too." My voice caught. I decided to leave it at that.

"Where are we going?" Graves piped up.

Christophe shrugged. "To clean up and rest. Milady needs food, and—"

"Don't call me that." The words bolted out of me. I hung onto the door as if I was drowning. "Jesus, Christophe. Please."

"What, no taste for formality?" We jolted over more washboard ruts, but the road was much drier. Of course, here on this side of the ridge the storm hadn't fallen so hard. "As you like, *moja ksiezniczko*. There's a decent-sized town not too far. We'll acquire transport and supplies; this car won't last long."

Great. "All our supplies were in the house." I sounded numb. The words wouldn't go together quite right. "Gran's house. They just . . . it's burning. There was so much rain; why was it burning?"

"Either they thought you were still inside, or it was fired to deny you shelter." His expression turned grim, no amusement remaining. He kept pulling at the cigarette, too, like it personally offended him. "Your *loup-garou* perhaps thought to hold them off by himself. Foolish."

Graves took the bait. "Fuck off." The command under the words—a *loup-garou*'s mental dominance—made all the space in the car shrink, hot and tight. I craned my neck, looking over my shoulder. He was sitting right behind Christophe, his cigarette held to his mouth and his other hand a fist against his tattered, mud-coated knee. "How do we know you didn't lead them here, *Reynard*?"

Christophe was silent, but his hand tightened on the wheel.

"Quit it. Both of you." I swallowed again. The tingling in my fangs was going down, thank God. I didn't have to hold my tongue carefully or try to talk with my lips kept stiffly over my teeth. "Let's just all get along, all right? And *not* do the vampires' work for them."

"Anything for you, Dru," Christophe said, level and cold. "And I mean that. Now be quiet and let me concentrate."

Graves stared at me, his eyes gone dark. He and Christophe were running neck and neck in the mad sweepstakes, it looked like. I'd never seen Goth Boy look so blackly furious.

"Hey." I worked my left hand free, reached into the backseat. "Graves. *Graves.*"

He was shaking, I realized. His long black coat was gone—had it been inside the house? He looked odd without it, kind of. But the skull-and-crossbones earring glittered in his ear. It gave me a funny feeling, seeing that gleam.

Like I'd lost something.

His T-shirt was a mess of rips and tears, and the bruising on his face was going down. Werwulfen, even *loup-garou* who don't get hairy, don't wear the damage long. Not if they can rest and eat. The physical injuries healed right up.

Now I wondered about the hurts inside, where that healing wouldn't reach.

Ash whined again, softly, in the back of his throat.

Before I knew it, I was up on my knees in the passenger seat, twisting around. "Graves. Look at me. *Look.*" He *was* looking at me, but I wanted him to see me. He looked . . .

Jesus. He looked angry, and scared, and like he was a short breath away from hurting someone. His irises were almost black, so dark I had trouble seeing what his pupils were doing.

"Dru." He rolled his window down, chucked the still-fuming cigarette. "Don't worry about me. Put your seat belt on."

Say what? "You look—"

A shrug, his shoulders moving under the wet, filthy T-shirt. A faint gleam of green came back into his irises. He shook his head, hard, like he was dislodging a nasty thought. Water flew from the ends of his hair. "Sucker-boy up there pisses me off. Mellow down easy, everything's copacetic."

"Graves—"

"Sit down." The rage faded. Now he just looked tired and irritated, and his eyes flushed with green glow again. His stubble had gotten thicker since this morning—I'd always thought half-Asians didn't get much in the way of facial hair, but it looked like he was changing all that. "Put your seat belt on. Don't make me worry about you while that asshole's driving, okay?"

I was too tired to fight. I did it. Then I curled up against the door and shook while Christophe drove, Graves seethed, and Ash eventually stopped making that noise. When we broke out of the woods and bumped up onto the highway, the sun burst out from behind the clouds, and I closed my eyes.

CHAPTER TEN

The **Holiday Inn** shower was a little piece of heaven. And afterward, dry clothes were a luxury. Just a black T-shirt and jeans, no underthings, but I wasn't complaining. You can always buy panties later, you just can't buy them if you're dead.

And Christophe had gotten the right sizes, too. That was food for thought, but I didn't want to eat it. I had enough to chew.

As soon as I was out of the bathroom, Graves nipped in. Christophe was still rubbing at his hair with a hotel towel, standing by the room's window and peering out through the small crack in the cheap curtains. A thin bar of sunlight striped his face, and he glanced at me. A faint smile touched his lips.

"You've bloomed." He didn't sound surprised. Just pleased, and congratulatory.

Well, hallelujah. At least *someone* noticed when my face changed and the rest of me did too.

Ash crouched in a corner. He was still covered in mud, and I had to figure out how to get him cleaned off just as soon as Graves was out. There was a stack of towels on one twin bed, I grabbed one and started working at my own hair. I had a comb in my bag, thank God.

"Yeah." To be warm and dry was pretty much all I could ask for right now. "I know, I look different. It's pretty weird."

"Weird?" He let the towel drop, dangling from his hand. He'd taken care of everything, getting a room, cleaning up a little and vanishing for twenty minutes while Graves prowled the room and Ash crouched in the corner and I stared longingly at the bathroom, reappearing with a few crackling Walmart bags and a brand-new messenger bag slung across his new black V-neck T-shirt. One of the shopping bags he'd pushed into my hands and told me to wash up. *We can wait. Go.*

It hadn't occurred to me to argue.

"You know, my face is all different. I look strange." I dropped down on the bed closest the wall; I was betting Christophe had put my bag there so I would stay where he wanted me.

Away from the door and the windows.

It was a sobering thought. To add to all my other happy-dappy thinking.

"You're beautiful." He said it so flatly I almost missed the meaning of the words. "As always, *kochana*. Room service should be up soon."

All the breath left me in a rush. "Christophe . . ."

He turned his back completely to the window. And even though he'd been working at his hair with a towel, he still looked impossibly *finished*, the blond highlights in his layered cut behaving perfectly. The faint traces of mud and damp still on him looked planned, too. "I'll ask for an explanation once you've eaten. Just so I know what's going on. But let's get something straight, first."

Mud still clung to his boots, and he paced across the room toward me, tossing the towel onto the other bed. Ash rocked back on his heels, watching carefully, his eyes flaring orange and his expression flickering between somber and . . . was it frightened?

I couldn't tell.

Christophe bent down, his booted toes precisely placed in front of my bare feet. A warm draft of apple-pie scent drifted across me. It was so familiar I could've started crying again. I'd gotten so used to that smell over the past few months.

I hadn't realized how much I missed him. Most of all, I missed the sense of someone watching, the sense that I could just relax and someone else would handle things. It's not that I'm weak.

Okay, well, maybe I am. But I don't think so. I just think, you know, I was Dad's helper. He told me what to do, where to stand, how to act. I missed knowing my place in the world. With Christophe there, I had a little of that back.

Just enough to start feeling like I could relax, maybe. A little. "I, um . . ."

"I don't like your *loup-garou.*" Even now he wouldn't refer to Graves by name. Christophe's nose was inches from mine, and his eyes were cold. Winter eyes, like Dad's but without the faint lavender lines in the irises. His skin was flawless, very faint shadows of grass stain looking like decorations instead of dirt. You can't really wash grass juice off without scrubbing. "He's deadweight you're better off without, and suspect besides. I envy him your loyalty. But I do not betray *anyone* to my father. When I want to kill someone, I kill directly. Do you understand?"

There wasn't enough air in the room, what with him leaning in like that. "Christophe . . ." I tried for another word, but my brain just up and failed me. "Chris . . ."

He touched a wet curl that had fallen in my face, brushed it back. His skin was warm; I could tell just by the heat of it reaching my own. He very carefully did not touch my cheek.

Instead, I felt his fingers on my wrist. He lifted my right hand, dropped something very small into my palm, and closed my fingers around it. Two something smalls, with sharp edges.

"I don't have to like your *loup-garou* for you to trust me, do I?" Whispered, his lips softly moving.

I wanted to nod, or shake my head, or something. Couldn't move. Could barely even breathe. He was so close, and the pulse in his throat called out to me. If I got close enough, if I drove my fangs in and felt his blood scorching my tongue again, would I hear him in my head the same way I heard Anna? Why didn't I *now*?

He leaned forward, and for one mad moment I thought he was going to kiss me. Instead, he pressed his lips to my forehead and inhaled. A shudder went through him.

"*Moj boze*," he whispered, his lips moving against my skin. I was shaking too, now. "Thank God you are still breathing."

Someone knocked at the door. I jumped, Ash twitched, and Christophe was across the room in a heartbeat. He was just so god-damn *fast*. "Relax." And he was back to sounding amused. "It's food."

I opened my fingers while he unlocked the door.

There, in my palm, two diamond studs glittered. I'd left one in my room at the Schola. It must have been how he tracked me, some-how. The other one I'd left on the table in Gran's house.

Gran's burning house. Christophe had been inside when they attacked? With Graves, maybe?

I closed my fist up tight. Ash was on his feet now, nose lifted and his eyes settling down, and Graves was deathly quiet in the bathroom.

He could probably hear everything Christophe said to me.

Great. Just . . . great.

* * *

I laid the legal pad on the table, suppressed a burp that reeked of bacon. Club sandwiches are pretty standard everywhere you go, and I'd wolfed this one so fast I'd barely tasted it. The french fries were all right, though, when doused with enough ketchup. "This is what I've got. Routes, alternate routes, stops to get liquid resources, the works."

Christophe glanced over it, riffling the pages. "Good work. You're heading to California?" He hadn't eaten, but he'd gotten enough food for six people. The bill was going to be sky high.

It was a relief to find something that really wasn't my problem. It was damn near Christmas, as a matter of fact.

Ash was busy demolishing the last plate of steak and eggs, crouched on the bed. Graves ate a bacon cheeseburger more slowly, each bite carefully chewed, watching us with narrowed eyes. He'd refused to sit at the table, folding himself down with his back braced against the bed closest the door.

I shrugged. "For now, yeah. I know how to run. There's . . ." I hesitated. "I'm not going back to the Order."

Christophe shrugged. He said nothing. Just watched me.

Oh, what the hell. I might as well tell him. "There's a hunter in Carmel. One of Dad's contacts. He hunts suckers with his gang. Figured he was the best choice out of all Dad's friends. I can't tell which of them were *djamphir* like August, or which would . . . well, I just figure Remy's safest. Plus he's all the way across the country, and we didn't spend long in California any time we were there. We were mostly below the Mason-Dixon. Hell, we spent more time with

August than we did . . ." I swallowed hard. *Plus, if I have to, I can go over the border to Tijuana and points south. Chupacabras and cockroaches and nasty things, but at least it'll be harder to track me there, and Juan-Raoul will help me.*

It was an effort to keep my mouth shut. I was doing the nervous-talky thing, and that never works out well.

Christophe nodded. "Good thinking. By tomorrow I'll have more cash and a car that won't attract suspicion; I've already disposed of the other."

I immediately fastened on that. "We're without transport tonight? What if —"

"I have a backup plan." He actually rolled his eyes, a very teenage movement. "Have a little faith in me. Besides, none of the *nosferatu* escaped yesterday. I'm fairly certain we have another night before we're tracked here." He flipped back to the beginning of the legal pad, drew the atlas over, and opened it to the page number I had listed next to our first stop.

"You're sure none of them escaped?" My palms were suspiciously damp, and not just because it was eighty-eight degrees and a hundred percent humidity out there. I'd thought my hair would frizz, but no. The ringlets lay sleek and veined with blonde, though if I braided them back they would slip free. I didn't even have a piece of string to tie them up with; the one I'd been using before was probably still up in the meadow, lying in the mud.

At least my hair covered up the diamond studs. Yes. I'd put them back in.

Why not? At least Christophe never wavered. He was always the same. Maddening, opaque, kind of creepy because he was so much older and stuck in a teenage body . . . but he never did a 180 on me. I never had to guess whether he liked me or not.

What are you thinking, Dru?

"I'm certain." He sounded so absolute. What would it be like to be that sure of everything? He never seemed nervous or like he was going to change his mind about me.

"Thanks." It sounded pale and inadequate even as soon as it left my mouth. "For everything."

"An honor, and a pleasure." He didn't even look up. "How did you escape Sergej?"

I shivered at the name. Ash looked up, watchful. Graves's shoulders hunched. He stared at his plate instead of me now.

Well, I guess Christophe had to ask. And an explanation was the least I owed him.

My mouth was dry. "Anna . . . she was there. And her Guard. They were all locked up. We . . . Leon was there too. I hit him pretty hard, I stabbed S-Ser—" I couldn't say the name. Not after the warehouse and that dark little room, where he'd just *appeared.* "I stabbed *him.*"

"With a lamp," Graves supplied helpfully. "Then we got the hell out of there."

He didn't mention me sucking Anna's blood. He also didn't mention coming back and shooting the king of the vampires.

Saving my life.

I found out I was twisting my hands together. My teeth tingled faintly, remembering, and I smelled smoke. "Graves came back for me. The whole place was burning. Anna and her Guard, well, they vanished. We were outside, and Ash found us."

"I should have followed the Silverhead." Christophe set the atlas down, flipped through the legal pad again. "God knows *he* can find you. Which is a mystery. And he is Broken no longer."

"That happened before. At the Prima. Right before Leon . . . He showed me . . ." I ran out of words. Pulled my legs up, bracing my heels on the chair, and hugged my knees. *He made me think you'd handed Graves over to Sergej. Because of me. And I believed it.* "Anyway, I got off the Schola grounds and you know the rest."

"Some of it." He kept looking at my handwriting. The pages riffled a little, because a tremor had gone through him. "We'd gone to rescue the *loup-garou,* but it was one of the decoys. You were headed straight for another decoy. It was a neatly laid trap."

Which brought up another question. "Did you find . . . Is Leon . . ." Yeah, Leon had handed me over to the king of the vampires, and I'd been pretty sure he was dead in that dark little room. So had Graves.

But still. He was *djamphir,* not sucker. I kind of hoped he'd made it out somehow.

"Dead. Or I would have finished him myself. My father fled, gravely wounded. I was convinced you were still alive. Perhaps the Order has finished searching the wreckage for your remains."

He said it so calmly. The club sandwich was revolving in my stomach. I swallowed hard, trying to convince it to stay down. "Does Bruce think I'm dead too?"

Christophe shrugged. He set the pad down. "It's almost sundown. I'm going to go make a few preparations. I trust I can ask you to remain here, and you'll listen?"

I nodded. "Unless more vampires show up." It tried to be a joke, fell flat. I hugged my knees even tighter. The T-shirt rode up. All my weight was distributed differently. I didn't even know who I was anymore.

But Christophe looked at me, blue eyes soft and direct. I'd never seen him look at another person that way. Even in the *true-seeins* where he looked at my mother like he wanted to . . .

Kind of like he wanted to eat her. No, that's the wrong word.

Like he wanted to *consume* her, pull her in and just assimilate her somehow. But he looked at me like he was *seeing* me. Really, truly seeing Dru Anderson, not just the shell I put up for the world.

He pushed his chair back and rose in one fluid motion. "I'll be back before dark." He scooped his new bag up and brushed past me. But his hand came down, and he touched my shoulder as he passed.

It was like he'd poured something hot and strong into me. A flush that worked down to my bones instead of staying on my skin like the *aspect*.

He paused at the door. Looked back over his shoulder, and it was as if we were the only two people in the room. "Keep this locked."

A blast of humid air, the sunlight flooding in as he stepped out onto the walkway, and he was gone. The air conditioning kicked up a notch. Down here in the valley with the concrete, it was approaching the hottest part of the afternoon-into-evening. Up on the ridges there would be some wind, at least, and the creek and the trees.

And a burned-out shell of a house. I now owned nothing but the land, and not even that until I was eighteen. I'd always had this thought of moving up there after I was finished with school or something, just retreating from everything. Maybe trading hex-breaking and stuff for food, like Gran had. You could just scrape by in that part of the country. Everyone up in the hills pretty much "just scraped by."

As life dreams go, I know it sucks. But it was my little dream, and now it was a charred mess. Just like everything else.

A wave of shaking slid through my bones, jostling around like my body hadn't decided whether or not it was going to pitch a fit.

Ash kept chewing, staring bright-eyed at me. He was still filthy, and I had to coax him into a shower somehow. Christophe had even brought clothes for *him*. He'd thought of everything.

"Dru?" Graves moved, like he was going to unfold himself from the side of the bed. "You okay?"

Don't ask. "I . . ." My eyes prickled. "I don't know."

He stripped his hair back from his face with stiff fingers. But he wasn't looking at me. "He was there. Right before the . . . the vampires hit."

"You lost your coat." I let my hair fall down, because the prickling turned to hot water and welled up. I couldn't blink it back.

Jesus. The crying needed to stop, and *now*.

Graves coughed slightly. "It's okay. It's a thousand degrees out there; I don't need it. Dru, we have to talk."

Oh, Jesus. Every time we have to talk, I end up more confused than before. I can't take this. "Not now." I bounced up, swiping at my eyes. "Come on, Ash. Let's get you cleaned up."

CHAPTER ELEVEN

t was another Subaru, but blue, and newer than the one we'd stolen. Power windows, power locks, plenty of cargo space, and it smelled faintly of vanilla from the air freshener hanging from the rearview. Dawn was gray in the east, the whole world was greenjuice fresh, and it was going to be another scorcher. You could just tell by the way your clothes stuck to you as soon as you stepped outside.

I didn't know if Christophe had slept. I'd curled up in the bed furthest from the door and fell into a darkness so deep I couldn't even remember any dreams. When I'd closed my eyes Christophe had been standing looking out the window; when I opened them he was in a chair at the table, writing on the legal pad. A chunky silver watch gleamed on his wrist, and the window was just graying up with the sunrise. He glanced up, and saw that I was awake.

We were out the door fifteen minutes later.

I folded my hands around the paper latte cup. Christophe turned the air conditioning up a bit. The tires made a low sweet sound on the road, and if I shut my eyes, I could almost pretend I was driving with Dad.

But the silence with Dad had never been this angry, or this dangerous.

Ash curled up on his half of the backseat, impossibly small. Graves hunched in his seat, holding an americano and staring out the window like the answer to world peace was in the passing scenery. I lasted about twenty minutes before flipping the radio on to fill up the silence, twisting the dial until I found an oldies station. Graves lasted about a half hour after that before he cracked the window and lit a cigarette. Christophe restrained himself, but I saw his jaw set.

It was a ways to California. Something told me this was gonna be a long trip.

* * *

"God," I moaned, with feeling. "Not pizza. Please. I can't take more fast food."

"What's wrong with pizza?" Graves wanted to know. "Lots of cheese, bubbling grease, pepperoni—"

"Ugh." I laced my fingers over my stomach. "No pizza, Christophe. No burgers either. I want to eat somewhere *nice*." My conscience pinched. "If we can afford it. Or hell, let's get a place with a kitchenette and I'll cook."

Yeah, I was desperate.

Christophe squinted through the fall of afternoon sunlight. It was hotter than hell, and the air conditioning wasn't helping as much as it could. Trapped in the car for ten hours with a few bathroom breaks, lunch had been McDonald's, and I was about ready to go nuts. It would have been hilarious if I was watching it on TV.

"Don't worry about that. We'll go somewhere nice," Christophe said wearily. "As soon as we find shelter for the night. We've made good time."

"Thank *God*." I realized I was sounding whiny, but right at that point I didn't care. I wanted out of the car, and I wanted a real meal. I'd settle for something unfried, or something that bore a resemblance to actual food rather than hockey-puck patties on anemic buns paired with soggy-ass extruded potato starch.

"In fact . . ." Christophe checked the exit numbers and eased us off the highway. "We can arrange pizza for the wulfen and I can find you some decent Mexican food. At least, if my memory serves me."

It sounded like heaven. "We can all do Mexican." I wasn't about to leave Ash somewhere he could get into mischief.

"Whatever you want." He didn't sound too thrilled with the notion, and he brought us to a stop at the light at the end of the ramp.

Graves coughed. "Pizza's fine. I'll run herd on Ash."

Say what? I didn't twist around in the seat to look at him, but it was close. "We should stick together. The vampires."

"They won't be after *us*. Besides, suckboy and I don't get along. We might as well split up for a bit." There was the click of a lighter.

How much was he going to smoke? I shifted in my seat again, all cooped up and itchy. "How much have you smoked today?"

"What are you, my mother?"

Well, if you're going to be snide . . . "Do wulfen get lung cancer?" I addressed the question to the windshield. Tucked a curl behind my ear.

"Never." Christophe stared at the stoplight, waiting for the left-turn arrow to change to green. "Most don't like the smell of burning, though."

"I wondered about that." Now I could casually turn my head, glance in the backseat. But Graves was staring out the window, his chin set stubbornly. "Come on, Graves. Mexican. I bet Christophe can even get us margaritas if he smiles at the waitress."

For some reason, that was the totally wrong thing to say.

"Underage drinking—" Christophe began.

"He makes my stomach hurt." Graves interrupted flatly. "Jesus, Dru. Give me some *space*."

"Space?" *Fine.* "I'll give you all the space you want, *Edgar*."

The instant it was out of my mouth I regretted it.

The arrow turned green, Christophe hit the gas. He was wearing a very slight smile. The golden light of late afternoon was kind to him.

Graves said nothing. I didn't dare look back now. I was already kicking myself.

But the anger had my mouth, and it wasn't backing down. "They had a file on you back at the Schola Prima." There. An explanation, to smooth things over. Maybe.

He wasn't looking for explanation. "Must've been good reading."

"I didn't read it. I just heard your first name." I felt defensive, and I deserved it.

"You were at school with me, you must've heard it before then."

It was official. He was looking for a fight. I was about half-tempted to give him one, too. "I didn't pay attention."

"Yeah." Now he sounded vindicated. "I know. Still don't."

I pay attention when you say you love me. Then I pay attention when you get all rejective on me. I pay plenty of attention, Graves. You just can't make up your stupid little mind. It took a monstrous effort to keep the words behind my teeth.

"*Be the bigger person*," Gran was always saying. But she'd never had to put up with *this*.

"That's enough." Christophe slowed down, getting a little closer to the back bumper of the Ford Explorer in front of us than I liked. "There's a good hotel around here. Be quiet so I can find it, children."

"We're not children." Graves bristled.

"Compared to me, you might as well be, psychological standards for *djamphir* trapped in teenage bodies notwithstanding." Christophe could've sounded more dismissive, maybe. If he tried. He glanced up at the signs around us, sighed.

Just like Graves could've sounded nastier, maybe. If he'd tried. "Including Dru?"

"Milady Dru is startlingly mature." Christophe hung a right. Concrete rose up around us, and we slid into welcome shade. Air conditioning doesn't help sometimes when it's *really* humid. "And she has plenty of time."

"What, to grow into dating you?" Graves actually laughed, a bitter little bark both like and unlike the sarcastic half-snort he'd used before. When he was a normal kid. Or at least a human kid.

Even I couldn't believe he'd said it. I sucked in a breath. Christophe slowed down, changed lanes, and the air inside the car was even more tense. Ash was completely silent, and I would've bet anything he was watching Graves and Christophe with bright interest, tipping his head back and forth like he was observing a tennis match.

"I'm not—" I began.

"That's really none of your business, *loup-garou*. Milady Dru does as she pleases, and owes us no explanation."

I really wish you wouldn't call me Milady. How the hell had this gotten so serious all of a sudden? "Look—" I began.

"I'd say it's my business." Graves exhaled smoke again. I smelled exhaust, concrete, and anger; my head began to hurt. "I'd say it's most *definitely* my business."

"And I would say you're lucky to still be breathing, dog." Christophe took another turn, left this time, stamping on the gas like it'd personally offended him. "After what I caught you doing."

"What?" I twisted in my seat, stared at Christophe. "Come on, both of you. This isn't the time—"

"Go ahead." Graves's cigarette was fuming and his eyes were dark again. Tension rippled under his skin, the Other shining through. "Tell her whatever you want. God knows half the shit that comes out of your mouth is a lie by omission anyway. Maybe I should tell her what *I* know, huh?"

"Certainly. Tell her what you think you know." Christophe simply checked the street signs. Traffic started closing around us. The air conditioner blew a steady stream of chill at me, but it wasn't helping with the hot tension in here. "And I shall tell her that you were preparing to leave her to the tender mercies of Sergej's assassins. Running away with your tail between your legs—"

I lost my temper. "Both of you *shut up!*" The car actually rocked on its springs, as if Christophe had touched the brakes. Ash let out a whimper. My mother's locket was a spot of soothing heat, and I found out I was outright clutching it. Like a maiden auntie with a string of pearls.

Wonder of wonders, miracle of miracles, they both shut their fool mouths. I couldn't even feel good about it.

Tense-ticking silence. My stomach revolted, acid eating through me. We crept through traffic. "This has to stop," I said, finally. "Or I'll ditch *both* of you and go on the run alone." *Or with Ash. He shoplifts, but at least he keeps his mouth shut.* "You're making it easier for the vampires every goddamn time you do this. I'm *tired* of it. Both of you can just go to hell as far as I'm concerned."

Something occurred to me just then. We had a whole continent to drive across. This was only the first day.

The Schola Prima was looking better and better all the time. At least there I had tutors and occasionally some time to myself. When I locked my door and hid under my bed, that is.

Of course, there I'd had to worry about who would sell me to the suckers next. And worry about Graves, missing and presumed tortured. And Christophe pushing me in the sparring room, and outside it shoving me in every direction except the one I wanted to go. Now Gran's house was gone, my last best card gone up in smoke. Nowhere left to go, nowhere to hide, nothing even remotely approaching a safe harbor.

"Shit," I muttered. I pulled my knees up onto the seat, hugged them. If I could just curl up small enough, maybe I could stop the feeling of the world spinning out from under me again. Since that cold Dakota night when I'd dreamed of Gran's owl and didn't tell Dad the next morning, the whole world had started whirling faster and faster. Every time I thought I found something solid, it was yanked away.

Time to grow up, Dru.

Except I'd never felt like a kid. Maybe with Gran, but she never believed in sugarcoating anything. I'd felt grown-up all this time, especially since she . . . died.

No matter how grown-up I felt, though, things kept knocking me around.

The rest of the world didn't think I could drive, or drink anything stronger than a Shirley Temple, or even vote or run my own life. Even though I could canvass the occult network in pretty much any city in the US, take out a poltergeist . . . or be Dad's backup in a house with bleeding walls and howling voices even *he* could hear, a house that was the haunted equivalent of a Venus flytrap.

We'd brought out the little boy who'd wandered in there and returned him to his family, and they'd paid Dad for it . . . but I'd still be treated like a criminal if the cops ever picked me up and found out I was under eighteen. Locked up or locked down, no matter that I was more capable than plenty of so-called adults.

I could face down the king of the vampires in a burning warehouse, but they'd stick me in *high school*. If I ever came to the attention of the authorities, juvie would be the only place they'd think of putting me.

But it wasn't just that. No matter how grown-up I tried to be, there was a place inside me where being grown-up didn't reach. That place was scared and cold and abandoned, and I didn't have the energy to push it down or keep it locked away right now.

Gooseflesh rose all over me in big shivering bumps, and it wasn't helping by the way I was sweating even under the blast of air conditioning.

Fear-sweat.

A draft of sticky cinnamon scent boiled up from my skin. Why was I smelling like *them*? Like Christophe, with his apple-pie cologne, and Anna, with her flowery reek of spoiled carnations.

And that was another thing. I'd heard Anna clearly, inside my head. She'd all but forced me to drink her blood. What the hell was *that*? Nothing Gran ever said prepared me for something like this. Not even drinking from Christophe's wrist while I almost died from a gunshot wound had given me a clue.

"Dru." Graves reached through the space between seats. His hand closed around my shoulder, gently enough I could ignore the iron strength running underneath his skin. "Hey. I'm sorry. It's okay, all right? It's okay. Don't."

Ash whined again, in the very back of his throat. *He* was depending on me, and I'd gotten Graves into this too. I was sucking at getting them out and keeping them safe, despite trying as hard as I could.

No matter what I did, no matter how hard I tried, it just wasn't enough.

Christophe glanced at me. There was a faint sound—he'd swallowed, audibly. "Graves." He shifted a little in the seat, took a left. "I apologize."

I put my head down on my knees. Tried to breathe deeply.

"No problem." At least Graves didn't sound angry. Or grudging. "I, uh, well. We'll get to a hotel soon, right?"

Christophe hit the brakes, eased up. The car crept forward. "Very soon."

"I'll keep track of Ash. We'll get room service. You take Dru and get her something good. Something nice, you know?" Graves squeezed my shoulder, but gently. I guess he was trying to be comforting.

Too bad I was past being comforted.

"I think she needs to rest for a while," Graves continued. "She's, uh, pretty broken up. About the house. The fire."

I'm right here, I wanted to yell. *Don't talk* around *me, for Christ's sake.*

But I didn't care. They could do whatever they were going to do. I had enough to deal with, keeping my stomach from emptying itself all over the dash. Keeping the screaming inside me locked down in my throat where it couldn't come out and break every window in the car.

"She . . . has had a difficult time of it." Christophe spaced the words evenly. Neutral.

The space inside the car relaxed. I kept breathing into my knees, my eyes shut tight. The engine purred along, smoothly, carrying us all.

We finally made a sharp right, tires bouncing a little.

Christophe let out a long breath. "Here we are. Four Seasons, at your service."

"Swank. Can we afford this?" Graves actually sounded grudgingly impressed.

"Of course. Nice rooms, discreet staff, quiet. Just the thing." Christophe brought the car to a stop, nice and easy. "Let me do the talking. Just stay behind me, and try not to look . . . well, never mind."

I made up my mind I wouldn't care. Breathed into the comforting hollow between my jean-clad knees, wished the dark could last forever.

"Dru." Mocking and businesslike, Christophe was back to his old self. It was almost a relief. "We're going to have to check in, *kochana*."

Graves's hand fell away from my shoulder.

I braced myself and looked up, blinking furiously.

It *was* swank. Money breathed out of the fake adobe, and there were valets already perking up to attention. The doorman, a tall man with chocolate skin and a snappy dark blue suit jacket, eyed our car. His tie was a vivid flash of red. All the colors were too intense, crowding in through my eyes and pressing into my brain.

Dad would hardly ever have stayed in a place this nice. He had some ideas about the constitutionality and advisability of valet parking. But occasionally, he'd take me so I knew what to expect and how to get in and out of a nicer class of hotels.

My voice wouldn't work quite right. My cheeks were wet. "I don't think I'm dressed for this." *We'll stick out. Oh, God, will we ever stick out here.*

"Don't worry." Awkward for the first time, Christophe actually patted my elbow. The awkwardness passed, and his face smoothed. He actually looked ready to handle this. "You look lovely. Stay here, let me open your door."

Chapter Twelve

Christophe took control, quietly and efficiently. One look from him and the doorman and bellhops snapped to attention, the valet took our car, and our luggage—such as it was—was unloaded with alacrity. The desk clerk had murmured something about a standing reservation, and we'd been whisked upstairs inside of two minutes. Christophe tipped the bellhop, saying something in a low voice, and pushed me gently toward the huge granite-tiled bathroom to freshen up. Clean clothes arrived like a genie had ordered them, so as soon as I got out of the shower there was a new pair of designer jeans and a navy-blue silk T-shirt. I used the hotel soap with abandon, scrubbing away the sweat-film, and tried not to cry. It didn't work. I was leaking.

The restaurant was Italian, within walking distance, and the type of place Dad wouldn't have touched with a ten-foot pole. The kind where they have eight different sorts of forks ranked alongside your plate, sneering waiters, and a ties-are-not-optional dress code.

The "Italian" extended to a sort of indoor courtyard full of lush greenery. I guess you could even call it a grotto, what with the statues. *Naked* statues, in glaring white marble.

The expensively suited maitre d' had held my seat and laid a green linen napkin decorously in my lap, discreetly not mentioning that I was on a slow leak. Christophe pretended not to notice, and as soon as he settled himself and the water glasses—actual goblets full of crushed ice and a paper-thin slice of lemon arranged just so— were filled, he picked up the menu and examined it critically.

I wiped at my cheeks. The tables were all screened off, either by potted plants or by trellises with climbing vines. All the trouble of air conditioning, and this place was still trying to coax plants to grow inside. I wondered who watered them, and a sharp high giggle died in my throat.

"The décor is awful," Christophe finally said, evenly. "But the concierge swears the food is good. Do you want wine?"

I shook my head. My hair, still damp, slid against my shoulders. It wasn't even worth tying back. The *aspect* was a warmth just under my skin, easing the cramping stiffness of sitting in a car all day.

I cleared my throat. The hum of conversation and clinking of forks against dishes was low music. "The clothes." I sounded rusty. "Where did you—"

One corner of his mouth quirked up. "I have my methods. Hmm. A primavera for you, probably. Something light. Do you object if I order?"

Another shake of my head. Christophe was immaculate again, and the maitre d' hadn't blinked at what either of us were wearing. Then again, the jeans were designer, Christophe's habitual paper-thin black sweater was obviously expensive, and Christophe himself had the easy elegance of a fashion magazine come to earth.

I was distinctly outclassed. And how creepy was it that he'd figured out my new sizes? Did they teach that at the Schola? How to size up a girl's hips with a glance?

Not that I was complaining, really. But still. It was another thing to try not to think about.

"I think *I* prefer steak. We'll start with bruschetta, unless you're a calamari fan . . . no? Very well. What do you want to drink, if not wine?"

"They won't give me wine." It was a scandalized whisper. I scrubbed at my cheeks with my fingers, trying to make the tears stop. Thankfully, they were drying up. "Jesus, Christophe!"

That earned me one amused glance. "They'll give you whatever I say. You worry too much. No matter. What do you want?"

"Diet Coke. If they have it." I didn't mean to sound snide. It was actually a relief that he looked so unaffected. The tight ball of panic inside me eased a little. It smelled nice in here—green and fresh and garlicky. Expensive. Quiet, like there was no way a vampire would ever burst in and tear the place up.

He just shrugged, still staring at the menu. "Ruins the palate, but all right. Dru—"

I was saved by a quick little brown penguin of a waiter rolling up to the table. He reeled off the specials in heavily accented English, and Christophe's eyes actually lit up. He laid the menu down, folded his hands, and busted out something that sounded like Italian.

The waiter looked shocked for a second, but then they started gabbling like old friends. A busboy in a snow-white jacket brought a plate of crusty, steaming bread slices and a little crock thing of butter, a decanter of olive oil and one of balsamic vinegar, as well as a small terra-cotta tub that reeked of heavenly roasted garlic. He also set down two wineglasses and vanished.

The table was going to get crowded if this kept up.

Christophe handed the menus back to the waiter, who actually *bowed* and backed away.

I grabbed for my water glass. It sloshed a little, because my hand was shaking. "What was all that?"

"He's Neapolitan; I wanted to practice. Just relax." Christophe glanced over my shoulder, and I realized he was sitting where Dad would've, if Dad could've been persuaded to set foot in here. I was tucked back out of sight behind a lattice full of what had to be grape leaves, but Christophe could see almost the whole restaurant, including the opening where the waiters and busboys flowed back and forth like minnows, with efficient little bustling movements. "Have some bread. They spread the garlic on it. *Nosferat* repellant."

"Really?" I perked up a little at that.

His face changed slightly. "No. It was a joke. Although the Maharaj have a prohibition against eating garlic. And leeks. But only for their few women."

I shivered. We hadn't covered Maharaj very much at the Schola— they were a third-year-class item, like command-and-control systems and the really in-depth Paranormal Physiology courses. And that was when you started learning combat sorcery, too.

The Maharaj were great at sorcery.

For a moment I remembered my bedroom in the Dakotas and the dreamstealer hissing, and the seizures locking every muscle in my body until Christophe threw water over me. I'd found out enough from my tutors at the Schola Prima to shudder at just how much his quick thinking had saved my life.

"*Moj boze.*" Christophe sighed, laid his hands on the table. Nice, capable hands, his nails clean and the chunky silver watch on his wrist glittering sharply. That was pretty new—he usually didn't wear jewelry. "I am clumsy today. Forgive me. I meant to make you smile."

I wiped at my cheeks again with my free hand, took a gulp of cold water. At least the slow leaking from my eyes had stopped. I let out a long shaky breath. Wondered how Ash and Graves were getting on in the cold, palatial hotel room. "It's not your fault. I just . . ."

I groped for words. He was quiet, head tilted, all his attention focused on me. I'd almost forgotten what that felt like, the way he leaned in and listened.

It was . . . comforting. I set the goblet down, condensation slippery against my tear-damp fingers. Reached for a piece of bread, even though my stomach was still a tight-clenched fist. "I wish you and Graves could get along." There. We could talk about that. Why not? It couldn't get any worse, could it?

I almost winced. It probably could.

Christophe looked down. Touched one of the heavy forks set at his place with a fingertip. "Why him?" He pushed the fork a quarter inch out of place, moved it back. The *aspect* slid through his hair, slicking it down and eating the blond highlights for just a moment before retreating. "Of all the creatures you could choose to have me vie for your affections with, why *him?*"

I really didn't think I had affections to vie for, Chris. But I knew what he was asking. The wulfen were second-class citizens at best, according to the *djamphir*. It bothered me.

A *lot*.

What could I say? That I was miserably confused? That I felt safe when Graves was around, because it felt like there was nothing I couldn't handle as long as he was there, steady as a rock? And that I also felt safe when Christophe was there, because he was scary—and completely on my side? That I'd wanted Graves so bad it hurt, and he'd backed off—and that my hormones staged a revolt and made me blush like an idiot whenever Christophe got close enough to touch me? They were oil and water, and I liked them both, but not together. Together they just messed me up even worse.

The waiter saved me by showing up with a bottle of red wine and pouring a ceremonial dollop for Christophe, who tasted it gravely and made a few comments. The waiter's nose gleamed. He proceeded to pour both of us a glass, set the bottle in a little empty silver bucket on a pedestal near the table, and vanished again.

I stared at the glass of wine like it might bite me. I didn't look anywhere near twenty-one. This was worlds away from jacking a bit of Dad's Jim Beam on nights he was out hunting and I was at home wondering if anyone was going to come back to pick me up.

I'd always been so good at avoiding Boy Tangles. It's easier when you move from place to place—you know not to get attached, and you slide away before a boy can really get his hands on you. But now . . .

Christophe picked up his wineglass. Took a sip like he'd been doing it all his life. Of course, he was older, right? A *lot* older. He set it down with a precise little movement. "I don't want to distress you. I seem to do nothing but. So. I apologize—again. Let's move to other things. Do you like the wine?"

I shrugged. My cheeks were hot. "I'm, uh. I don't know. I've never had it."

"No worries. They'll bring you soda in a moment or two. Take what you like, Dru." He lifted his gaze, and the piercing blue stare was uncomfortable. To say the least. "Take whatever you like. It's all yours. You haven't seen the good side of our world yet. You have time."

What could I say to that? I did try a sip of the wine, but it tasted like paint thinner and I was glad when the Diet Coke showed up. By then, the appetizers had come, and Christophe was asking me about routes and highways. So things got to sounding a little more natural, and I didn't feel like crying.

At least, not much.

CHAPTER THIRTEEN

I came back from the bathroom to find the table cleared, a fresh glass of Diet Coke, and Christophe gazing at another menu with a serious, critical expression. He didn't look up as I lowered myself back onto my seat, praying I hadn't committed any huge crimes against etiquette. They even had mints in the marble-and-watered-silk bathroom, wrapped and gleaming in a fluted-glass dish.

We'd hashed out the next few days of travel and arrangements. If I thought about that—the next few steps—everything else seemed manageable. Especially since Christophe was like Dad. He asked questions without making me feel stupid, decided things pretty fairly but definitely, and listened to my objections and suggestions. There wasn't a lot of waffle in either of them. Gran would've liked that about Christophe.

The thought pinched under my breastbone. I picked up the Coke in its tall, sweating glass and took a long, long gulp.

A funny metallic aftertaste lingered for a moment. Restaurants are like that; there's always something that goes off, even at the most primo place.

"Have you ever had tiramisu? Or do you prefer chocolate?" Christophe lifted the dessert menu a little, offering it to me.

I flattened one hand on my stomach over the silk, as if I had an ache. "Nah, I think I overdid it on the bread. Good food. I don't have much of a sweet tooth, anyway."

"Are you sure?" He looked so hopeful, eyebrows up and his sharply handsome face open and relaxed, that I actually grinned at him.

"All right, I'll take a look. But no promises." I took another few long swallows of Diet Coke, set the glass down. It was seriously metallic-tasting, and I made a face.

"Is something wrong?"

"Nah, it just tastes a little weird. They probably need to change the syrup in the machine." I studied the menu. Half the stuff on it was described in terms that could've won an award for obfuscation. "Who writes this stuff? And what the hell is a compote? It sounds like a car part."

Christophe actually laughed. "Fruit boiled down and sweetened, I believe."

My eyebrows drew together. "And they do this to rhubarb and . . . " I blinked. The letters looked a little fuzzy. "They have chocolate cake." My tongue felt a little fuzzy. Maybe it was the garlic.

"Are you all right?" Christophe tensed.

"Yeah, fine. I think I'm just tired. It's been a long day." I handed the menu back. "Go ahead and get what you want. I might steal a bite of whatever. Although I never did like rhubarb much. It's stringy."

"Very well." He tilted his head, and the waiter reappeared. Christophe watched me while his mouth moved, liquid streams of words in another language. The waiter bobbed again, looking absolutely thrilled but strangely fuzzy too, like I was seeing him on a bad TV set.

I blinked again, furiously, trying to make sense of this. The metallic taste got stronger, breaking over my tongue, and a shiver went down my spine.

Something's wrong.

Christophe didn't seem to notice. He just kept talking to the waiter and finally handed the menu back. Then he folded his hands neatly on the table where his plate had rested, and watched me. Half his glass of wine was still there, and the surface of the liquid trembled.

"Dru?" Now he sounded concerned. "You're pale."

I slumped in the chair, my hands turned to gripping fists on the arms, and the metallic taste crawled down my throat.

Something moved behind me, in the trellis. Christophe said something very softly, but not in Italian. Sounded like Polish, but he pronounced things differently than Augustine. Augie always sounded like he was swearing, and Christophe sounded precise, even with his mouth handling the funny sounds.

I was too occupied trying to stay upright. Someone came around the trellis, stepped up to the table on my side. Someone tall, and slim. I caught a flash of red and my heart leapt into my throat.

It was a caramel-skinned boy with dark glossy hair and liquid dark eyes. He was sharply handsome, but not in the way that yells *djamphir*—the shape of his cheekbones was different, and he had a pointed chin and a proud beak of a nose. A thin gold hoop gleamed in one ear, nestling against the softness of his hair. He wore a loose red T-shirt and chinos, and he spoke in English.

"Slow and sloppy, old man." His accent was different than Christophe's, too. *Indian, maybe. Subcontinent, not American,* I realized through the fuzz my brain had become. "We have three or four minutes. Don't worry. She's just immobile for the moment. Be reasonable, and she'll be none the worse for wear."

"She" means me. *Immobile?* I tried to move, couldn't. Every muscle had seized up. I could barely breathe.

Christophe's eyes flamed with blue. The *aspect* slicked his hair back, and his fangs dimpled his lower lip. He stared at the boy next to me, and his left hand had suddenly tensed, cupped against the trembling table.

It wasn't the table. My legs were shaking, and I had my foot braced against one of the table supports. The shaking communicated itself through the wood, the liquid in Christophe's wineglass sloshing now.

"I came to warn you," the boy continued. "Will you be reasonable?"

Christophe's tone was low, even, and deadly. "If you've harmed her—"

"So it's true, the monk has taken a fall." The boy laughed. "As long as *djrirosha* is administered in the next ten minutes, she'll be fine. Listen, Gogol, for I bear news. Take your *svetocha* and hide as deeply as you can. The Elders have made treaty with your father, and count it well worth the cost."

Gogol? But I knew. That was Sergej's last name. And Christophe's. My heartbeat stuttered. Darkness crept into my peripheral vision.

"The Maharaj and . . ." Christophe actually looked stunned. Blond slipped back through his hair as the *aspect* retreated. "You're mad. Or lying."

Maharaj? A faint, dozy alarm spilled through me. Along with sorcery and breeding nasty things, the *djinni*-children go in for poison. In a big way. And I'd swallowed a bunch of the Coke.

"No, just a traitor to my own kind by telling you this. The Elders have decreed, so the rest of us are helpless. But I bethought myself to come warn you. There are those among us who believe the smaller viper is one we can live with."

"The *Maharaj'rai* are breaking with the Order?" Christophe had gone a weird gray shade under his perfectly polished skin. He looked actually *stunned*. "You're *certain?*"

The boy nodded. His earring winked at me. I strained against the cocoon of fuzz holding my arms and legs down. Sick heat began in my toes, rising up my calves an inch at a time. My fingers felt like sausages in a pan, swelling.

Now I knew what being paralyzed was like. My arms and legs were rigid, concrete instead of flesh. The table had stopped shaking. My breath came in short sipping bursts, my heart fluttering like a hummingbird's wings, and sudden fear that whatever was keeping me from moving would stop me from being able to get any air in at all made me strain to move even harder.

The guy next to me leaned forward a little, and a draft washed over me. Sand, heavy clove spice, and burning. He smelled like he was going to burst into flame at any moment. The *touch* throbbed inside my head. *A heavy, bright blue perfumed flame that would send up ribbons of heavy smoke. That smoke would creep into my lungs and shut them down, and it would turn into a green-glass snake with bright cruel eyes and feathery wings —*

"One moment." The boy made a quick gesture. There was a snap of glass breaking, and Christophe half-rose, the table jolting as he hit it. A cold wind blew over my face, brushing my hair, full of the smell of roses. The iron bands around my chest eased, snapping one by one, and the tingling in my fingers and toes washed away all at once. "Huh. Look at that, her lips are blue. And yet she's still pretty. Pleasant travels, Gogol."

Christophe swore, but the boy vanished on a draft of spice-laden wind. So it wasn't just *djamphir* who could do that. I'd have bet money nobody in the restaurant had even noticed him.

I slumped in the chair, pins and needles ramming through my

limbs. Then Christophe was on his knees, both my nerveless hands in his, his skin so warm it burned. I made an unhappy little sound, a kittenish mewling, had to stop halfway through because I didn't have the air.

But I could breathe again. The back of my throat tasted like metal, and roses. The numb rigidity in my arms and legs started to drain.

Christophe's lips moved, soundlessly. The world went away on a rush of gray tinted with rosy pink, and the *touch* tolled inside my head like a bell.

Maharaj. This is bad news. Seriously bad.

The world came back like a pancake flipped over on a griddle. Christophe, saying my name.

"Dru? Dru. Open your eyes. You can breathe; it's all right." He still had my hands, so hard my bones creaked. I coughed, weakly. Everything was too bright. I swayed a little in the chair.

"Whaaa—" My tongue wouldn't quite obey me. I sounded drunk. Great. We were in a restaurant, I'd just been poisoned or something, and now I sounded three sheets to the wind. *Dad would have a total cow.*

The hard pinching sensation in my chest reminded me that I didn't have to worry about that. Not right now. Not ever again.

And oh God but that was the wrong thing to think.

Something cool and damp touched my cheeks. I blinked. The penguin waiter was dabbing at me with a wet linen napkin, babbling something at Christophe, who gave short choppy answers. He watched me closely, and when I started pulling weakly at his hands, he finally relaxed a bit.

"There, *kochana*. All's well."

Oh, I don't think so. I don't think this is at all well. "I think I want to leave now." It was a high breathy sentence, like a little girl savagely embarrassed at a party or something. "Before something else happens."

"No dessert?" But one corner of his mouth lifted slightly. How he could make an almost smile look so grim was beyond me. "Very well. Come. You can stand. And if you can't, I'll help."

"Will *la signorina* be—" The waiter was having some trouble with this. I didn't blame him.

Christophe said something else, with a rueful expression.

Amazingly, the round brown man chuckled. "*Amore!*" He kissed his fingers and fluttered them in the air and rolled away, still laughing.

Christophe's face fell. "Idiot." He threw some money on the table and practically dragged me out of there.

I didn't have a chance to protest—the ground was heaving underfoot, like a dog's back trying to shake a flea. The wet sticky darkness outside enfolded us, and the jasmine bushes planted outside the restaurant threw their cloying all over me. My stomach revolved, settled unhappily. "Jesus," I whispered. "What did you tell him?"

"I told him I'd proposed to you and you fainted." Christophe sighed. "*Moj boze.* The Maharaj."

"You *what?*" I almost fell over, but Christophe yanked me back onto my feet. Whatever the boy had sprayed in my face had taken care of the poison, I guess—but I wasn't sure, and I didn't like not being sure about something like that.

"It was all I could think of. Come, *moj maly ptaszku*, the open street is no place for you. I must think."

"Who the—what the *hell*—" I couldn't even frame a reasonable question.

"That was Levant. He wanted to be sure I wouldn't attack him until he could give his tidings." Christophe paused. "He is . . . a friend, in his way. As much as a Maharaj can befriend those not of their kind."

"Some friend." My arms and legs began to really work again. My brain kicked over into high gear. Every inch of me tingled unpleasantly, the *aspect* smoothing down over me and burning a little, like I was having a reaction to shellfish or something. "The Maharaj—the dreamstealer, back in—"

"Yes. Their ruling council has thrown in their lot with my father." Christophe's jaw was set. "I must think, Dru. Please."

"I'm not stopping you." I was soaked with sweat, I realized, and shivering uncontrollably despite the heat. Everything was too bright, the streetlamps miniature suns and the half-moon behind scudding clouds like a searchlight. My eyes watered; I kept blinking. "Wait, what? They . . . your *father*? King of the vampires? Don't they—"

"The Maharaj hate us. As far as they are concerned, every scion of the *nosferat*, no matter how distant or how noble, is fit only for extermination. Bruce had convinced them we were the lesser evil, and the more likely to win the war." He set me on my feet again as I stumbled. Breathed something in what I now guessed was Polish, something I was *sure* was a curse just from the way he said it. Then he put his arm over my shoulders and pulled me close. "God and Hell both damn it. This changes things."

I began to get a bad feeling. Or, I guess, the bad feeling I already had got about ten times worse. "What? What does it change?"

He shook his head, sharply, as if dislodging something nasty. "I need to *think, kochana, moja ksiezniczko*. The Order must be warned. And . . ." Maddeningly, he stopped.

"And what? Christophe, come *on*! I just got *poisoned*!" *By the fucking Maharaj! My first one I've ever seen, and he . . . oh, man. Man alive, that was something.*

"Hush." He stopped dead on the street corner. Cars crept by, gleaming, and the hotel rose like a huge white ship a block down. My teeth chattered, and he looked down at me. His face, half-shadowed, was drawn. "I may have to do things you will not like. Do you trust me?"

What a completely ridiculous question. But I guess it wasn't so ridiculous. Less than a week ago I'd yelled that I hated him, and I'd been all ready to believe he'd handed Graves over to . . . to *Sergej.*

The name sent a glass spike of pain through my temples. Why hadn't the *touch* warned me not to drink? I could usually pretty reliably tell if food was safe; there was that one time in Pensacola when Dad had been about to take some tea from a very nice old lady who ran a pretty good occult store. I'd knocked it out of his hand right before she'd started snarling and gibbering in a dead language that made the hair all over me stand up now just remembering it.

She'd thought we were from the Gator Dude—the guy she had a running feud with. We weren't; we'd just been passing through. Now I sort of wondered if I'd made her think we meant bad business instead of just chalking it up to paranoia and the fact that Dad made a lot of people awful nervous.

The metal taste and the reek of roses faded; I turned my head and spat without thinking, to clear it. A shiver broke over me, and I *felt* the drug burn off. Sweat stood out on my skin, acrid as I metabolized whatever he'd dosed me with. Everything on me tingled even more fiercely.

Jesus.

Christophe's arm tightened on my shoulders. "Never mind," he said brusquely, and stepped out into the crosswalk just as the white walk sign flashed. My mother's locket chilled against my chest. "It doesn't matter. Come."

I was exhausted, covered in sweat, and just happy to be breathing. My feet were like concrete blocks, and all I wanted to do was lie down.

Maybe I should've said something, I don't know. But maybe it wouldn't have mattered anyway.

CHAPTER FOURTEEN

The air conditioning was silent, and the room was an ice cube. I didn't mind. Clean and dry, I snuggled under the comforter, crisp white sheets like a cloud, the pillow just right and my knees pulled up.

It felt *great*.

Graves sprawled in a chair near the window, his legs loose and easy, his head tipped back so far it looked like it might fall off. A glimmer of green showed between his eyelids every once in a while. Ash was curled up on the floor, under a comforter pulled from the other bed, the whole messy package wedged into the furthest corner from the door.

Christophe sat cross-legged and straight-backed on the floor at the foot of the bed closest the door, his head bowed as if he was meditating. The shotgun lay in front of him, its blued barrel gleaming slightly in the dark. His *malaika* were arranged, one on either side of him. It should've looked ridiculous.

It didn't.

My tongue stole out, touched my lips. My right hand was curled around my mother's locket. Every once in a while I would rub my thumb over the sharp etching on its back, the weird runic symbols I couldn't decipher. It was usually soothing.

Right now, not so much.

A flash of green from beneath Graves's eyelids. Like he was checking the room.

"Graves?" I whispered.

He didn't move.

"I can tell you're awake." I moved a little bit. The pillow scrunched itself up even more perfectly. "Why don't you lay down?"

He sighed. But quietly. Ash was breathing in deep soft swells, sometimes making a little murmuring sound like a kid in a dream.

"First place they'll shoot if they come through the door," Graves murmured. "Plus, I wanna think. Go to sleep."

Great. The two boys who could talk to me both wanted to "think" and the one with the kindergarten vocab was dead asleep. I guess by the time I got changed and brushed my teeth they'd done all the talking; at least, it looked like Christophe had explained whatever he was going to. Because Graves's face had set itself and his shoulders had come up, and he looked at me dark-eyed and sullen like I'd done something awful.

Again.

The only thing I'd done was go to dinner and get poisoned. Was he going to blame me for that?

The room was dark, but the bathroom light was on and the door pulled mostly to. So I could see Graves's jawline, stubble showing up on his planed cheeks. He still looked a little gaunt; it pared his face down to the bone and showed his high cheekbones. The suggestion of epicanthic folds around his eyes made him exotic, and his hair was a wildly curling mess in the humidity. And the way his mouth turned down at the corners was just as grim as Christophe's.

"Can't you talk to me while you're thinking?" I couldn't help myself. "Please?"

He sighed again and shifted in the chair. "'Bout what?"

Abruptly I was conscious of Christophe, sitting so straight and still, facing the door. He was probably listening. What could I say to Graves with him there?

I rolled over onto my back, stared at the ceiling. The sprinklers were recessed, but you could still tell it was a hotel room. It was the way it smelled, mostly. And the give of the mattress underneath me, unfamiliar even if comfortable. "Never mind." The words stuck in my throat. "Sorry." I shut my eyes, hard, tried to count the tracers of color whirling in the dark.

Graves shifted in the chair, a whisper of cloth. "You know, I'd been waiting for a chance to talk to you. That day. When I saw you skipping."

I threw my arm over my eyes. Mostly it was to hide the stupid smile that showed up, my lips stretching before I could stop them. "After Bletch nailed you to the wall in American History?"

He groaned, but softly. "Don't remind me." And there was my sarcastic Goth Boy. "Best day of my life was when you gave her a heart attack."

That managed to kill the smile. I'd hexed that teacher and almost killed her. The *touch* thrummed softly inside my brain. I was getting used to it feeling so . . . *big*, like I could probably drop out of my body and see the whole city if I wanted to.

Why hadn't it warned me about poison in my drink? Whatever the seal-sleek brown boy had sprayed in my face was probably an antidote. At least, if it was some other slow-acting thing . . . Christophe said it was okay, to quit worrying and rest.

Why hadn't *Christophe* known something was off?

"I didn't mean to." Well, I *had* meant to hurt the teacher, but not the way it ended up. "So you'd been waiting? To talk about what?"

"Just to talk to you. You weren't the usual sort of new girl, Miss Anderson." Now he was smiling, I could tell. "Figured you'd be interesting. To say the least."

I was now toasty warm all over. My arms and legs were heavy, relaxing. "I felt bad Bletch had picked on you." A short silence. "That was the day Dad . . . disappeared."

"No shit." Now he sounded thoughtful. "So you just . . ."

"Waited for him to come back. When he did . . . he was a zombie." I'd never said it quite so baldly before.

Like a kid, I hadn't wanted to make it true by saying it out loud. Because if you don't say it, there's still a chance God, or someone, or *anyone* will notice the mistake and fix it.

"Goddamn. Now I feel stupid, offering you cheeseburgers."

Oh, Lord. How could I explain? "You saved my life." Quietly, as if it was a secret. "If I'd been at home when Ash showed up, and that burning thing . . . well." I paused, but Ash didn't stir. He just made another one of those soft sleepy-time noises. "It wasn't just a cheeseburger."

"Really?" Graves shifted in his chair again. "Good. I mean . . . good. That's good."

The tight knot inside my chest eased. As long as he was here, I could handle it. I could even handle the funny unsteady feeling all over me when I thought about sitting in that chair unable to breathe or move.

Maharaj. There's bound to be a reason why they're a third-year subject. That sort of stuff is seriously bad news. "I'm scared," I whispered.

"We all are." Graves sounded very sure. "Just go to sleep, Dru. We're all together. It'll be okay."

I don't know if he was lying, or just trying to soothe me, or what. But it worked. I rolled back onto my side, and before I could think of anything to say, darkness took me. I fell into a soft, restful sleep like a down blanket. Just before I tipped over the edge, though, I heard Christophe's voice. But different, without the businesslike mockery.

"*Loup-garou?*"

"Yeah?" Graves replied.

"Thank you."

The darkness, just then, was kind.

*   *   *

Ash's growl dragged me up out of unconsciousness, just like a hook will drag a fish. I sat straight up, my right hand shot out, and I had both my mother's *malaika* by the time my sock feet hit the floor.

"*Quiet!*" Christophe snapped, and wonder of wonders, the deep thrumming cut itself short. My heart hammered, and I began to wake up. Copper filled my mouth.

"What—" I began to whisper.

The phone, all the way across the room on a business table with a modem jack and a pile of stationery, not to mention a vase of silk irises, shrilled. I let out a shriek, Ash whirled—he was crouched in the corner, his irises glowing orange in the dim predawn gray—and leapt. He landed on the bed, the mattress groaning sharply, and hunched his thin shoulders. He'd wormed his way out of his T-shirt again, and his pallid narrow chest gleamed.

Christophe was suddenly *there*, right next to the phone, resolving out of thin air with a chittering sound. He scooped up the receiver before it could shrill again. Lifted it to his ear and waited, silently, a statue.

Graves was at the window, peering out through a slit in the heavy curtains. Both the shades and the curtains were mostly drawn, and now I knew why someone had left those two inches of space there. It meant you could look out without twitching the curtains and giving yourself away.

"Where?" Just the one word, clipped and short. Christophe held the shotgun loosely, pointed at the floor, and not a hair was out of place. Did he ever sleep?

Two knocks on the door. Crisp, authoritative, precisely placed. I actually gasped.

Christophe laid the phone down in its cradle. "All's well," he said over his shoulder. "Lights."

I suppose he meant it to be a warning, but I still wasn't ready when he flicked the switch by the door and undid the locks. I blinked, tasted morning in my mouth, and hoped I hadn't been snoring.

The door opened. I tensed, and Ash growled again.

"Chain the dog, Dru-girl," a familiar voice said. He sounded like Bugs Bunny—half Bronx, half Brooklyn, all New Yawk. "We come in peace."

What the hell? "August?" I sounded squeaky. "*Augustine?*"

"In the weary flesh. We have to get her out of here, Reynard."

Christophe didn't stand aside, blocking the door. He still had the shotgun, and his shoulders were tense. "Who's with you?"

"Hiro and some of the wulfen. We're all that could be spared. We're being hit on all fronts, and this entire area is crawling. Somehow they're *everywhere.*"

"Augie?" I took two steps forward. *How did they find us?*

"Thank God," Graves said, softly.

I glanced at him. He'd turned away from the window, and his entire face had relaxed. Why? Jesus, it was someone from the Order who'd turned him over to Sergej in the first place—

"Ah." Christophe stepped back, opening the door. Ash was still growling, and everything in the room rattled. "Dru, calm the Broken down. Enter, Dobrowski. I presume the *loup-garou* was calling *you*, then?"

Golden-haired Augustine looked just the same as always—white wifebeater, red flannel overshirt, jeans and heavy engineer boots, and not a day over twenty-two. He'd hit the drift late and looked old for a *djamphir*. There were bruised-looking circles under his dark eyes, though, and that was new. "Calling us? We got wind of her through the wires. A cop and a grocery store manager—hey, Dru." It would've been impossible for him to look any more relieved. He pushed past Christophe, who shook his head and swung the door closed. "You've *bloomed*. Thank God. Sweetie, can you get him to stop that? I don't want to have to hurt him."

I gathered myself. I couldn't even feel gratified that Augie noticed I was different now. "Ash." Just the one word, but it cut off the growl like flicking a switch. Then Christophe's meaning caught up with me. "Wait, hang on. Graves?"

"I couldn't think of anything else to do." His shoulders sagged, and his eyes were so dark. "So I was going to call them."

My brain froze. "Wait. When was this?"

"When you went to town. With Ash. I went down the road looking for a cell signal. Then, while you were at dinner, I called an Order drop-line." Graves hunched his shoulders. He was *shaking*, actually, and I wondered why. "I'm sorry, Dru. I just . . . it's best. They can protect—"

I stared at him. "You *called* them? Well, great. What the hell. Maybe that's how the vampires found—"

"Dru." Christophe's voice cut across mine. "He did the right thing."

"They found you?" August pushed past Christophe into the room, sweeping the door shut behind him. "When?"

Christophe had things he wanted to know, first. He locked the door, then slid past August and stalked into the room. "An incident with the police? Dru?"

I stopped dead. Stared at Graves.

You shouldn't trust me.

No. I couldn't think it. I just *couldn't.* "Where did you get the cell phone? If you were looking for a signal, Graves, where did you get the phone from?"

His irises were black now, no trace of green. His hands in his pockets, his shoulders slumped. "Stole it out of some lady's purse. That WalMart in Pennsylvania."

"Oh, so that's where Ash learned to shoplift, I bet?" My hands curled into fists. "God *damn* it, Graves—"

"Dru." Christophe was suddenly next to me, his hand curling around my shoulder. "Leave it. If he had not called the Order, *I* would have sooner or later. You *must* be protected."

"Yeah, real bang-up job they've been doing of it so far." I tore away from him. "Who died and left you in charge of me, huh? I'm *not* going back to the Order. I'm heading we—oh." I shut up. Telling August where I was headed was not a good idea. Except I'd already spilled the beans to Christophe.

Christophe grabbed my arm again, his fingers sinking in. His eyes burned blue. "The Maharaj have decided to ally with my father instead of with us. For what reason I cannot guess, unless they know something we do not and wish to treat with the victor instead of the vanquished. The Order will have a difficult enough time fighting on two fronts, and if the *djinni-ji* are watching for you as well, I prefer you safe within the Order's defenses. Gather your things."

All this time I'd been wishing for someone else to show up and take charge, and now that he was doing it, I seriously wanted to smack him. "The Order's not going to protect me." I tried yanking away from him again, but his fingers bit down and I stopped, glared at him. "Or Graves. Look how well *that* turned out. Why should I give them another chance to screw up and make my life miserable, huh? At least out on my own I know who to depend on!"

"Oh, I don't think you do." The *aspect* settled over Christophe, his hair slicking down, the blond highlights eaten by darkness. He looked as grim as I'd ever seen him. "I think you trust entirely the wrong people, *kochana*. Now." Either he was shaking or I was, I couldn't tell. "If you do not pack your things, August will, and I will drag you to whatever extraction point they've managed to hold in this city. Do you understand me?"

I stared up at him for a long moment. Ash whined softly, deep in his throat. The entirely mad idea that I could use the *touch* to make him jump Christophe floated through my head, but that would be stupid.

Still . . . the thought had some merit.

"Dru." Augustine stepped forward, avoiding Christophe's *malaika* on the floor in front of the TV. "Dru-girl, princess, *please*. There's me and Hiro. And your wulfen friends. Reynard's right, if the Maharaj are playing fast and loose we need to get you under cover. I know you're scared, but please. Listen to us. We've *got* to get you out of here. There are *nosferat* all over the city; they've been on your trail since the warehouse. I don't know how you've stayed alive so far—"

I don't know either, Augie. It's been a hell of a ride. For the first time, August was talking to me like I was a fellow adult. I couldn't even feel happy about it.

"Let go of me." I didn't sound like myself. Christophe eased up a little, and when I took my arm away from him I could feel the *aspect* smoothing over bruises his grip had left. "Thanks, Augie. You're the one who *asks* me instead of tells me whatever-the-fuck to do."

He actually looked shocked. "Language, kiddo." It was the same thing he would have said during the month I spent with him while Dad was up hunting something out Canada way—hunting, probably, for Sergej. I'd figured out that much later, at least. "Come on. Please?"

"I think we ought to move it along." Graves stood, his hands in his pockets and his head cocked. "Whatever we're going to do." He sounded . . . weird. Flat, monotone, and a little bored.

The words had a completely unexpected effect. Christophe tensed, raising his head and staring at him. August let out a long soft breath, the *aspect* flickering through him too and his fangs growing with a slight crackle, touching his lower lip.

"Bad." Ash weighed in, a thin whisper. "*Bad.*"

I half-turned, and he was staring at Graves. Ash's eyes glowed orange, and he braced himself, legs tensing and shoulders hulking up as he crouched on the bed.

"Because *I am Broken*," Graves continued in a low uneven singsong, his eyes now black from lid to lid, "I can't fight *him* much longer. *He* wants her captured, or dead." His head tipped back, and the Other—the thing wulfen use to change and *loup-garou* use for dominance—swelled through him, a colorless tide that smelled of strawberry incense and smoky fury. "And if *he* has to use me to do it, *he* will."

CHAPTER FIFTEEN

I t happened so *fast*.

Christophe shoved me, *hard*. My *malaika* flew out of my hands and I hit the bed, going down with Ash in a tangle of arms and legs. We spilled over the side, hitting the floor, Ash letting out an *oof* that would've been hilarious if I hadn't clocked my head a good one and got an elbow deep in my ribs. We rolled, Ash supple as a writhing snake, and there was a sickening crunch. A couple of thumps, a shivering crash, and it was official: we were making a lot of noise.

"Don't—" August sounded breathless. "Reynard—*Christophe*. No. She won't thank you for it." A low grunt of effort. "*No.*" Then a long string of foreign words, the *k*'s and *z*'s all sharp as a *djamphir's* fangs.

I struggled. Ash flowed away and I leapt to my feet, my T-shirt flapping where it had torn along the collar. My boxers were all messed up too, and air conditioning lay cold and slick against my shivering skin. I was *freezing*, every inch of me coated with ice. *Oh, Jesus, please—*

I had no idea what I was about to ask for.

Graves lay, flung back under the window, his long frame curled up around an invisible beach ball. His eyes were closed, and he was deathly still. The paleness under his coloring turned him a weird chalky yellowish color, and I let out a half–sob.

The television's screen was starred with breakage. August had Christophe's arms pinned. He had a pretty good full nelson on him, and Christophe's shotgun lay on the peach carpeting. August's boots slipped as Christophe surged to the side, and that sound was Christophe's voice cracking as he ranted in that odd, unlovely foreign language that colored all his words.

"No!" August yelled again. "Settle *down, moj brat*, killing him solves *nothing!*"

Killing? Everything snapped together behind my eyes, and I dove for the shotgun. Christophe's voice broke as he kept raving, and the hiss-growl of a very pissed-off *djamphir* rattled everything in the room.

My fingers closed around the shotgun's stock. I grabbed it and skidded aside, blinking through space. The carpet burned my bare feet; I racked the gun and put it to my shoulder.

Pointed right at Christophe. And August, I guess—you can't hit just one person with a shotgun, not when the two you're aiming at are holding onto each other.

Christophe froze. So did August. They both stared at me, Christophe craning his neck with an odd sideways movement that threatened to make my stomach unseat itself. They were both in the *aspect*, their eyes glowing, August's hair streaked thickly with butter-yellow against the gold. For the first time since I'd known him, Christophe's hair was wildly mussed, even slicked down with the *aspect*.

He didn't look so perfect now.

My heart pounded like it wanted to bust out of my chest. I backed up a step, two, until my bare heel touched something soft. Graves's hand, outflung on the carpet. I didn't step on his fingers, but I carefully brushed my foot against them. His skin was warm, and the *touch* filled my head with the sound of muffled wings beating.

Christophe had hit him pretty hard, and he was unconscious. But he was alive; that was the main thing.

"Back up." I was amazed at how steady I sounded. "Both of you. Back *up*."

Christophe's lips peeled back from his teeth. His fangs were out, and even though boy *djamphir* fangs aren't as big as full-blown *nosferat's*, they still mean business. Even with his face twisted up and those pearly-sharp gleaming canines out, he didn't look ugly. No, he still looked beautiful. The way a tiger or a cobra looks beautiful — deadly, complex, and dangerous all at once. "Let me go," he whispered fiercely. "August. Let go of me, or I will *kill* you."

I shook my head before August could reply. "No way, no day, Christophe. Augie, you just keep hold of him. I'll shoot you both, I swear to God I will."

Christophe twitched; Augustine tightened up on him. They both stared at me. Christophe was breathing raggedly, his ribs flaring. Spots of ugly flush stood out high on his flour-pale cheeks.

He looked pretty uncomfortable. I was having trouble caring.

The hiss-growl in Christophe's chest petered out. When he spoke, it was level and cold. "He is *Broken*, Dru." He twitched again; August hauled him back. "Sergej is looking through his eyes—"

"Then we'll take him along and *un*-Break him." I swallowed hard, only tasted bitterness and the peculiar I've-slept-long-enough-to-have-bad-breath that tells you it's early or late enough for no sane person to be awake and moving around. "I did it for Ash. I can do it for Graves." It was pure bravado—I didn't even know how I'd brought Ash back, but I was so not going to let Christophe do whatever it looked like he was fixing to do to my Goth Boy.

Don't you point that gun if you ain't prepared to shoot, Dru. Dad's voice, steady inside my head, the first time he took me out to plink at cans with a .22 rifle.

Sweat stood out on August's pale skin. "He's not completely Broken. He's fighting Sergej. And *nasze kszniczki* will not thank you if you harm him. We have restraints. We'll take him along. Put the gun down like a good girl, Dru. Longer we spend here, worse it gets."

I shook my head. Curls fell in my face, but the gun was steady. An owl's soft passionless call echoed in my head for a brief moment, and feathers touched my face and wrists. My *aspect* trembled over me like oil heated in a griddle, just before it starts smoking. *Think fast, Dru.* "You two are going to back up. You're going to wait in the hall. I'll get dressed and get us packed. Ash'll help me. Then we'll—"

"No." Flat and final, from Christophe. "Let go of me, Dobrowski."

I piped up in a hurry, just in case August decided to do as he said. "You are *so* not giving any orders right now, Chris. You're gonna wait in the hall. I'm not letting you do *anything* to Graves." *Not if I can help it. And right now I'm the one with the gun.*

But am I really going to shoot him?

I didn't want to find out. Still, the longer I stood there, the more sure I was that if August let go of Christophe, things were going to get hell-in-a-handbasket in a helluva hurry.

Ash peeked up over the edge of the bed. "Bad," he said softly. "Bad now."

Well, at least he wasn't trying to tell me what to do. "You just stay right where you are," I told him. If he decided to go crazy, we were looking at a Situation. I gave Christophe my best level stare—*Dad's* level staredown before the throwin' down. I searched for something to say, settled on the absolute truth. *"I am not going to let you hurt him."*

Christophe struggled once more, but August choked up on the chickenwing and held him. Just barely, though. Augie kept sweating, great beads of water standing out on his skin, but Christophe looked all too ready to keep going until he was free to tango.

And I didn't want to shoot him. I *didn't*.

But for Graves, I would. Certainty settled under my skin, and I hoped it showed on my face. I wanted Christophe to believe me and settle down.

Maybe it was Mom's voice that came out of me next, I don't know. Maybe I just decided to try another tack. Maybe the *touch* plucked it out of the air and laid it in my brain.

"Christophe. Please." Very soft, very reasonable. Not even caring if I was begging. "Help me. If you care about me at all, *help* me."

I stared into his mad, cold blue eyes, searching for the Christophe I knew. The one who held a knife to his own chest in a dilapidated old boathouse, his fingers scorch-hot against mine, and told me not to hesitate if I really thought he was a threat. The one who had leapt into a burning Schola for me and fought off the *nosferat* afterward in the bloodfog. The one who had been there, in one way or another, saving me in the nick of time over and over again. The Christophe who settled on my bed at the Schola Prima and talked to me for hours, who held me while I cried, who told me just to give him a chance. The *djamphir* who was completely scary and utterly maddening but was still—and here it was—the one person I always believed would come for me, no matter what.

I've been left behind like luggage so many times in my life, never really knowing if someone would return and collect me. I don't know quite when it happened, but that part of me always left wondering had decided that Christophe *would*. I could rely on him.

I stared at him, and willed him to prove me right.

Tension leaked out of him. He blinked, twice. The skinned-back grimace eased. His breathing evened out. He coughed, once, as if something was stuck in his throat. Finally, a husky rasp of a sigh slid out of him. "Very well."

I glanced up at August, who was looking at me like I'd grown another head. I nodded, but I kept the shotgun tight against my shoulder and my finger on the trigger. Accidents happen when you keep pressure on the trigger, yeah — but Christophe was *fast*, and I needed every split-second edge I could get on him.

August's hold on him eased. Ash shifted slightly, making a little whistling sound as the crackle of the change touched him and retreated. Christophe straightened, tipped his head back, swallowed hard. His Adam's apple bobbed. He rolled his shoulders back in their sockets precisely once, then his chin came down.

I braced myself for whatever he'd do next.

For a moment he just stood there and looked at me. When he spoke, it was with chill certainty. "Dobrowski. Fetch restraints, and whatever wulfen you have. Have Hiro clear an exit for us. I presume we have an extraction point?" He didn't look away, and I could have sobbed with relief. Because he sounded like Dad, when Dad decided a situation had gone critical and the only thing left was to move as fast as we could.

"Ready and waiting." August sounded as relieved as I felt.

"Go."

Augustine backed up, avoiding the *malaika* in the floor with a *djamphir*'s eerie grace. He gave me a Significant Look, but whatever it meant was lost on me. I kept the gun pointed and steady. The door opened and closed, and he was gone.

The shaking began in my legs. I denied it.

Christophe's hands hung loose and easy. "Ash. The *loup-garou*. Stand guard."

"Do what he says," I added. Probably unnecessarily, but better safe than sorry. *I'm trusting you, Christophe. Come on. Please.*

Ash scuffed against the carpet. He slunk over and crouched next to me, facing Graves's unconscious body. I stepped forward, rolling through so I was balanced all through the motion, covering the angle.

Christophe took a step, too. Toward me. The shaking was all through me now, but the gun was steady. I was only shaking inside, where nobody could see.

Where I was flying apart, and someone new was rising through the pieces of the girl I thought I was.

Silence settled around us. My cheeks were flaming hot now. My mother's locket warmed against my chest, but only faintly.

Christophe slowly, deliberately, took another step. His boots crushed the carpet, eerily soundless.

I couldn't move.

"Tell me." Another step, just as slow as the first. "If the *loup-garou* had me at his mercy, would you do the same for me?"

Well, first of all, I really doubt Graves would try to outright kill you. But there was no way I was going to say that out loud. The wooden grain of the stock was smooth and warm against my cheek. "Do you even have to ask?"

"I do." Another step. He was so close, and if my finger slipped on the trigger . . .

"Yes." What else could I say? "Yes. I *would.*"

He reached up, very slowly. I locked my fingers outside the trigger guard, let him pry the shotgun away from me. He lowered it, pointing the business end very carefully at the floor, and what he did next surprised me.

His free hand touched my shoulder. Slid under my hair, curled over the back of my neck. He pulled me forward, and I went gladly. The shaking turned outward, and when I laid my cheek against his sweater, he sighed, hard. His breath touched my hair, because he'd lowered his chin and was breathing on me.

"Dru," he whispered. "*Dru.*"

I didn't say anything else. I couldn't. I shut my eyes and leaned into him, for just a few moments. Clinging to him, but I suppose it was okay. He was clinging to me too.

And right then, it was enough.

CHAPTER SIXTEEN

ess than ten minutes later, we were packed up and the room's phone shrilled again. Christophe scooped it up before it got halfway through the first ring, held it to his ear. His face didn't change.

Graves was still out cold, curled up next to the window. Ash rocked back and forth slightly, watching him.

Christophe laid the phone down gently. "They'll bring him. We need to go."

"I'm not—" I began, but he brushed past me and was suddenly at the door. The locks chucked aside and it opened, and a familiar pair of cat-tilted blue eyes peered past him.

Nathalie barely paused, barging straight in. Her sleek dark head bobbed, her blue eyes were spangled with little bits of yellow wulfen glow, and I braced myself for anger or worse—disappointment.

After all, I'd been a raving bitch to her the last time she'd seen me.

She threw her arms around me, and her odd musky perfume

wrapped around me too. As usual, she looked impeccable, from the royal-blue scarf twisted around her neck to her long dangling key-shaped earrings, her jeans torn just right and her espadrilles fashionably frayed.

"Nat!" I almost got a mouthful of her hair. "I'm so sor—"

"You *moron!*" She hugged me so tight I could feel a wulfen's strength in her. My bones creaked. "You're an *idiot!* I would've come *with* you! Don't ever *do* that *again!*" She eased up enough to hold me at arm's length and shake me, three times, precisely, then grabbed me again and hugged me so hard the air whoofed out of me. "Moron! *Dumbass!* Jesus, Dru!"

"Skyrunner." Christophe sounded grimly amused. "A little quieter, if you please."

More familiar faces. Shanks slid by Christophe, his lean face set and his legs looking longer than ever. He pushed at the emo-boy swoop of dark hair over his forehead and glanced at me, then at the window, where Ash still crouched. "Sheeeee-yit," he drawled.

"Is that Graves?" Blond, anxious Dibs crowded past him. "Is he hurt? I've got the restraints. What *happened?*"

"He's Broken." Christophe swept the door mostly closed. "Get him prepped for travel and be cautious. Milady Dru won't leave here without him."

Damn right I won't. "Oh my God—" I almost got another mouthful of Nat's hair. She was holding on for dear life. "Jesus, guys, it's good to see you."

"Hey, Dru." Dibs shuffled past, carefully not looking at me. Clashing, jangling silver dripped from his hands, but I was too busy hugging Nat to really see what he carried. "We were worried. Bobby almost had a heart attack."

"Not me." Shanks hopped up on the bed I'd been sleeping in,

folding down into an easy crouch. "Benjamin, though, he looked about ready to have kittens. You went right out the damn window and vanished, Dru. Congrats on never being boring."

Which was as close as he'd ever get to telling me he was happy to see me.

Nat sniffed and let up on me, patting at her cheeks. "Crap. Now my eyeliner's probably ruined. We were *worried*, Dru. Don't ever pull a boner stunt like that again, you hear me?"

So she wasn't mad. Thank God. The terrible knot inside my chest eased slightly. "I'm so sorry—"

"Can we move it along here?" Christophe's tone could have sliced solid granite. "This is an emergency."

Dibs crouched next to Graves. The silver turned out to be thread-thin glittering restraints, and I swallowed a sick feeling as he quickly, efficiently had Goth Boy trussed up like a Christmas goose. "These work on wulfen." Dibs ducked his head, talking to the floor. "Should work on him, too. Unless he convinces someone to take them off."

"Which is why Nat and me're here." Shanks cocked his head. "Dru, what the hell happened?"

"He saved my life." It was suddenly important to get that out first. "Came back with a gun while I was fighting off S-S-Serg—" I couldn't finish the name. "*Him*. While I was fighting *him* off."

"Come, children, let's move." Christophe had the shotgun, the two *malaika* hilts poking up over his shoulders. Nat was already buckling me into my own *malaika*-harness, and I caught sight of a familiar shoulder holster peeping out from under her blue linen jacket. Shanks scooped up the two duffel bags of gear and clothes, Nat's quick efficient fingers gave a yank at the strap of my messenger bag to make it lay right, and she gave me a little shove toward the door.

"Dibs'll handle the *loup-garou*," she said. "Come on, you go right after Reynard. Hey, you know, he's cute."

"What?"

"Graves." She fell into step behind me. "He's cute. You didn't mention that."

"For Christ's sake, Nat, he's unconscious." Something bitter crawled up into my throat. Was it . . . yeah, maybe a little. It was jealousy. I mean, Nat was so pretty.

Jeez. So not the time to be worrying about this, Dru.

Christophe checked the hall. "Stay close, *milna*."

"No worries about that." I wished for a gun, but if we ran across vampires the *malaika* were the better bet. Plus the fact that I was toxic now. That would help.

But Sergej had gotten close enough to Anna to get his fangs in. She was *svetocha* too. He got close enough to my mother to kill her, despite her toxicity to suckers. Still, I'd tangoed with the king of the vampires a couple of times now and came out ahead.

That doesn't mean your chances are good next time. Don't get cocky.

The hall was eerily silent, directionless lighting and a leggy expensive table with a flower arrangement down at the end. I wondered if anyone in the rooms around us had called down to the front desk because of the ruckus.

I glanced back over my shoulder. Shanks hefted the duffels easily, and blond little Dibs had Graves's lanky form over his shoulder. Wulfen are way stronger than human beings, but it was still thought-provoking to see slim Dibs carrying Goth Boy like it was no big deal. Just a bulky package. Ash followed, padding silently in Dibs's wake, his eyes still fixed on Graves.

Christophe headed away from the elevators, toward the service stairs. His shoulders were set, and the *aspect* flickered over him in deep swells like ocean waves.

"Christophe?" I whispered.

He tilted his head slightly, letting me know he was listening.

"Shouldn't we wait for August?"

"He'll be around. Quiet, *kochana*, let me work."

Well, all right. Just because I wouldn't see Augie didn't mean he wasn't around. Got it. Felt like an idiot. Great.

The stairs were like every other set of industrial stairs all over—concrete, layers of chipped yellow paint on the handrails, every sound magnified. The *touch* shifted uneasily inside my head, but whether it was everyone's uneasiness, or the nervous adrenaline rabbiting under my heartbeat, or actual danger, I couldn't tell. There was too much static. It was as if all the filters that had been on the *touch* before had been stripped away, and I couldn't get a clear signal.

Was that why I hadn't sensed the vampires before? I wished Gran was alive to tell me. Except she'd probably be pissed as hell about her house burning down, and . . .

My mother's locket cooled, metal suddenly icy against my chest. I stopped dead on the stairs, head cocked. *What was that?*

A faint scratching, claws against concrete. But stealthy; they didn't want to be heard.

Christophe had halted, too. His head was tilted, probably at the same angle mine was.

"Did you hear that?" Nat, whispering. There was a sound—she'd drawn her Sig Sauer.

Christophe muttered something, but so softly even I couldn't hear him. Then, "Up. Go up. Robert?"

"Shit," Shanks breathed. "You're kidding." But he turned sharply, pushed against Dibs. "You okay, Dibsie?" Ash hopped back two steps, staring.

"He's too thin." Dibs was careful not to bang Graves's hanging head on the yellow-painted handrail; Ash somehow slid aside so he was behind Dibs. "I could carry him all day."

"Don't say that," Nat chided, around a half-swallowed laugh. "Come on, boys. Less talk, more move."

"Ash?" I whispered.

"Bad," Ash whispered back.

Christophe almost ran into me. "Dru." A fierce hot whisper in my ear. I was trying to focus past the sound of their movements. There was *another* sound—skitterings, and feather-brushings, and tiny little tapping. "We must move. Now."

"I hear it," I whispered back. "What—"

"Maharaj, most likely." He pushed against me; the contact made my legs work again. He was always herding me around. "Don't worry. I won't let them near you."

Gee, that's comforting. I opened my mouth to whisper something, God alone knows what, because just then the lights died. The blackness was a wet towel against my eyes, and the scraping little slithers crested like a wave, a few floors down.

"*Move!*" Christophe whisper-yelled, and I grabbed for the railing. Judged where Nat was by the soundless warmth in front of me, matched her step for step. Christophe managed to be right behind me without tripping me, and when his hand touched my back, I didn't jump. Flat-palmed, his fingertips just below my bra strap, the warmth from it flushed all through me and made my cheeks burn. He didn't push, just kept his hand there, and I wondered how he was hanging onto the shotgun and negotiating the stairs at the same time with one hand off the rail, and—

The whispering slithers drew closer. Ash and Dibs both made small sounds, and I knew without being able to see that Shanks had transferred the duffels to one hand and moved up to help Dibs. A door banged open and suddenly it was just me and Nat and Christophe.

"Graves—" I didn't have enough breath to yell.

"They'll take care of him!" Nat tossed over her shoulder. *"Move!"*

Christophe was now swearing. At least that's what it sounded like, a steady stream of filthy-sounding words in a foreign language. A chill moved along my skin, and I tasted that faint maddening ghost of citrus.

Vampires. Or just something big and dangerous.

Go figure—all I had to do was get scared enough running up a dark staircase and the *touch* came through loud, if not clear. Why was the danger candy failing me? Because I'd bloomed.

Great.

My sneakered feet slapped the concrete, and I gave up trying to be quiet. It didn't matter now. Still, it was hushed, and I realized there had been no slice of light through a door when Dibs and Shanks peeled off.

Where are they taking him? Oh, God, take care of him, please. I know I've been sucking at the praying lately, but please, dear God, please—

"Next floor!" Christophe sounded only faintly out of breath. How fast were we going, anyway?

"Got it," Nat barked back, and the tiptapping scraping behind us became a rumble. The handrail vibrated under my skating fingertips; Christophe pushed and I found a fresh burst of speed. We clambered around a tight turn, then Christophe shoved me across the landing, Nat hit the door like a bomb, and we burst out into dimness that seemed scorch–bright after the absolute black of the stairs. Emergency lighting glowed, and Nat skipped aside, gun up and braced, pointed behind us. Christophe shoved me again, so hard I almost lost my footing, and whirled. He tossed something small and gleaming metallic through the door behind us, just before it whomped back closed. A shower of metal from the hydraulic over-head hit the carpet in a patter—Nat had busted it off its hinges.

"Fire in the hole!" Christophe yelled, and tackled me. Nat hit the floor at the same moment, rolling with sweet natural wulfen grace. My head bounced against carpet, all the breath knocked out of me, and there was a massive, grinding explosion.

What the hell? But I knew that sound even as I curled up and clapped my hands over my ears. Grenade.

Jesus. Where had he pulled *that* out from?

My ears rang, I shook my head. Choking smoke billowed; the door listed on its hinges. Then Nat was pulling me up, Christophe flowing to his feet with *djamphir* grace, his eyes burning blue in the gloom. He said something I couldn't hear; I shook my head. My hair had gone all crazy.

My ears cleared all at once with a pop, as if I'd just come up out of the pool. "—fine," Nat said. "No bleeding. Dru? You okay?"

I coughed, the acrid smoke tearing at my throat. "That was a *grenade!*"

"Pays to be prepared." Christophe was actually grinning, a fey smile. "Come, that won't hold them long. End of the hall, ladies. We're going to fly."

I had a sinking sensation he wasn't kidding. Nat brushed at me, quick swipes like Gran when I'd come home dusty. "You all right? Dizzy?"

I managed to shake my head. "That was a *grenade!*" I repeated, like an idiot, and Nat grinned. The yellow in her irises glowed too, and I wondered what my own eyes were doing.

Come on, Dru. Do you really want to know?

I found out I didn't. Nat got me going; we set off for the end of the hall. There was a window there, its curtains moving slightly on a breeze from nowhere. I smelled a sudden mineral tang, right before the sprinklers burst into cold drenching life.

"Oh, *shit!*" I half-yelped, and Nat laughed.

"This is going to ruin my outfit!" she yelled, and Christophe leveled the shotgun at the window. The door behind us creaked, and I snapped a glance over my shoulder.

Little dried husks of things were shoving themselves through the broken door. Smoke roiled. The things had long scuttling insect legs, hard shiny carapaces, and little red pinprick eyes.

The *touch* flexed inside my head. The things were a hex all right, but one so delicately built and so massively powered it was leagues beyond anything Gran had ever managed to teach me. I *saw* the thin blue and red lines holding it together, complex knots cradling threads of force growing like a living thing, self-referential and hungry. Like a virus, or a geometric cancer in the messy fabric of the physical world.

It was beautiful.

Cold water sprayed from the sprinklers, hissing as it met the insects. They swelled in a steaming wave, and the door crumbled. Nat dragged me along, laughing like she was having a great time. The shotgun's roar was tiny compared to the massive noise of the grenade's explosion, and the window shivered into a glittering fall of safety glass. The flower arrangement on the table underneath it exploded.

Nat let go of me. She screamed, the change rippling through her, and bulleted forward. She took the window and a good chunk of the wall on either side with her, flying out into the night. I dug in my heels.

Oh, hell no. No way!

Christophe pivoted. He glanced behind me and his face changed. His free hand jerked, and he lobbed another silvery thing underhand. I was trying to slow down, skidding against wet carpeting. But Christophe grabbed me, completing a full 360, and headed for the window. His arm was around me, he grabbed the waistband of my jeans, and I got a good faceful of his apple-pie smell. The blood-hunger woke, every vein in me lighting up like a marquee, and we hit the hole in the wall at warp speed.

Falling, weightless, I expected us to fall a lot longer but the jolt came before I was ready. Christophe took most of it, the *aspect* snapping over both of us like a stinging rubber band—*djamphir* can land very lightly, but I wasn't ready. There was just so much I wasn't ready for.

A huge grinding noise burst above us. We rolled, Christophe taking most of the momentum, and he might have been screaming. Or I might've. I don't know, because the wall around the window twenty floors above us was a blossom of greasy orange flame. We fetched up against something, hard enough to jolt the breath out of me, and I walloped in a deep lungful of clean night air. The screaming stopped, my ears popped again, and I just lay there for a second.

It was a roof. We hadn't fallen far—I mean, not far for a *djamphir*. Still, I could've killed us both by not being ready. I stared up at the fireball as it belched up, smoke streaming, and thought, *That's a helluva lot of noise.*

Christophe, yelling something. He braced himself, and I realized I was staring over his shoulder because he was flat on top of me. For once, the thought didn't make me blush. I was too busy looking at the fireball and the plume of black oily smoke.

He levered his weight aside, yelled again. "Are you *hurt?*"

I couldn't find my voice. Shook my head, my hair moving against concrete. He grabbed the straps of my *malaika* harness and pulled me up, I kept staring, goggle-eyed. Fine thin threads of hexing unraveled, seeking hungrily, digging into cracks along the wall like veins. "Jesus," I finally whispered, my lips shaping the sound, my fangs tingling as they lengthened, delicate little points.

He actually shook me. My head bobbled. "*Dru.*"

The snap of command pulled my chin down. He looked worried for a half-second before I blinked. The world came back into focus. Nat melted out of the shadows, her sleek hair ruffled and her linen jacket torn. The *aspect* smoothed down over me, an oil-balm working in through my skin, easing away hurts. Erasing the bruises.

"What?"

"She's fine," Nat snapped. "Let's move."

But Christophe paused. He still had his shotgun, for crying out loud, but his free right hand smoothed my hair back, tucking curls behind my ears. "All's well, *skowroneczko moja.* I won't let them catch you."

That's awful nice. I couldn't make any words come. I just stared like an idiot. But he seemed okay with that. He touched my forehead, brushing lightly with the pads of his fingertips. Then a trailing down my cheek, very soft, infinitely . . . tender.

Yeah. Like he hadn't just thrown us both out a window.

"Come now," he said quietly, under the noise. I heard sirens, the whooping of a fire klaxon, and the rushing suck of flame devouring oxygen through every hole it could find, like a kid sucking on a straw. "We must move quickly."

I found myself nodding. "No kidding." I sounded calm and businesslike. It was a surprise, but I was imitating Dad. Had he ever felt this unsteady, this lost?

You're not lost. Christophe's right here.

It was more comforting than maybe it should've been. I grabbed Christophe's hand, squeezed hard. His eyebrows came up, but he immediately looked away, scanning the rooftop. "Let's go."

And not a moment too soon, because a high chill hateful cry rose in the distance, slicing through all the other noise. It dug into my brain with sharp glass spikes, and I flinched. Nat inhaled sharply, her head upflung, and she actually sniffed.

Testing the air.

"*Nosferatu*," she breathed.

Yeah.

Christophe pulled me across the rooftop, my fingers linked in his. His skin was warm, and the *touch* drank in the fierce calm surrounding him. There was a fire escape and a breath of roasted garlic—the restaurant was around here somewhere. Nat was right behind me, crowding close.

Thank God Graves is out of this, I thought, and then I was too busy to think anymore. There was a fire escape going down into an alley, and as soon as we hit the alley we began to run.

Because another high, nasty whistling screech-cry echoed from far closer—the hotel's roof, I was guessing. Christophe swore softly, and I put my head down and concentrated on keeping up.

CHAPTER SEVENTEEN

The rest of that run is a patchwork of confusion in my memory. Bolting across streets, into alleys, up fire escapes, rooftops blurring underfoot, Christophe more often than not hauling me along because I wasn't moving fast enough to suit him. I wasn't about to complain.

It wasn't dark, but it wasn't light either. We stuck to pools of shadow, flitting from cover to cover, streetlights and city glow suddenly enemies instead of friends. The suckers wouldn't use guns—not likely, Christophe said, but the Maharaj were another proposition. Once someone opened up on us with an assault rifle, and the sound of the bullets chewing into the street behind me still sometimes shows up in my dreams.

Christophe hanging and twisting to kick in a window, Nat blurring between changeform and girlshape as she ran, random reflections of light picking out iron grillwork on a balcony or the pattern of bricks on a restaurant's facade. The moon, behind low scudding clouds and smiling like a diseased coin. The glow of Christophe's eyes as he scanned a rooftop, Nat crouching and panting a little while she rested for ten seconds before we were off again, her hair ruffling in the breeze. A car's headlights throwing our shadows against a graffiti-tangled concrete wall.

"Got any more grenades?" Nat yelled merrily, and Christophe swore in reply, with breathtaking inventiveness. I levered myself up over the roof's edge like I was muscling out of a swimming pool. My hair fell in my face and the bloodhunger burned all through me. The fangs dug into my lower lip; I had to be careful or I'd bite out a chunk of myself and they'd have a blood trail.

I was so glad, for once, that *svetocha* only have teensy top fangs; boy *djamphir*'s are larger and only on the top too. Sucker fangs are top and bottom, and they are serious business. I'd seen pictures of what those teeth could do. The jaw distends like a snake fixing to take down a huge egg, and sometimes they tear flesh to get at the liquid inside.

"Door," Christophe said, as close to short of breath as I'd ever heard him. Nat's boot had already thudded onto the metal door's surface; it crumpled like paper. "Could you be any *louder*, Skyrunner?"

"I could," she shot back cheerfully. "Would you like me to? Up. We're almost there."

I was glad. My ribs heaved; sweat stood out on my skin. We were just a jump ahead of the *nosferat*. There were so *many* of them, no time to take a breath, just the running and Christophe and Nat bantering back and forth like they were at a party or something. I'd heard Dad use that sort of humor before, with other human hunters.

I was too occupied running and not doing anything stupid to contribute. Plus, I couldn't find anything witty to say.

I mean, *oh God oh God we're all gonna die* doesn't really fit the definition of *banter*, now does it.

The suckers kept screaming, hunting-cries echoing all over the city. I wondered what normal people were thinking of this, if they'd even hear, if they'd blame it on a neighbor's television or something. There were sirens everywhere too, and fires. I wasn't sure how much of it was just big-city warfare that happens on any normal night, and how much was suckers torching places where maybe *djamphir* or wulfen were fleeing—or trying to buy us some time to escape.

I didn't know how many of the Order were in the city. Things sounded bad, and the terse questions Christophe threw at Nat when we weren't scrambling were thought-provoking and terrifying all at once.

Inside, there were more stairs. I actually groaned before I could help myself, and Nat laughed. "Good for your ass!" she barked, and took them two at a time. Christophe's hand closed around my arm. I didn't need it—the *aspect* was still reliably doing its job. I'd been weaker and slower for so long, though, that I was kind of afraid of going all out. I couldn't pace myself.

"Just a little further." He'd gained his breath back, even though I could see the sweat drying in his hair. The soot and grime striping him looked like it was placed for maximum effect. "Extraction point's on the roof. We'll be safe in ten."

I found enough breath for a single word. "Okay." Then I concentrated on not being a hindrance. Our footsteps were in such close tandem they sounded like a single pair.

"Clear of the zone we'll get a plane; we'll land in Houston. There's a Schola there—hot food and a good bed. Protection for you. They'll have the *loup-garou* there, under restraint." Christophe pushed me in front of him. "Keep going."

I did. Nat sometimes leaned forward, her palms slapping the stairs as she flowed through changeform and back, stretching and leaping so gracefully it was enough to make the heart hurt. She was down to her last clip of ammo; I knew because she'd merrily informed Christophe of the fact three and a half minutes ago.

Up, and up, and up, breath tearing in my lungs and the *aspect* blurring everything around me. When Nat gathered herself in the middle of the last flight, I barely slowed. She extended in a fluid leap; another metal door crumpled and she rode it down. Leapt free, twisting in midair to land on her boots and skid to a perfectly-controlled stop.

"Ta-*da!*" she cried, and the helicopter crouching on the rooftop, in absolute defiance of any codes or regulations, whined as its motor started. It looked vaguely military, dull black and *huge*, and there, in the opening on the side, was a familiar face.

Hiro crouched, his lean caramel-colored face set as it usually was. He half-rose, fluid *djamphir* grace evident in every line of him, his black hair writhing in spikes as the *aspect* poured over him like a river. He was on the Council, and he was scary—but he was also the most patient and approachable out of any of them except maybe Bruce. His winged eyebrows rose slightly, and if he was surprised to see us it didn't show.

His hand shot out, bracing him as he half-stepped down and stretched his other hand toward me.

We were so close.

The glare was sudden and immediate, klieg lights switching on. Nat whirled, snarling, the white light tearing through my dark-adapted eyes. I flung up a hand, and there was a whining roar.

Hiro leapt, a small black shadow. The helicopter made a grinding noise, and the missile hit it squarely.

"*Get down!*" Christophe shoved me, *hard*. I fell, losing skin on my palms as I tried to catch myself, skidding across the rough pebbled surface of the rooftop. Then the world turned white and rolled over, lifting up away from me. Every other massive noise that night paled in comparison. A giant warm hand scooped me up and flung me, air suddenly hard as concrete, and I skidded right off the edge of the roof. Somehow my body twisted, saving me without thought, claws dug into the side of the building with a terrific jolt almost breaking my wrists, my shoulders grating with pain. I hung, and it was a good thing, because flames belched over the lip of the roof and my hands let out another agonizing shriek of pain.

The *touch* swelled, a pipe organ of agony as *nosferat* shrieks cut through the din like hot knives through soft butter. The *aspect* was scorching, flowing over me, and my toes scrabbled against the side of the building, seeking purchase. Nothing, they just slipped, my arms tensed. My wrists and shoulders shrieked as I tried to haul myself up, but even with superstrength the angle was wrong. I smelled copper—thin rivulets of heat slid down my arms, soaking into my T-shirt.

Blood. *My* blood. The hunger woke up, fueling a burst of unhealthy strength. I let out a *huuungh* of effort, lost but still embarrassing under all the other racket. Managed a couple of inches, but my arms were shaking. My claws were ripping, little bit by bit, out of my fingertips.

Have you ever had your fingernails slowly torn off? It's not fun.

I tensed again, everything focused on bending my arms. But I was tired, we'd run a long way, and the smell of blood wasn't just taunting me. It was filling my head with smoky rage, hard to think, and my strength was bleeding away too.

I felt instead of heard the *skkkkritch!* as my claws slipped, and then I was plummeting like a star, eight stories passing in an eyeblink. Spinning catlike in midair, got my feet under me, and the *aspect* flexed, snapping like a rubber band over every inch of skin I owned.

Landed hard enough to jolt the breath out of me, but nothing broke. My hands were raw pieces of meatpain; I lifted them both to my mouth and got a faceful of bloodscent. It sent me to my knees on a drift of garbage, and I spun aside instinctively as flaming wreckage began drifting down into the alley.

What the hell? But it was obvious. Someone had blown up the helicopter. With a *rocket*, no less. Just waiting for us to get there before they opened fire.

Hiro. Christophe. Nat. Oh, God.

Nosferatu hunting-screams rose like bright ribbons in the night. They jabbed through my head, iceglass spikes, and my back hit the brick wall of the alley. It was filthy down here, and the heat and humidity just made it worse. I heard muffled wingbeats, and Gran's owl filled itself in. It soared down, dodging falling bits of fiery refuse as they cartwheeled silently into the alley. The bird was a charcoal sketch, its feathers just suggestions of paleness. It made a tight circle over me, kept gliding.

Can't go back up there; they could have other guns to pick everyone off. Think, Dru!

My thinker sputtered like an old engine. *Houston. He said Houston. You're in enemy territory, there's mad hexers and a bunch of nosferatu roaming around, and you're bleeding. You've just run halfway across the city and anyone who might help you is probably running for their life too right now.*

Yep. It was official. I ruined everything, I was a disease. No matter how bad shit got, there was *always* worse coming down the pike.

I braced myself against the wall. I didn't have much time—the suckers were going to get here any second to mop up whatever was left. Going up to rescue anyone was impossible, and idiotic too. But Christophe. And Nat . . .

Get the hell away from here. That's the first step.

I coughed, hard. Cleared my lungs. My hands were moving, flipping up the flap of my messenger bag. The *aspect* burned against my fingertips, soothing and repairing. I found the switchblade by touch and fished it out. It snicked open, and I suddenly felt much calmer.

This is a test, Dru. You don't have anyone else to take care of now.

Gran's owl zoomed away. I bolted for the mouth of the alley, following it and dodging flaming wreckage.

And I vanished into the night.

PART TWO

CHAPTER EIGHTEEN

I t probably says something for American cities that a teenage *svetocha*, covered in grime and soot and with blood streaking her arms, can pass largely unnoticed. Just what it says ain't nice.

I wasn't on autopilot, but I wasn't quite myself either. The *touch* was a loosely waving anemone around me, steering me away from the edges of trouble. I crouched for a good fifteen minutes in a dumpster once, peering out between the lid and the lip of it, my feet slipping a little on greasy crud and my eyes watering from the stench. It covered up the thick aroma of cinnamon rolls boiling up from my skin, though. And while I watched, gagging every few moments and trying desperately not to throw up, I saw things.

Dogs built of smoke and fine hexwork, thin red and blue threads coalescing in steam vapor as they ran through the streets, searching. Little tiny flying things, that same red and blue hexwork, hanging from threads like puppet butterflies. And the black paper-cutout shadows of suckers, blurring through and trailing bright spangled streaks of hatred.

This is a lot of trouble for one little svetocha, *don't you think?* I held down my gag reflex by sheer will, again. My sneakers slipped in crud, and a thin cold finger of liquid touched my ankle. *Oh, gross. So gross.*

I found a residential section, and it took me a good hour to find a car worth stealing. It was a Jeep Wagoneer, spare ignition key left under the front floor mat—don't ask, some people *are* just that dumb—and this time I didn't stop to see if there were insurance papers in the glove box. Because the hunting cries were still rising all over the city in crystal chill columns of hate, the more frequent the closer dawn came. The eastern sky held a faint tinge of gray, but not nearly enough to suit me.

Gran's owl circled overhead, and with it floating in front of me I penetrated a tangle of side streets and—luck or the *touch*, I'm not sure—found a freeway on-ramp. 75-86 South; that would take me to 65 South. Then I'd cut west, and I'd be in Houston in a couple days if the car held out, less if I pushed it and drove the whole, what, fourteen hours or so?

Just get clear of the blast zone, Dru. Then hole up somewhere and do some thinking. I'd say this requires some heavy thought, at least.

I jammed the accelerator down. The Jeep picked it up, and the sound of the freeway filled my ears because I had the front windows down. I was never stealing a car without power windows again, dammit.

I wiped at my cheeks, but I found out I wasn't crying. It was some kind of occasion—everything going to hell and a vampire attack, and for once I wasn't leaking.

Hooray.

* * *

There's a town near Mobile called Daphne, which is a really pretty name if you don't know the legend behind it. On the outskirts there's an abandoned house, set back from the Gulf and slowly sinking into sandy soil. Something underneath the small white frame house is giving way an inch at a time, and the development it was a part of way back in the sixties is a ghost town. Nobody thought that the ocean would start taking nibbles off beneath this particular piece of the shore, but I guess the sea had its own ideas.

All the houses are crazy cockeyed by now, roofs slumping and walls buckling. The whole neighborhood is condemned, and I guess the developer who went out on a limb to convince people this was a great idea ended up shooting himself in one of the homes. Which one, Dad and I never found out.

Sometimes the dead *do* just leave. It happens.

Johnny Cash's mournful voice shut off when I cut the engine. The Wagoneer was filthy with dust from the little bit of offroad needed to get here, and for once the Gulf smelled fresh. Just before noon, the sun was up, it was hotter than hell, and even the breeze coming off the water didn't help. Salt smell filled my nose, I blinked and rubbed at my eyes. Unbuckled my seat belt.

This particular house was familiar. The freshening breeze moaned through half-open windows and whispered through sea grass, and I inhaled deeply. No trouble anywhere, the *touch* loose and quiescent like a sleeping cat. Gran's owl had faded out with the dawn. I was grainy-eyed and still smelled of soot and ick, but at least I'd washed the worst of it off at a gas station once the sun was safely up.

It might not even be here. I bit gently at my lower lip as I studied the house. *Don't rush it, even if you think there might be nothing there. Take your time. You're on your own, no safety net. Do it right.*

Same white house, sloping to one side, same broken windows.

Same cold breath against the nape when you approach it, your feet crunching on sand and bits of shell scattered from the walk that used to be snow-white. The pavement is cracked; the streets have gaping potholes that could break an axle. I was kind of surprised I'd found it—I'd been navigating on memory and gut instinct alone.

I almost expected to see Dad in front of me, walking soft and easy like he was heading into enemy territory, gun drawn but down. He never approached a cache without gun in hand.

Because if you're coming back to a cache, things might be bad, and if things are bad, the chance of someone waiting there for you had to be seriously considered. Still, he and I were the only people who knew about this place, right? And two can keep a secret if one is . . .

. . . dead.

Don't think about that. Get in, get the cache, get out.

I supposed I should be grateful we'd spent so much time below the Mason-Dixon. At least I knew what I was about down here, and I would be in comfortable territory even over into Texas.

Of course, I'd been in comfortable territory at Gran's, too, and still managed to screw that up hardcore. I didn't even know *how* I'd messed up so bad. It'd just happened way too fast to take back.

I toed the door open, a *malaika* in one hand. A razor-sharp wooden sword was hardly the worst weapon to have around, I guess, but I would've preferred a gun. I'd had to unbuckle the leather harness before I got out to pump gas, for God's sake, and my back wasn't too happy even under the *aspect*'s smoothing heat. Driving with a pair of *malaika* strapped to your back is one way to end up feeling like an arthritic old lady.

The door creaked. The floor rolled in rotting humps, and the white noise of the ocean filled my head. *Come here'n take a look at this, Dru-girl.* Dad's voice, calling through the shaky halls. Sharp rotting tang of mildew, each inch of wood swelling, drifts of paper trash in the corners. Looked like nobody had crashed here for long, thank God.

Even normal people can sometimes feel the creepy-chill. And stay away.

I cased the entire house, moving ghost-quiet, working the sight-angles like Dad had taught me. Sometimes he had me sweep a house with him, sometimes on my own while he timed me and offered pointers afterward. I'd never really considered it not normal. I mean, I knew other kids didn't do what I did, but no kid ever thinks their home life is weird. It's just . . . there. Like your breathing, your heartbeat.

Like gravity. Only all my gravity was gone and I was spinning.

You're a disease, Dru. You're bad luck.

My sneakers tracked in the sand, and when I finally made it up the tottering stairs a second time memory filled my head like gasoline fumes. Dad showing me again how to move quietly on steps, how to test each board, how to walk only where he did and the signals to use when I felt something weird. Of course, he could usually tell just by looking at me—I guess I got *that look*, the one that gave him the singing willies, a lot. *You go white as a sheet and your eyes . . . well, they look like your ma's,* he'd told me once. I think he'd had a little too much Beam that night.

He generally had to have a little sauce before he would talk about Mom.

Upstairs in the smaller bedroom, the closet was propped open. The carpet in here was rotten clear through, probably black with mildew underneath, but the day was hot enough that it didn't soak my knees with yuck when I went down cautiously and felt around inside the closet. It smelled truly ferocious in there, and by the time I found the notch I was halfway to throwing up again. I was glad I hadn't eaten anything.

The slice of flooring was swollen from the morning damp, but I got it worked up. And hallelujah, the ammo boxes were still there. Four in a row, neat as you please. Which meant I was now armed, had some extra cash, and probably had some ID, ammo, and MREs in there too.

"Oh, thank you," I whispered, not sure who I was thanking. God, maybe, or Dad for laying down the cache in the first place. There was another cache on my way to Houston, but this one meant I could breathe and I wouldn't have to stop to gather liquid resources. "Thank you. Holy . . ."

I stopped, my head coming up. Was that a soft footstep? The *touch* unfolded, swept out in concentric ripples, little waving fingers combing the air, searching for danger.

Nothing. The sooner I got out of here, though, the better. I didn't stop to look inside the ammo boxes, just loaded them in the Wagoneer's trunk and piled in, spun the wheel, and left only footsteps and a roostertail of dust as evidence.

CHAPTER NINETEEN

By the time I reached Biloxi I was about ready to lay down and die from exhaustion. The second time I almost veered out of my lane after blinking, I decided it was time to find a hotel. My eyes ached, the rest of me wasn't far behind, and my mother's locket flared with alternate ice and molten heat.

Plus I felt like I could eat every trashy bit of fast food I could lay my hands on. With the cardboard it was wrapped in. *And* the bag. Extra fiber, yum.

I should have driven further. But really, wrecking the Jeep was *so* not an option. The sun was westering, dipping behind an inky veil of clouds, weather moving in from the Gulf on indigo wings with furnace underlighting. Looked like a storm, and a doozy too. But it would probably make things fresh and clean in the morning. I found a Walmart and used up some of the cash from the cache—the bills smelled of mildew but were otherwise all right—to buy jeans. Panties. T-shirts, a couple tank tops, a couple sports bras I was sure would fit me now, and a couple pairs of cheap sneakers. And, finally, some elastic bands for my stupid hair. If I could just stop losing all my luggage things would be swell. Or at least, better.

Still, better losing some gear than losing my life. Right?

That silver lining was wearing away right quick.

The Comfort Inn had palms in the driveway and a sleep-eyed clerk who didn't even glance at my fake ID. Which was a relief, since I looked nothing like the picture anymore. The Dru on the ID Dad had put in the second ammo case had darker, almost-frizzed curls, a different-shaped face, and a shy young smile that didn't quite believe it was being photographed. She was twenty-one according to the birth date.

I was getting older all the time.

I ever catch you usin' these to buy booze, Dru-girl, I'll tan your hide.

He sometimes threatened that, but he'd never swatted me even once. Neither had Gran. It was just something they said. And seriously, the threat kept me in line.

I know better than to make waves when someone can just disappear on you.

I'd looked at the little plastic-covered card and felt a funny sensation all over my skin, like I was vanishing.

I rubbed my thumb over the picture before I stuffed it back in the cheap wallet Dad had packed with it. As if it was my mother's photo in Dad's billfold—the only picture of her we'd had, and gone now.

Sergej probably had it. And I was so tired I didn't feel anything at the thought.

I thanked the sleepy clerk kindly and took my room key with a tired flourish. At least I only looked road-grimy, and smelled bad but not bad enough for a normal person to notice.

The lobby was done in the particular type of pink florals that will give you a headache unless you're an eighty-year-old bleary-eyed grandma who thinks overstuffed couches are *cute*, but the rooms weren't bad. Quiet, at least, and the sheets were clean. The water pressure was decent too, and I stood half-asleep in the shower for a long time. The clothes I'd been wearing were useless; I tied them up in a plastic Walmart bag and would dump them in the morning.

It was weird to be alone.

At the Schola I'd had to work to get some time to myself; driving with Graves and Ash meant I was always listening to and anticipating them, and traveling with Christophe meant I was always following him around.

You can hide from them, but not from me.

Was he dead? Possible. Not very likely, Christophe was tough . . . but still. He'd either meet me in Houston or he was on my trail right now. And Graves, his eyes turning darker and darker, tied up or . . .

I tried not to think about it. Failed miserably. How deep was Sergej's hold on him? Why hadn't I *known*?

Dru! Dad's voice barked, and I jerked, my hand hitting the side of the shower. *Quitcher woolgatherin'! You're asleep on your feet like a mule. Come on, now.*

By the time I was in a clean T-shirt and underwear, yawning and scratching and standing in front of the microwave while a Hungry-Man dinner revolved inside, I was well on my way to fretting. Sometimes it gets that way when you're tired—nothing stays in any sort of proportion.

Of course, I had a bunch of vampires trying to kill me and everyone who hung around me for any length of time got blown up or tortured. Even if I was losing some of my sense of proportion, I figured I had cause.

I had to eat with my fingers. It didn't bother me much, except it's hard to do with mashed potatoes. I turned on the television and watched the news while I polished off two more frozen dinners, scooping up the taters and licking them off my fingertips like icing, tearing chunks off the slices of processed turkey. The marionberry crisp was soggy and cold on the first two trays by the time I finished the third, but I ate it all anyway.

I left some of the corn. Never been big on corn.

Nothing on the news about explosions or suckers or sorcerers in Atlanta. That didn't surprise me much. The air conditioner made a racket, so I turned the TV up a bit. Not a peep about shenanigans in Georgia. Just the regular cavalcade of crime, human interest, and a weather report saying "expect a thunderstorm." Well, any fool could look out the window and see *that*.

Rain started in spatters as I brushed my teeth. I spent about a half hour checking the gear from the cache, and when I went to bed I had everything stowed away nice and shipshape.

And I had a loaded baby Glock on my nightstand, carefully pointed away from the bed. I'd cleaned and checked it just like Dad taught me, and everything seemed to be all right. I'd pick up more ammo tomorrow. I was working through soup by then, so tired the urge to yawn just about threatened to crack my jaw. I held off— you shouldn't yawn while cleaning guns. Then I dragged my sorry carcass up and warded the walls. It took a while. I had to start over two or three times because my concentration kept wavering, the thin fine blue lines slipping through my mental grasp. By the time I finished, I was actively yawning more than I was breathing, the *aspect* smoothing down over me in soft blurry waves.

I wondered sleepily why warding was blue, and the hexing I'd seen was blue and red. Gran would've been interested in that. I felt like I was missing something, but damn if I could think of *what*. I was just so tired.

The last thing I did was fish the diamond earrings out of my bag and put them on. Just because . . . well, I figured it couldn't hurt. Nothing could, at this point.

I was ready for anything.

Or so I thought.

The long concrete hall stretched away into infinity. I saw him, walking in his particular way, each boot landing softly as he edged along, and the scream caught in my throat. Because it was my father, and he was heading for that door covered in chipped paint under the glare of the fluorescents, and he was going to die. I knew this and I couldn't warn him, static fuzzing through the image and my teeth tingling as my jaw changed, crackling—

—and Christophe grabbed my father's shoulder, dragged him back, away from the slowly opening door. The sound went through me, a hollow boom as the door hit the wall and concrete dust puffed out.

BANG.

CHAPTER TWENTY

By the time the long roll of thunder faded I was on my feet, scooping up the gun. The *touch* flared inside my head, and in the flickering blue-white glow from the muted television I sensed more than saw the brushed-metal doorknob jiggling.

The *touch* spilled free of my skull, but told me nothing much. There was something weird—interference. Odd static fuzzed over the TV screen, swallowing the black-and-white movie that had been watching me while I slept. The white noise filled my skull, bouncing around like a pinball.

What the hell? I pulled back, shaking my head.

I ghosted to the wall partitioning bedroom space off from hall-and-bathroom space, gun held low and fingers locked outside the trigger guard. Thunder boomed again, filling the sky, and the thin blue lines of warding in the walls shivered. They were reacting to whoever was outside the door. And not in a good way—whoever-it-was smelled like cloves and sand, and their mental fingers picked at the wards like a kid undoing a sneaker lace.

My mouth tingled, the faint taste of oranges filling my throat and a chill sliding down my spine. I knew that chill.

Brace yourself, Dru. Shit's about to get weird.

There was the gun. Was I actually going to shoot whoever was coming in?

Fine time to be doubting that, Dru.

The warding sparked, resisting. I almost thought of grabbing hold of it from my side and giving whoever it was a snap, like popping a rubber band hard against their mental fingers. If you hit someone just right like that you can give them a helluva headache. Maybe even knock them out.

But if they could unravel wards like that, they were probably more skilled, and I'd be the one with the headache. My best bet was keeping the *touch* inside my head and using the damn gun.

Better be ready. Do it like Dad taught you.

The door opened, silently. The wards unraveled, whispering off into nothing like smoke. Soft regular thudding; my ears picked it out. Two of them, and I was hearing their heartbeats.

Well, isn't that useful. My own heart was in my mouth, warring with the ghost of citrus and the tooth-aching cold. Why just two of them, if they could spring a trap with a rocket launcher on top of a building a couple states away? An advance team? More coming in the windows or watching the hotel?

Now, Dru. It was Dad's voice, or I might have moved too late. *They're walking right into your angle.*

At the last second, the gun jerked down. I got lucky—the first one folded when the bullet shattered his knee. A one-in-a-million shot, and Dad would've yelled at me for not taking the body shot. *Don't point that thing if you ain't prepared to kill somethin'!*

The roar of the gunshot was lost in a thumprattle of thunder, lightning lit up the room, and the television screen flashed. The second guy—tall, dark-haired, gold glittering in his ears and at his throat—pitched forward, his hands flying out and the hex sparking red and blue like a firework.

There's a few different sorts of thrown hexes; this was one of the flat fizzing Frisbee types that make a *zshhhhht!* noise and go whirling.

My left hand flashed out. In a hex battle, you're either quick or you're toast. Dad and I had run across several practitioners over the years, and once or twice it'd been Gran's careful training that saved both our bacon.

So it was Gran's owl, now, filling itself in with swift streaks, that burst into being as the hex singed my fingers. The owl hit the second guy in the face with a crunch, and the red and blue hex spun as I caught it like a nail-studded baseball, sharp edges biting my skin.

As long as I wasn't going head-on, I had a good chance of bending the hex around. Like *t'ai chi*—stepping aside from the force of the punch and deflecting it, instead of meeting it with equal strength.

I may not be brawny, but I'm *fast*.

My left arm came back, I whipped it forward as if I was tossing the Frisbee back at him, and the guy lost his hold. Which was another miracle, because generally it's harder to wrest control away from someone who's taken the time to build such a pretty, malevolent piece of work as a really good hex.

And this one was a lulu. But I guess the guy was having a hard time focusing with his face full of talons and feathers. The owl exploded, a rain of white down popping out of existence just before his bleeding face came up—

—and his own hex crunched squarely into his lean midriff.

He folded up just like a spider flicked into a candle flame and was actually flung back into the hall, golden electric light shining off a spatter of blood that hung in his wake right before there was another photoflash of lightning and the power failed. Darkness like a wet bandage pressed against my eyes, and in the aftermath of another huge roll of thunder I heard ragged breathing and someone muttering cusswords.

"Bitch!" A boy's voice, breaking. "You shot my *knee!*"

He sounded fifteen, tops. Where were the adults who were supposed to handle this thing? Did they even exist? Was he old, too, and trapped in a young-sounding body?

You're goddamn lucky it wasn't your head. I said nothing. The emergency lights came up, a dull orange glow, and the hex in the hall was still sparkling and digging into a prone form. Hot acid boiled up inside my throat. *He wasn't looking to leave me a Christmas card. Get moving!*

The guy on the floor kept cussing while I stepped into my jeans and boots. I buckled my *malaika* harness—a trick to do one-handed while you're covering a squirming guy on the floor. He could have had a gun too, but if he hadn't shot me by now, I didn't think he would.

Duffel in one hand, gun in the other, I made it to the wall near the window. Let out a long, shaky breath.

"What did you do?" The boy on the floor had stopped cussing. I wasn't sure I liked it. He was sounding mighty sharp and focused for someone who'd been shot. "How can you do that? How can you use the *jaadu?*"

I'm not going to hang around and chat with you, you know. The *touch* slid free of my skull, little invisible fingers questing for danger. He choked, but I didn't have time to worry about it. No rain against the windows—it was heat lightning; no wonder everything was all staticky.

Three-floor drop. You can make it easy. I didn't want to get trapped inside the rest of the hotel, and I didn't know if these guys had backup. Maybe they were expecting me to go out the window; I didn't know.

But I also wouldn't have gone out into that hall, and stepped past that body and the crackling, nasty hex, if you *paid* me.

"Wait." The boy on the floor was moving, rolling around. "*Rajku-mari*, wait. For God's sake, *wait—*"

Too late. Glass shattered, the stifling hot night full of ozone, wet heat, and the smell of Gulf rot closed around me, and I was gone.

* * *

Thank God I hadn't been stupid enough to park the Jeep in the hotel lot. I still had a couple of bad moments getting to the side street I'd left it on. I kept jumping at shadows. Can you blame me?

The rain started just after I threw the duffel in, hard quarter-sized drops thudding into dirt and concrete. More lightning played in the billowing clouds like huge veined hands.

I was getting awful tired of thunder. But at least there was nothing unnatural about this storm. My left hand hurt like hell—I wrapped it up in a chunk of fast-food napkins. I didn't smell blood, but it was weeping, and it burned like I'd held it in boiling water for a while.

And I'd only touched that hex for less than a second. What would it have done if it hit me? For a couple seconds I braced my forehead on the steering wheel while my ribs heaved with deep ragged gasps.

But Dad's voice inside my head was pitiless. *Move it along, honey. You ain't out of the woods yet.*

I flipped the wipers on and got out of there. Seven and a half hours later I was in Houston. But by then things had already gone even further to hell.

CHAPTER TWENTY-ONE

Finding the Houston Schola wasn't hard. I mean, yeah, I stopped on the outskirts of the city and bought a map, a bag of peppermints, some boiled peanuts, and some dental floss, and made a quick and dirty pendulum from a wrapped peppermint and the floss while I munched the peanuts and drank some warm Yoo-Hoo. The pendulum gave me the general location—a wedge of the northern part of the city, a slice of expensive real estate if the tingle in my good right-hand fingers told me anything. Close enough, and I was sure I could find it from there.

As it was, I could. But it was a matter of getting close enough and following the sirens while a column of black smoke billowed up. Traffic was snarled, and we slowed to a crawl. As a result, I got a good eyeful.

The good news was that the Houston Schola was kind of still there.

The bad news? Was the *kind of*. If by *kind of* you mean "shells of charred and smoking buildings arranged around a scorched quad that might have been pretty gardens if someone hadn't taken a flamethrower to them." Emergency personnel were still swarming, and black smoke hung everywhere.

The Jeep crept through heat shimmering up from the pavement and the traffic snarl created by a bunch of what Dad would call lookie-lous, cars slowing down to gawk.

I stared. Little crackling strands of red and blue hexing crawled over every surface. The knots that had held them fast while they did their dirty work were unraveling, and I could almost *see* how they did it, how they pulled the two strands together and made them work. Gran had never told me about anything like the red strands, and if I just knew a little bit more about the Maharaj I could probably take a stab at untangling it. Or even duplicating the effect.

The *touch* hurt whenever the red strands got too close, like sunshine on already-burned skin. My left hand throbbed, blistered and raw. I'd disinfected it and wrapped it in gauze, and the rawness didn't look to be spreading. It was only my left hand; I'd deal.

The main building of the Schola here had actually faced a city street without a lawn and a wall. Its long colonnaded front now looked like a bomb had gone off. Even the wall enclosing the rest of the property was scarred and pulled down in places. There were other buildings, but they were all smoking and laid waste too. At least, all the ones I could see.

"Goddamn," I whispered, under Jerry Lee Lewis on the radio making his way through *High School Confidential*.

Dad had always made a face when I turned that song up. The sound track of my childhood is the oldies stations you can get all over America. No matter where you land, Casey Kasem is rockin' 'em up and countin' 'em down. He's a cottage industry. Long live rock'n'roll.

I was almost past the Schola. Traffic was horrible. I had half a tank of gas and I had to think.

It took me an hour to get to the freeway. Heatshimmer bounced off the pavement, Houston like a big dozing concrete animal ready for another long guzzle at the oil teat. The *touch* jumped like a nervous animal, my brain stroking at the problem of the red and blue threads.

What am I gonna do now?

I stopped outside the city limits for gas and a load of road food. A couple hot dogs, more Yoo-Hoo—this time it was cold—more peanuts, and a couple Tiger Tails. I never liked them, but Dad did, and I put them on the counter before I thought about it. I had to use a basket to carry everything; my left hand was swelling something fierce.

The tired old woman running the register didn't even blink, just subtracted the total from the leftover of the mildew-smelling fifty I'd given her for the Jeep's gas and handed me my change, blinking at the television, blaring some talk show, set further down the counter in a nest of Slim Jim cartons.

I found myself thinking of where Christophe would expect me to go so we could meet up, if he'd survived the rooftop. But it was idiotic to expect him to come riding in to save me, even though it was nice when it happened. I told myself several variants of this as I got in the Jeep; the engine turned over softly. Whoever'd had this car had taken care of it. It was holding up just fine.

Not like me. I was two steps from meltdown.

People were *dead* because of me. Not just the guy I'd hit with his own hex. There was also Piggy Eyes Lyle. Had he survived what I'd done to him?

I was a risk to everyone. I was a goddamn plague.

And Graves and Christophe . . . Jesus. Shanks and Dibs would take care of Graves. Ash too. They would take him out to their people and see if he could be reclaimed. They'd probably have a better idea of how to do it than I ever did. I didn't even know *what* I'd done to Ash to un-Break him. Maybe he'd just done it himself.

If Christophe had survived, he was probably tracking me. But.

There were a whole lot of *buts* flying around.

What if . . . just what if, mind you, a hypothetical…

What if Christophe or Graves—or both of them, let's talk worst case—what if they were . . . dead?

There it was, the thing I'd been trying not to think. You can't ever run away from a thought like that. It always finds a way to slip the knife in before you can get far enough. It plays with you like a cat with a mouse, letting you run just so far before it claws you but good.

The Maharaj were seriously bad news. From what it looked like, they could throw hexes even Gran would've had a hard time with. Poison and sorcery, and they were backing up Sergej and his vampires. I might have a chance of hiding from the suckers *or* from the *djinni*-children, but both? That was a whole different ball of nasty wax.

Especially since I had no safe place left to run to. California, yeah . . . but Remy and his team were human hunters. They cleaned out sucker nests, sure, working the edges. Could they go up against Sergej? The name sent a glass spike of pain through my temples.

No way.

Was it even faintly responsible to bring trouble to their door? Was it what Dad would've done?

California was never anything but a pipe dream. You knew it. You knew some damn thing would happen, and you'd bring danger to someone's door. Dad would kick your ass for leading Sergej right to your fellow hunters. My heart hurt, a piercing, stabbing pain. I'd been dragging Ash and Graves along because I'd been hoping Remy would be able to tell me what to do with both of them.

Way to go, Dru.

I shook my head, dropped the Jeep into gear, and headed back for the freeway.

It occurred to me then, something I should have thought of already. Atlanta. The rocket launcher and the helicopter. Maybe the Maharaj were just that good, maybe the Order had slipped up—I mean, a helicopter on a roof isn't exactly *subtle*, you know?

But there was also the possibility that someone had sold us out. Again.

The Jeep's interior filled with the soft sound of wingbeats under the radio playing Creedence Clearwater Revival. There was a bad moon rising, and she was me.

Gran's owl didn't show. It was just softly audible, the wingbeats keeping time with my frantic pulse.

I hit the freeway and just headed north. I had to decide what to do, and I had to keep moving while I did it.

Except in the end, it didn't matter.

* * *

The outskirts of Dallas are not a good place to get caught by the cops. I was going the speed limit, but the red and blue lit up like Christmas in my rearview and I had to make a decision: gun it or pull over?

For a few seconds I thought he was just going to go past me, on a call somewhere else. But no dice. I pulled over, edging as far onto the shoulder as I could, and he followed. Small rocks scattered on the shoulder crunched under our tires, and he was going to run the plate number soon and find out this car was hot as hell.

Great. I added everything up—the *malaika* still strapped to my back, the gun I wore, the gear in the back, the cash, the two sets of fake ID—and subtracted the cost of having to lose the cops, ditch this car, and steal another one.

It wasn't even a contest. I waited for the cruiser's driver's door to open. Light traffic, dusk had already eaten the sunlight, and it was muggy and hot as hell. I was gonna miss this Jeep.

The *touch* resonated inside my head like a plucked string. As soon as the door opened, I turned the wheel and stomped the gas. I could almost hear Johnny Law cussing as he piled into his car again.

The Jeep swerved out three lanes; I corrected and drifted back. The *touch* sparked, I jammed the pedal to the floor and the *aspect* woke, my fangs tingling as they lengthened, scraping against my lower lip. A bolt of pain went up my left arm, I was squeezing the wheel *hard* with both hands. Red and blue lit up my rearview and the siren whooped on.

Dad would've just *killed* me. Sure, he'd taught me how to get wheels if I needed them—but it's always a fool's game, because getting in a chase is one of the stupidest things you can do. The cops have *radios*. And *computers*. And a whole *hell* of a lot of know-how when it comes to outsmarting dumb criminal drivers.

But I wasn't a criminal. And I couldn't risk losing all my gear and being in a cell when the vampires or the funky sorcerers showed up. I just *couldn't*. So it was this, or nothing.

My head rang and Gran's owl exploded into being right above the Jeep's hood. Feathers puffed, torn away in the slipstream. I actually jumped and let out a shriek, and the Jeep swerved crazily. Years of Dad teaching "self-defensive drivin' " kicked in. The *worst* thing you can do in a situation like that is overcorrect and turn your car into a flying pancake.

The owl jetted forward, and the Jeep leapt to catch up. The engine thrummed, the tires actually lifted off the pavement when we breasted a short rise, and if I had to do something I was going to have to do it quick before Johnny Law got on the radio and reinforcements showed up to box me in.

CHAPTER TWENTY-TWO

Ditching the Jeep was a little easier than I'd expected. It was a good car, but two of her tires were busted and she was making a wheezing noise by the time I killed the lights and scrambled for the backseat. I kicked the rear passenger door open, bailed out with the duffel, and was on the roof of a nearby abandoned warehouse by the time the chopper found the car again, its bright white beam stabbing down like a shot from an alien abduction film. They'd get my prints, probably, but I couldn't do anything to help *that*. The empty ammo boxes in the back next to the can of gas would perplex them a bit, too.

And there went the Tiger Tails, too. *Dammit*.

I shrank into the shadow of a big silver HVAC unit. It wasn't humanly possible to get up here, so the cops should ignore it. I'd gone straight up the side of the building like I was a fish being reeled in, the *aspect* smoothing down over my body like hot oil and my wrists aching as my claws sank into the lip of the roof, my arm tensing to pull me and the duffel over. My left palm was a searscorch of pain, but that didn't slow me down.

Landing with jarring force, sneakers skidding, and I'd actually crashed into the vent and stayed there. I almost didn't think to twitch the duffel back out of sight against my feet, everything in me rabbit-jumping as if I still had to run.

Don't be stupid now. Be smart. Be still.

My pulse dropped now that I was reasonably safe. It was *hot*, an oppressive wet blanket full of smog-taste and the reek of cooling pavement. More sirens bayed in the distance as more cop cars arrived, bouncing over the train tracks and sending up spumes of oily dust. I kept my eye on the chopper, though, lighting up the fenced railyard next to the warehouse. It was a good guess—through the busted-out parts of the chain-link fencing and among the confusion of the yard and the scrubby kudzu and trash wood was pretty much the only way to run with a hope of losing them.

For a human, that is.

I wasn't even breathing hard. I watched as the cops swept the area, more of them arriving all the time and searching through the rail yard. The warehouse was locked up below; I know because they circled the whole building looking for a way in. Just in case.

Well, gee, that was easy.

I was just congratulating myself when my temples gave a flare of pain and a ghost of citrus wandered across my tongue. It wasn't danger candy, but it was enough to make me stiffen.

In the distance, a high glassy cry rose like a spiked silver ribbon.

Suckers.

Shit.

Were they after me, or just hanging around? That was a hunting cry, but it was a long ways away. The suckers could be chasing someone else. Who knew I was here? Who could've tracked me when *I* still wasn't sure where I was going?

You don't know, and you can't take a chance. Get the hell out of here.

Still . . . I was hidden, and the cops were still spreading out and searching. It could be unrelated.

Yeah. And monkeys could fly out your butt, Dru. Come on.

But I waited. I watched them swarm over the Jeep and look for me.

If I could go up a wall like this, evade the cops this easily . . . wow. It was a weird feeling. Creepy. Scary.

Powerful.

Was this what Graves was talking about when he said he didn't want to go back to being normal?

Then I thought about finding a place to sleep tonight, getting a fresh set of wheels, and figuring out where the hell to go next and what to do while suckers were trying to kill me. I thought of the burned-down hulk of the Houston Schola and wondered if anyone, *djamphir* or wulfen, had died in the flames. I thought of a broken body lying in a hotel hall with red and blue hexing crawling all over it. I thought of Piggy Eyes Lyle slumped against the news-paper box like a mangled toy and how *easy* it had been to tear up a cop car, how easy it would've been to pull the trigger on that poor county sheriff. I thought of Dad, and Mom, and Gran's house burning down, and Graves's eyes turning black as Sergej reached through him. Of Ash screaming while he tried to change back into his human form.

I don't want this. I never wanted this.

I didn't even know how to fight back without hurting someone who didn't deserve it. Or who might've deserved it, like Lyle or the hex-kid, but who might not've deserved how much of it I dished out.

Another high piercing cry, this one much closer and shading up into what had to be ultrasonic. It drilled through my head, but I was pretty sure the cops clustering around wouldn't hear it.

Get the hell out of here, Dru. The need to be moving rose under my skin. I couldn't tell if it was more rabbit-jumping, or if it was the *touch* warning me. If I started doubting the *touch* I was dead in the water, but I was also dead if I tired myself out running when I should've been staying put and resting so I could run when it was absolutely necessary.

"All right," I muttered, and took a look around. They were starting to lose hope over in the train yard, and apparently nobody seriously thought I would've gone this way. The warehouse slumped under an oppressively heavy sky, hard diamond points of stars trying to pierce the orange glow that was citylight trying to replicate sunset and failing miserably. Other warehouses crowded close, some empty and others just locked up. The spaces between them weren't overly wide. Not for a *djamphir*, I guess. Which meant not for a *svetocha*.

I eyed the closest building, the one that would set me up for leapfrogging to another one, and another. My eyes picked out the likely route with no help from me, and the *aspect's* warmth was a balm even under the oppressive heat. My left hand stopped smarting and settled into a heavy ache.

First things first. Wonder if I can jump to that rooftop over there? Well, no time like the present to find out.

* * *

A half-mile away I dropped the duffel and peered down into the street. It's amazing what a difference so short a distance can make. A neon sign down the street—a pair of legs in fishnet stockings—blinked blearily on a post lifting it up like a sacrificial victim. Underneath it, a red-roofed windowless bulk crouched. The place was called the

Lustee Ladee, and I immediately crossed it off my list of Places I Might Conceivably Want To Hide.

On the other hand, there were cars clustered around it like shiny little piglets hooking up to a sow. It was a veritable smorgasbord. A good chunk of people who worked around here were probably parked there, having what I supposed might pass for a good time to a certain type of grown-up dude. I realized my face was squinched up as if I tasted something bad at the thought.

I crouched on the nearest warehouse roof, a muggy breeze touching my messed-up braid but not cooling my forehead one bit, taking my time. You can't just pick *any* car. It has to be right—something with some legs and pickup, but that won't get you pulled over. You also have to consider that a parking lot isn't the best place. Too much chance of someone strolling out or a bouncer getting nosy, a security camera or something messing everything up.

I was still eyeing my choices when the *touch* twitched inside my skull, and my head jerked up. My left hand jerked, palm filling with molten pain. There was a low weird sound like silk tearing, and my heart dropped into my stomach with a splash, somersaulted, then leapt up into my throat and did its best to strangle me.

The red and blue sparks came out of nowhere, birthing themselves from the static-laden wind. Swirling, they coalesced, and the shape gathered strength. Long and low, a lean muzzle and four slim legs, a gleam of eyes as smoke appeared too, filling in the spaces between the sparks. The knots resolved too, complex threads catching and holding fast.

It would have probably been awesome if I could just stay still and watch how it was being built. You always want to pick up new stuff where you can.

For a few precious seconds I froze, staring at the thing. I've seen extra-weird in plenty of flavors all over the US, but this was . . . Jesus. To do something like this at a distance—was it even at a distance? I didn't *smell* any Maharaj around.

Would I know it if they were sneaking up on me, though? The aura—the wax-citrus taste that used to tell me when something was off—had deserted me. Probably because I'd bloomed. I'd have to find other ways of staying alert.

The blisters on my left hand ran with hot prickling painful tingles. The sense of force building was familiar, my eyes hot and dry and my solar plexus tightening. *Get up a head of steam and hit that thang before it gets solid, Dru-girl.*

My right hand flashed up, touched a *malaika* hilt. Hawthorn wood, good against lots of things in Gran's universe. My left jabbed forward, and the *touch* flared. If you can grab the point at which something unphysical is coming through to build itself in the tangled, snarled fabric of the real, you can disrupt it. I'd done it before, most recently with a big red tentacled thing in the girls' locker room at the Schola Prima.

Now *that* had been a doozy.

The hex-dog snarled, crouching as it solidified. Well, maybe *solid* wasn't the word, because it was built of smoke and knots of hexwork. But its teeth were chips of obsidian, glittering as its insubstantial lip lifted, and the snarl rippled through it. The knots were tying themselves together with quick jerks, and I didn't have much time.

My left-hand fingers cramped together, weirdly twisted like I had the rheumatiz. The *touch* grabbed, slipped, grabbed hold again, and I flung myself backward as the hex dog finished its crouch and sprang. Another ripping sound, this one like wet meat shredded in iron claws, and the thing let out an agonized howl that scraped along every nerve ending I had. My back hit the rooftop, my head bounc-ing, and the dog exploded in a rain of smoke and icy flashing pellets of something that stung as it showered down.

I couldn't even feel good about that. Because another sucker hunting-cry lifted, spearing the muggy night, and it was so close I scrambled up, shaking the little bits of almost-ice away. The raw blis-tering pain in my hand eased a little.

A burst of cloves and incense belled out from the hex-dog's vibrating, fading "fingerprint" on the snarled tangle of the fleshly world, the smoke shredding. I grabbed the duffel, slinging the longest strap diagonally across my body.

I was not losing my gear again, dammit.

I took off across the roof, sneakers whispering. The smoke wanted to cling to me, but when Gran's owl hooted softly and arrowed over my shoulder, its wings snapping down and almost brushing my hair, it shredded the vapor away. My body moved smoothly, the world slow-ing down, encased in the hard clear plastic of supernatural speed as I gathered myself and leapt, flying over the street below and landing soft as a whisper on the top of a gas station's roof. A short hop, get-ting some height as my feet touched the hood of a vent, and I was airborne again.

It was like flying. It used to be I'd have to strain every muscle to keep up with Gran's owl. Now it was the world turning under my feet doing all the work, my sneaker soles touching down to propel me in different directions. Like running with the wulfen through Central Park's leafdapple shade, feeling like a complex part of a speeding machine. That was the difference, I guess, between running now and running with them: with the wulfen, for a few minutes as we ran, I felt like I belonged.

Now I just wanted to get *away*.

The owl, glowing white, veered sharply to the left and dove. I followed, hitting the pavement a little harder than I liked and taking off. Behind me, like infection pushing up against the surface of a wound, I *felt* them.

Suckers. My breath came fast and light, sudden knowledge blooming inside me. I didn't have the taste of danger candy to warn me, I just had intuition now.

Great.

Gran's owl let out a soft *who, who?* Wings snapping, it braked, *hard*. I skidded to a stop, and the bird turned in a tight circle over me. Part of me was on the ground, ribs flaring and squeezing down as I breathed, and before I knew it I'd reached up and the warm satin hilts of the *malaika* were in my hands. The duffel was going to weigh me down, but I didn't have time to drop it.

Because the black-paper cutouts of suckers boiled out of the darkness.

There were so *many* of them. Two females closing in fast, their irises turning black as the hunting-aura closed over them in a blot of cold fire, both wearing dark jumpsuits, one blonde and one dark-haired but both with ponytails that bounced smartly as they pulled up short. The rest were males.

None of them looked a day over sixteen, but the hate on their young-old faces twisted them up like dripping, nasty tubers. I dropped into first-guard, the *aspect* rising over me like a cobra's hood.

I was fully-bloomed and deadly to them. But they had numbers. Which meant I had to think fast. But my thinker was busted. There was just nothing left to do, nowhere to go, and nothing to depend on to save me.

If I'm going down, I'm going down fighting. I swallowed, hard, and then did either the stupidest or smartest thing I could.

I gathered myself, took a deep breath, and screamed as I launched myself at the ones in front of me. If I could break through their ring I could lead them on a chase, and when it came down to that I'd rather be running full speed when the nasty hits me.

I almost made it, too.

Chapter Twenty-Three

For a long time there was a whining sound, a bumping and buffeting. I drifted in and out of consciousness inside something cold and metallic. I couldn't move—my wrists were held down, and my ankles.

Restraints, I realized through a fog. My left hand burned dully through a chemical haze, like I was drugged or something. *And I'm in a box.*

My eyelids fluttered shut. *Thank God I don't have to pee,* I thought hazily, before the dark swallowed me again. After a long while I was vaguely aware of a bump and a screech, and I figured out I was on a plane. That was all I knew. Then the dream came out of nowhere, and this time I was tied down and I had to watch.

The concrete hallway stretched into infinity. I saw him, walking in his particular way, each boot landing softly as he edged along, and the scream caught in my throat. Because it was my father, and he was moving toward that door covered in chipped paint under the glare of the fluorescents, and he was going to die. I knew this and I couldn't warn him, static fuzzing through the image and my teeth tingling as my jaw changed, crackling—

—and Christophe grabbed my father's shoulder and dragged him back, away from the slowly opening door. The sound went through me, a hollow boom as the door hit the wall and concrete dust puffed out.

BANG.

"You shouldn't be here," Christophe hissed, his eyes burning blue. "Are you mad, or simply an idiot?"

Dad shook him off. "What the fuck—"

Christophe shook his sleek dark head, the aspect laying on him in a crackle of static electricity. His fangs were out and snow clung to his knees, clumping on his boots. "Get out of here. Go."

"You're him. The man on the phone." Quick as a wink, Dad had the gun raised. "She told me—"

"Elizabeth told you somewhat of me, yes. But I'm not what you think." Christophe shoved him, hard. "Get out of here. He will rise soon, and you're worse than helpless here. Go home!"

"I don't have a home," Dad spat back. "They took my home when they killed her, goddammit! All I've got . . ." But he stopped there, eyeing Christophe suspiciously. Maybe he'd been about to say something about me? I longed to know. "What are you doing here?"

The door at the end of the hall quivered hungrily. Run! I wanted to yell. Both of you, quit arguing and RUN!

"Paying my debt to Elizabeth Lefevre." Christophe's smile wasn't nice at all. In fact, it was chilling. "You're all that remains of her. A stupid, silly human."

Dad regarded him narrowly, his blue eyes at least as cold as Christophe's. "Then let's go down there and kick some sucker ass."

"You're worse than useless. Come on." Christophe moved forward, *as if to grab Dad and drag him out by force. I silently cheered, static buzzing through me as the vision held.*

I'd wanted to know, of course. I'd wanted to know what happened to Dad. And not-wanted at the same time. I'd already seen what happened when vampires killed. The pictures of the blasted oak tree in front of the yellow house we used to live in, something not even human-shaped anymore hanging in the branches, still whirled through my nightmares.

Dad pulled the trigger. A burst of white noise rammed through the image, and my scream lodged in my throat like a rock. I couldn't breathe, couldn't move, couldn't cry out. I was a fly trapped in amber, howling on the inside while Christophe's body jerked, bright red blood flying.

Dad's bootheel scraped as he turned and took off down the hall. He was a big man, but he was light on his feet. He vanished through the door as Christophe struggled back up to his feet, face twisted with pain and eyes burning.

"NO!" Christophe yelled, and another burst of static roiled through the image. I held on, my mental grasp slipping as the vision fought me.

No. I want to see. *Stubbornness rose inside me. I* have *to see!*

Christophe pushed himself up. Gunfire popped and crackled behind the door, yelling and a rising glassy roar. Christophe's hands turned into fists. He stood there for a long ten seconds, head cocked as blond highlights slipped through his hair, the aspect flaring and retreating, indecisive. Snow fell from his knees, hitting the floor without melting, and his face was a mask.

Then he turned and walked away, while my father's dying screams echoed from behind the door that was even now closing like a Venus flytrap on its prey.

I sat straight up, clawing at thin cold air. Metal clashed. My wrist was jerked back as I tried to roll off the hard surface, and I ended up halfway on the floor, my arm stretched above me like I was performing an enthusiastic wave.

What the hell?

A dim stone cube of a room greeted me. An iron door, a shelflike metal toilet, no windows. Light leaked in around the door, through the barred rectangle of an observation slit. Electric light, nice and golden, but not nearly enough of it.

The clashing metal was a short chain attached to the wall and hooked up, probably to keep me from falling off the bed. If I unhooked it, I could just reach the toilet.

Which I did. Hey, you've got to be practical when you're chained to a wall. At least it flushed.

I smelled faintly of cinnamon rolls, and my skin was still sticky from Dallas citysweat. My mouth tasted like zombie dust, but all in all I felt oddly good.

I shuddered, stretched the chain and my arm as far as they would go, and couldn't peer out the slit in the door.

Dammit.

I was in sock feet, my T-shirt, and jeans. My hair was unbraided, a wild curling mass.

There went all my gear. Again. Dad was always going on about caches and gear, and about how replacing shit was the cost of seriously being on the run. Looked like he was right.

Not that I'd doubted him.

I rattled the chain, examined the plate it was attached to. Bolted to the wall, nice and solid. I even lay on the bed, got both my feet up, wrapped my hands in it, and *pulled*. My blistered hand shrieked with pain, but I kept at it. The chain groaned a little, but the plate stayed solid. I braced myself carefully, then, inch by inch, put more pressure on the chain. The *aspect* grew warmer, closing around me until thin curls of steam rose from my skin in the damp chill.

The chain creaked; my breathing quickened. I finally had to loosen up a little. The hook the chain was hung on might have given me some leverage, but it was pretty flimsy. Looked like it could snap . . . but maybe I could tear it out and turn it into a weapon?

Yeah. I'll stab them to death with an itty-bitty hook. Great idea, Dru. I lay there and contemplated the chain. The cuff clung to my wrist, so small it wouldn't slip off over my hand even if I tried to take some skin with it. Featureless, light, powdery-silver metal, but it was *strong*. My claws couldn't even scratch it, and my wrist ached after trying.

The bolt on the door clanged, a huge echoing sound. I found myself crouching on the bed, my back against the wall and the chain rattling musically. A burst of thick cinnamon boiled up as the *aspect* coated me, my jaw crackling a little as the fangs slipped free. My mother's locket was a chip of ice against my breastbone.

The door creaked theatrically as it opened, and a tall figure stepped through. His eyes were black, pupil and iris both swallowing the light coming in from behind him. I blinked twice, not quite believing it.

"Graves?" I whispered.

A flash of green filled his irises, was gone as soon as it appeared. Swallowed by the darkness. His hair was freshly dyed, too. Dead black, hanging over a gaunt, expressionless face. A black dress shirt with pale bone buttons, sleeves rolled up to show muscle in his forearms. New jeans, and a pair of black Converse sneakers. He stood there, head cocked like he had a good idea, those dead eyes focused about three feet above me and his mouth a straight line instead of tilted in a half-sardonic, half-pained smile.

The *touch* chilled through me, crackling like ice cubes dropped into boiling water, and another shadow moved.

He was shorter than Graves, and curly-headed. A faint hint of swarthiness to his skin, and his profile was purely classic. You could see the similarity to Christophe when he turned his head, both of them in perfect, old-fashioned proportion. Like statues buried in dark volcanic ash for a long, long time. Preserved.

He didn't look any older than eighteen—until his gaze, sucking-dark from lid to lid, hit you like a wall of floodwater, battering away all resistance.

My left hand seized up in a cramp, and the bolt of pain up my arm was a lifeline. My mother's locket was so cold I had a vivid mental image of the metal freezing against my skin. Of ripping it free, a centimeter at a time, and the blood running down . . .

"Little bird," Sergej said. His accent was far more pronounced than Christophe's, and he sounded absolutely, chillingly *jolly*. Like he was having a hell of a good time. "Securely caged. You see, I've learned not to underestimate you."

Bullshit you have. My mouth was dry. I heard the click as I swallowed, convulsively. "I don't think you have." *After all, I'm still breathing.*

It was pure bravado. But shit, man, I didn't have a lot of anything else left.

Thank God I'd emptied my bladder. Looking at that handsome, cheerful, predatory face under its mop of honeybrown curls might just have made me embarrass myself.

His grin widened, fangs sliding free. He wore, of all things, a thin navy-blue T-shirt and new, very dark jeans. And cowboy boots.

The king of the vampires, and he was wearing shitkickers. Shiny new ones; they looked like Tony Lamas.

I got the feeling he'd dressed up for this.

My left hand cramped. Sergej stepped forward, brushing past Graves. Goth Boy flinched slightly, swaying aside. His Connies squeaked a little, a forlorn sound. I tensed, the chain clinking.

Another step. Bootheels clicked on stone. There was a drain set in the middle of the floor, and a shudder worked through me when I thought about why. Sergej was still staring at me, but as long as I kept squeezing my raw-blistered left hand the spiked pain kept me from falling into those horrible black eyes.

The *aspect* heated up. Like standing in front of an oven on a hot day, only the heat was a balm, smoothing away pain. I hoped it wouldn't heal my hand completely, I needed the spike of acid hurt to keep me from drowning. His eyes were so *black*, and the sheen on them was just like an oil slick. Almost rainbow-y, but without the nice colors. This rainbow was all the different gray shades of hate and suffering and the weird joy some people seem to get from nastiness.

Sergej halted. He leaned forward as if into a heavy wind, and inhaled sharply. The *aspect* flared, and he choked and stepped back, almost mincing in his clicking little boots.

I was still toxic. Thank God.

I actually let out a little sobbing sound of relief, and the snarl that crossed Sergej's face shoved me further into the wall. He surged forward, but the *aspect* flared with heat again, and he actually turned purple, the snarl stuttering as he throttled up again. He had to back up and gasp in a couple breaths, his hands tensing, sharp scythelike amber claws sliding free of his fingertips. A tremor rippled through him, and the black of the hunting-aura raveled out from the corners of his eyes in thin gray vein-strands. It looked like crow's-feet on his weirdly young face, and for a moment I saw the ancient, *hungry* thing that lived inside his skin.

I choked too, as if he was just as toxic to me. Wingbeats filled the space inside my skull, and the *touch* flexed. I realized I was trying to backpedal *through* the wall, forced myself to go still again.

He'd been able to get close enough to my mother for long enough to kill her. And close enough to Anna to get his fangs in her throat. Why wasn't he able to get close to *me*?

Not that I wanted him to.

Graves just stood there and stared, vacant. Every once in a while a flash of green would go through his eyes, lighting them up. It was eerie, but right now I was more worried about Sergej, who straightened and shook his hands out, the claws crackling as they slid back in. He tilted his head way back, his coppery throat working, and when he brought his chin down again, his curls falling in a perfect choreographed mess over his face, he was pretty again. A faint shadow lingered around his neck, as if the mottled purple flush had bruised him somehow.

I hope that hurt. Trembling roared through me in waves.

"I won't kill you yet," he informed me. "The other *svetocha* was of little use, and now she is of no use at all."

For one lunatic second I had no idea who he meant, then it hit me. "Anna . . ." The word fell flat in the stone cube, lay there gasping.

"Dead." Just like someone else would say *moved to Wyoming* or something. Like it didn't matter at all. "No matter, though. I have *you*. And you will help me walk in sunlight, darling *maly ptaszku*."

I shook my head. Anna'd been alive when her Guard—the boys in the red shirts, as if nobody ever told them about *Star Trek*—took her out of the burning warehouse. And before that, she'd all but forced me to drink her blood.

Was that why I heard her in my head sometimes? Or was it just because I was getting a little crazy with the Cheez Whiz? How could you stay sane with everything you ever depended on whacked away from underneath you, again and again?

Sergej laughed. It was a genuinely delighted little giggle. "Oh, yes. You'll help. I have plans for you. Do you like my new Broken?" A tilt of his curly head, and Graves flinched again. "He's really quite resourceful. Fought me the entire way. But I think, when I wring the last drop of blood from you and I feel sunlight on my face for the first time, he'll stop fighting. And he'll prove to be valuable. So much more decorative than his beastly little cousins."

Bile crawled up into my throat. I actually retched, and it echoed in the stone cube.

That just seemed to make Sergej's day. At least, he chuckled again and turned on his heel. He glided out of the room, silent as death, and Graves followed just as quietly. The door swung shut, the room's darkness closing around me like a mouth, and the chain jangled as I slumped down on the metal shelf and wrapped my arms around my knees. My left hand still hurt, a hot prickling pain.

I put my face down, my hair closing the entire world out, and I just shook for a while.

Graves.

He hadn't known me.

He'd just *stood* there.

CHAPTER TWENTY-FOUR

don't know how much later it was. Time loses a lot of meaning when you're locked in a box. Cold shadows sometimes moved over the little golden rectangle, little tiptapping footsteps too slow or way too fast to be human, drafts of bright-spangled hatred making the door groan each time. I kept bracing myself in different ways, working on the chain and the cuff.

It was my only option. Unfortunately, it wasn't one that had even a hope of turning out okay. Even probing at the cuff with the *touch* told me nothing.

There was a long silent time, and I started singing to myself while I yanked this way and that on the chain. My wrist felt bruised and itchy underneath it. I even sweated a little in the damp stony chill. At least I didn't smell bad. I still reeked like the cinnamon-bun place at the mall, which was a blessing because I hadn't had a shower in a while.

When the bolt on the door clanged again, I scrambled up to crouch on the shelf-bed, my cheeks guiltily hot. My back hit the wall and I didn't make a girly little fear-sound.

But it was close.

He eased in, leaving the door open behind him, and did a strange thing.

Graves crouched, right inside the door. He laid his hands flat on the floor and looked at me, and his eyes were back to green. My heart hammered. He even *smelled* right—a stray breath from the hall brought me a tang of moonsilver wildness and strawberry incense over the dry-fur nastiness of vampires. The bone buttons on his shirt glowed a little, and he looked . . . feral.

Dangerous.

Heat prickled in my eyes. I watched him, braced against the wall, heart thundering.

"*He's* asleep," Graves finally whispered. "Thinks he has me down. Like a good little dog."

The rock in my throat moved. I made a sound.

"Dru." He stared at me. A muscle in his cheek flicked. It hit me again, how different he was from the gawky, bird-thin, almost-ugly Goth Boy who'd bought me a cheeseburger and saved my life in a hundred ways ever since. Maybe they weren't overt, like Christophe's, but they were just as real. "Say something."

Yeah, sure. Like I had a whole list of things just lying around to say. My mouth opened. "Ash? Shanks? Dibs?"

He flinched as if I'd hit him. "Dibs is here. The others . . . I don't know."

I let out a shaky breath and settled for the obvious. "How do we get out of here?" I even sounded halfway normal, instead of scared out of my mind.

He twitched a little, and the green glow in his irises dimmed for a moment. His whole body tensed, shoulders hunching and the clarity of the change blooming around him. The Other shone out for a brief moment, and sweat sprang up on his caramel skin. Under his coloring, he was pale. A shudder wracked him, and he dug his fingers into the stone like he was going to start kneading bread.

"Dru." As if reminding himself who I was. "You gotta trust me."

I don't have a whole hell of a lot of options. I nodded. Curls fell in my face. "Okay."

That brought up a ghost of a smile. It wasn't anything close to my Goth Boy, but it made me feel a hell of a lot better. Relieved, even. My arms and legs actually went weak for a second, and I sagged against the wall.

He stared at me for another long moment. "They've got him. Reynard. Christophe."

I actually gulped. "Is he—"

"Alive. Thought I'd warn you. It's pretty bad. But you *gotta* trust me, Dru. I'm Broken, but . . . please."

"I already said okay." The urge to roll my eyes was incredibly strong. "Graves—"

"Never figured out why you did." He hunched even further. "Tell me. Now, while I can hear you. Why did you even . . . why *me?*"

For a second I didn't know what the hell he was talking about. Then it hit me.

If I had a chance to tell him something, this was it. And it couldn't be like all the other times, when everything I ever wanted to say to him jammed up in my chest like a ball of snarled yarn and I ended up spitting out something so stupid it made me cringe for days afterward to even *think* about it.

Make it count, Dru. I searched for the words. And, wonder of wonders, they came.

"Because you're brave," I told him. "You're the bravest person I've ever met. Because you didn't walk off when it looked like I was in trouble. Because you stuck around even though the Real World's scary and Ash bit you. Because you made everyone come back to that first Schola while it was burning, to get me out. Because you came back the last time we tangoed with *him*." *With Sergej*, I meant, and Graves shuddered. *Hurry up.* The words tumbled out over each other, faster and faster. "Because I *get* you. I like your jokes and I like you and I feel like I can handle anything when you're around. Because . . ." I took a deep breath and took the plunge. "Because you're beautiful and I love you. Even if you drive me up the goddamn wall with the back-and-forth and not wanting to be my boyfriend or anything. Okay? That's why. Because you're a rock, Graves. You're a total . . . rock."

Oh, crap. I started out good and ended up lame. Story of my life.

Graves crouched there, looking at me. His face worked like the gears behind it had gotten snarled. His eyes flamed green, and the high-voltage humming going through him was so loud I was afraid everyone in the world would hear it. He stared for what felt like forever while I tried to think of something else to say. The chain rattled as I shifted, and that shook him out of whatever he was thinking.

"Trust me," he repeated, and was gone in a heartbeat. The door clanged shut, the bolt shot home, and I slumped against the wall.

"I do." My whisper barely stirred the air. I thought about this for a few minutes, and I found out I was shaking. My hands vibrated like I was holding onto a weed whacker and my legs gave out. I sat down on the shelf-bed with a thump that clicked my teeth together, hard.

I waited for him to come back. But after a little while, I started working on the chain again. I trusted him, sure.

But it would be even better if I was ready to go when the time came.

CHAPTER TWENTY-FIVE

got exactly nowhere. When Sergej came back, he had a black-eyed Graves lock my other wrist down with a short chain attached to a wheelchair. Then he edged closer to me, stretching out his hand, and did something—and the cuff on the chain attached to the wall unfolded in complex clockwork. The *touch* shivered uneasily, and my stomach growled. I felt light-headed but clear.

And thirsty. The bloodhunger scraped at the back of my throat. I could *smell* it in both of them—the candy-rotting reek of red blood cells dying inside Sergej's veins and the sweet red fluid in Graves's.

"Poor little dear, growing weaker." Sergej retreated to the door. "Hungry, are we? And thirsty too, I'll wager. But you're ever so much more tractable this way."

Just give me an opening, asshole, and I'll show you "tractable." I glanced at Graves, but his face was set and pale, and those black holes where his eyes should be were creeptastic. I lowered myself gingerly into the chair and decided not to say anything.

At least now I was chained to a wheelchair instead of a wall. The chain might be durable and the cuff made of something space age, but wheelchairs are pretty fragile when it comes down to it. Things were looking up.

At least, they were looking up until Graves clumsily buckled the leather restraints over my wrists and ankles. The vampire stood and watched, clicking his tongue occasionally when Graves slowed down. Goth Boy was sweating a little, tiny diamond drops of water standing out on his skin. He kept his head down, his hair shaken into his face.

When it was done, Sergej whooshed past and was out in the hall in an eyeblink. Graves grabbed the back of the wheelchair and began pushing. After the dim stone cube, the hall was a glare, and I blinked several times. Hot water swelled in my eyes as they adjusted. The hall sloped up, and the wheelchair squeaked as Graves set off, following Sergej's soundless steps. But his right hand came down and touched my shoulder. For a second his fingers dug in, a brief squeeze. Then he took it away.

I was shaking again. Sitting down, though, meant I could put my game face on. My left hand squeezed against itself, knotted up into a fist, and the spike of raw blistered pain was welcome. Even though my hand wasn't healing from the Frisbee hex, I wasn't going to complain. Not while it gave me a tool I needed to fight off Sergej's snakelike stare.

The hall went up, and up, and spiraled. The stone gave way to regular walls, but it still felt underground. Dead air and the sense of weight pressing down on you, all over your body, echoes not quite behaving the way they should. Graves was breathing hard, slowing down as he pushed the chair. Sergej didn't glance back, but he made another one of those clicking sounds, like he was hurrying up a horse or a dog.

Graves sped up a little. I concentrated on breathing, and on not hearing the soughing of blood in his veins. On not feeling the blood-hunger rasp against the back of my throat, my veins drying out like red sand. The emptiness in my middle, worse than hunger.

I've been hungry before. I've been plenty scared, too. But this . . . this was . . .

The hall ended in a pair of doors. Big dark wooden doors bound with rusting iron, spattered with crusted, metallic-smelling fluids I didn't want to look at. Sergej reached up, his slim hands shocking–pale against the rough black wood, and pushed. The golden electric light ran down his curls, and if not for the quicksilver inhuman grace of his movements he would've made a pretty picture. He shoved, casually, and the heavy doors swung wide.

A burst of warmer air slid down the hall. The *touch* filled my head with shadowy pictures, sounds coming through static

Screaming, begging, please don't, no. Bright eyes glazed with avid glee over the black of the hunting-aura, claws shearing through bone, blood hanging in the air before it splashed on white and black tiles. High crystalline laughter, murmurings brushing the skin like razors, sobbing victims dragged across the floor and—

My head snapped to the side as if I'd been punched. The *touch* was much stronger than it had ever been, and it twisted inside me, the cathedral-space suddenly bursting with images. They roared through me in a torrent, and my left hand tingled with fresh hot pain.

That damn cinnamon-roll smell rose from my skin, and now it had a new tang. Warm perfume, a familiar smell.

Be brave, baby girl. A familiar voice. I could feel her breath against my cheek, could feel her arms around my small body as she lifted me. *Be very brave now.*

My mouth fell open. My fangs lengthened, scraping my lower lip. *Mom?* But I didn't say it. I *couldn't*.

Because Graves pushed me through the door, the wheelchair squeaked, and a vast space opened up around us. Circular, floored in white and black marble like a cross between an old-timey diner's linoleum and a high-end hotel's tiled lobby; tiers of seats rose in coliseum arcs to a stone-ribbed dome. The light was low and bloody, drenching every surface and making every edge weirdly sharp.

The seats were crowded with vampires. Bright eyes, fangs out, their young faces twisting up as they hissed and snarled. They were in every conceivable teenage shape and size, and they were all beautiful in a weird, stomach-clenching way.

I blinked furiously, their hatred scraping hard against the thin skin keeping me separate from the world. The bloodhunger rose, flooding my veins, and it took a second before the shapes I saw snapped into a picture behind my eyes.

At the far end of the circular space, a ragged human shape was spread-eagled, chained to the wall with familiar silvery metal. His head was down, dried blood stiffening his hair, and every inch of bare skin I could see on him—feet, hands, chest through the rips in his shirt, legs through the torn jeans—was battered and covered with tiny cuts. My heart leapt up into my throat, pounding thinly in my wrists and ankles, even behind my eyes.

It was Christophe.

CHAPTER TWENTY-SIX

leaned over and retched, even though my stomach was empty.
I couldn't help myself. A swell of nasty laughter cut through the
snarling.

In the exact middle of the circle, there was a table and a chair.
The table had equipment stacked on it, tubes and glass canisters.
The chair was a monstrosity of whipped and curlicued iron, spikes
screaming up from its back.

On the other side of the table, a familiar golden head. Dibs
crouched, pale and slack-jawed, bruised up one whole side of his
face, his dark eyes terribly empty. He was barefoot too, but his blue
polo shirt and jeans weren't torn up. He rocked back and forth a
little, his hands clapped to his ears, trying to shut out the din.

My heart squeezed itself up into a rock. Poor Dibs.

Sergej raised his hands, and the sound coming from him
shocked everything into silence. It petered out, a high glassy scream
that trembled in the ultrasonic and speared the tender meat inside
my head. The cry drained away, leaving every surface quivering, and

the assembled vampires—there were so *many* of them, my God— were still as statues.

Across the room, Christophe's head lifted fractionally, dropped. A gleam of blue showed through his tangled, crusted, hanging hair. It was a shock to see him so dirty and battered. Yet another thing that made me feel like I'd stepped through a door and into an alternate universe, where nothing was right anymore.

I let out a tiny, sobbing sound. It shivered and died in that silence like a small animal crouched in a trap.

Sergej half-turned and grinned at me. Those black eyes sparkled on their surface, and it was then that I figured out what made him the closest thing to a king the vampires had. All the rest of them were made of hatred, true. But Sergej? He was hate boiled down to its bones. He didn't need a *reason*. Christophe had told me something had happened on an old battlefield in Europe, and after that his father had . . . changed. Had drunk so much blood, maybe, that something in him swelled up and burst like a tick. Maybe it was the part of him that had stayed human enough to get close to someone and father a kid. Or maybe it was just the part that made every other vampire recognizably human, even if psychotic and killcrazy.

Most suckers were mad dogs. But Sergej was a foaming-at-the-mouth dog who *liked* it. Gloried in it, even.

"Children." Sergej spread his fingers. The tips of his claws lengthened, elegantly. "My darlings. Look at what I bring. A *svetocha* who has eluded us all these years, the one we have been hunting, the scion of two great Houses. She is ours, and our plans are coming to fruition." He paused, and a swell of murmuring delight went through them. They stared. Some of them whispered to their neighbors, their young-old faces incandescent with hurtful delight.

Dibs had raised his head. He stared at me, his jaw dropping

further, and the naked horror on his face hit me right in the chest. Behind me, Graves was trembling again. The wheelchair's handles groaned faintly as he gripped them.

Wait a minute. Two Houses? And years? What? Gran had to have suspected something was—or several somethings were—after me, the way she kept me scrubbed down and smelling like something else, all those floor washes and strings of wild onion and garlic all around the house. And Dad had kept us moving around, like in Florida before we went to the Dakotas. So something couldn't get a lock on us, he said, and no more.

I hadn't asked.

"I will walk in daylight," Sergej announced. "And when I do, my children, so shall you."

There used to be a *djamphir*, a long time ago when the vampires could go out in sunlight. He was called Scarabus, and he killed their king, making sure they could only come out at night. But the way he did it was by drinking a *svetocha*—his own sister—dry. The stuff in my blood that made me toxic and drove boy *djamphir* a little crazy was the same stuff that could give Sergej the power to go out in the sunshine.

That was why vampires hunted *svetocha* down so hard. Either they killed us before we bloomed and got toxic, or they wanted to empty us out like Capri Sun pouches and go wandering around during the day. And Jesus, that thought was enough to send anyone reasonable almost catatonic with fear.

Without the sun to help the Order hold them back, their hate could eat away at the regular world like a cancer.

Christophe's chin came up. The mad blue gleams of his eyes shone in the dim ruddy light. His fangs were out, and the *aspect* moved over him in waves. But slowly, sluggish. I could smell how badly he was hurt. The chains holding him against the wall like a fly on a windshield rattled a little, a warning.

That attracted Sergej's attention. He blurred across the intervening space, coming to a halt a bare three feet from Christophe. The nasty air-tearing sound, like little voices laughing, echoed in the cavernous space. It was the same sound as when a *djamphir* used more-than-human speed to vanish, and if I'd had anything to eat that would have brought it up in a tasteless rush again. As it was, I was working against the leather cuffs feverishly, my left wrist cold under the metal of the cuff and its length of chain.

"My son." Sergej didn't sound so happy now. "What will it take to break you?"

Christophe spat something. It sounded like Polish, and definitely didn't sound like *good morning*. The words bruised his lips and turned the air darker. Or maybe it was just the helpless rage in them, beating a frantic consonant-laden tattoo before falling to the black and white marble.

Sergej leaned forward a little, on the balls of his feet. All the same, there was another tension in him, pulling back.

He's scared, I realized. *Of Christophe*. The bloodhunger surged, pounding in my veins, the *aspect* trickling hot strength into me. But too slowly.

"I wonder." The king of the vampires sounded chill and contemplative. "When I drain the last drop from her, my wolf, will that quench this rebellion?" He swung away, and the hurtful glee came back. He clicked his bootheels as he stalked across the floor and Christophe surged against the chains, fighting.

It hurt me to see. Blood dripped, each plink hitting the floor loud in the magnified silence. If he kept this up, he was going to hurt himself even worse, and anger crested inside me for one red-hot moment.

"Christophe!" I yelled. The light flashed, brighter, crimson instead of low red, and a draft of cinnamon and perfume roiled up from my skin. *"Stop it!"*

Dibs let out a soft little hurt sound. The vampires were still, staring. Sergej halted as if slapped.

Christophe sagged against the chains. Sergej made a noise like trains colliding.

Sergej was suddenly *there,* leaning into the sphere of toxicity the *aspect* gave me. His face mottled purple, and he hissed, everything in him twisting. Maybe it was because Christophe had listened to me — or maybe it was just because he wanted to be the only one doing the talking.

He's a garden-variety bully. For a moment I felt a surge of hope, of strength, of something warm and comforting. You don't stumble through the jungle of the public education system in sixteen different states without learning about bullies.

But then the hope crashed. He wasn't *just* a bully. He was the king of the vampires, and I was in deep shit. We all were.

And I couldn't see any damn way out.

Sergej backed off a couple steps. His entire body twisted, shoulders shaking, and he drummed his heels into the stone floor with little cracking sounds. The mottling retreated as he hissed, the sound shaking everything around us. Everything rippled, even the floor. The wheelchair groaned, and I squeezed my left hand. *Hard.* The sunburst of pain jolted up my arm, cleared my head, and I twisted, working against the straps.

No use.

Sergej's head tipped back down. He made another one of those little clicking noises, and the wheelchair shook as Graves's fists tightened again.

He pushed me slowly across the acres of checkerboard squares, closer to the table. I looked at the stuff on it, and swallowed dryly.

So that's what he's going to do.

It made a kind of sense. The happy stuff in my blood that drives boy *djamphir* a little crazy pretty much only functions when it hits the air. But it also breathes out through my skin, and that's what makes me toxic to suckers now that I'd bloomed and could reliably use the *aspect*. If Sergej, for some reason or another, couldn't get through that shell, if my blood was even more toxic when it hit oxygen and he couldn't get his fangs in me the way he had with Anna, well . . . the best solution was to make sure the blood didn't hit the air, right? And there was a good way of doing that.

It involved needles and tubing, and something simple to push the blood.

A transfusion.

Sergej must've seen it on my face. "It has a certain symmetry, does it not? I was not able to drink from your mother; I had to settle for merely destroying. But you are heir to all her strength, and whatever remnants of dear sweet Anotchka you stole before she died, and a bastard strain of the *djinni* themselves. I will have it *all*. This is only the beginning. It will take me weeks to wring the last drop of strength from you." He indicated Christophe with one short stabbing gesture. "And my son will watch every session." Another hideously jolly chuckle, and Sergej dropped into his iron throne. He laid his hands along the chair's arms, and clicked his tongue again.

Graves wheeled me toward the table.

CHAPTER TWENTY-SEVEN

thought he'd make Graves stick the needle in my arm. But instead, Sergej tapped his fingers and stared at Dibs. I yanked against the restraints. Nothing. The wheelchair threatened to tip, but Graves steadied it. He was breathing hard, his pulse ratcheting up into redline, fighting.

It didn't matter.

"You." The king of the vampires sounded bored. "Ready the transfusion."

Dibs rose, slowly. He was still staring at me, his pupils pinpricks and his hair wildly curling over his forehead. High bright flags of color stood out on his cheeks, and I saw the messy fang marks on his neck. Little bruised holes, crusted with dried blood.

Oh, God.

His ribs flared with sharp shallow breaths. He looked scared to death.

"No."

Even I couldn't quite believe he'd said it. Everyone was staring at him instead of me now, and despite the relief, I suddenly cast around for something to do to get them to stop looking at him.

Because Sergej's face changed by a couple of millimeters, and everything in me went cold and loose. Still, he just sat there, staring at Dibs, and when his gelid black gaze drifted over to me I was pretty sure I knew what he was thinking.

He was thinking of how easy it would be to find someone else to stick a needle in my arm and get the whole show on the road. Which meant Dibs would be superfluous.

"Dibs." Hoarse and weary. The bloodhunger twisted inside me, and my working against the restraints wasn't conscious by now. I was rubbing and twisting to get loose any way I could. It was useless, but that didn't stop me. "Do what he says."

"What's he gonna do, kill me?" A short, choppy laugh, and Dibs folded his arms. Maybe it was to disguise how he was shaking. He was flour-pale, except for those fever spots on his cheeks. "If he does that, he doesn't have anyone else who knows how to run this. Graves? Don't make me laugh. He's not medically trained."

"He'll find someone." I swallowed hard, saliva rasping against the bloodhunger and leaving me dissatisfied. "And, Dibsie? Sweetheart." The echo of Dad's hillbilly accent teased at the edges of the words. I never thought I sounded Southern, but right now I could hear it. "He might not kill you. He might do worse."

Dibs's pupils flared. Sergej's stare was a cold weight against my skin.

"I don't wanna hurt you," Dibs whispered. The utter hopelessness crashing into him was terrible to see.

"It's okay." Soothing, quiet, like I was talking to a nervous horse. "It's okay, Dibs. Really."

The chains across the room clashed as Christophe stirred. I

hoped he wasn't about to do anything stupid. Unless it was tearing himself free and kicking everyone's ass and getting me out of here. That would *not* be stupid.

But it was stupid to hope for it at this point. What I had to do now was get them out of this alive.

Good luck with that, Dru. You're not getting out of this one.

Well, okay. But if I could get *them* out, or even get them some more time, it was worth it. One small way to make up for being a plague, since if I hadn't been around, Dibs would be safe at the reform Schola, Graves would be living in his hidey-hole at the mall, and Christophe? Who knew? But he probably wouldn't be chained to a wall in his dad's Sooper-Sekrit Evil Hideout.

Which, by the way, had no taste. Gran would've called it overdone. Dad would've called it a horror-movie whorehouse, most likely.

A funny urge to laugh rose up inside me. I quashed it, but it made me feel . . . not better, I guess, but stronger. Like I could do what I had to.

It was like a jolt of cold water. Everything got very, well, basic.

Dibs was shaking even harder. The shudders went through him in waves. *Sub*, they called it. Submissive. He wasn't built for this.

Give him something to focus on. "Dibs." I wished I could snap my right-hand fingers. "Ash? Shanks? Do you know where they are? And Nat?"

His arms dropped, his hands curling into fists before releasing. The change rippled through him, wiry golden hair moving in fluid streams . . . and retracting. The fang marks on his throat glared. So did the huge circles under his eyes. He looked awful tired. "I . . . Alive. Last I saw."

I almost sagged with relief. "Then they're going to bust the doors down soon. Don't worry. Just do what you have to, right now. Don't worry about anything else."

"Are you . . ." He didn't glance at Sergej. Great pearls of sweat stood out on his pale skin. But the shaking was going down in him. Thank God.

The king of the vampires tapped his claws against the arm of his iron chair. The reptilian clicking turned my stomach into a bowling ball.

I summoned a grin. It felt tight and unnatural, like the skin on my face was cracking. "I'm sure, Dibs. Everything's gonna be okay."

I was lying to him, I knew. But he dropped his eyes and took a sliding sideways step toward the table. There were even little packets of alcohol wipes set out, and things in sterile packages.

Sterile. Like I might get infected. The thought called up another screaming lunatic giggle that died in my throat.

I wasn't going to make it out of this. I was pretty damn sure of that. You'd think it would be the sort of thing that would reduce a girl to the screaming meemies.

But for Dibs's sake, I was going to be brave. I was going to lose a little blood here.

I just hoped I had enough in me to buy the rest of them some more time.

Chapter Twenty-Eight

Sometimes I have nightmares about what happened next.
They always start out with the smile on my face, cracked and
faded but plastered there, and my encouraging nods every time
Dibs glanced worriedly at me. Then there's the sting of the needle and
the aspect flaming into life, every muscle in me tensing against the
intrusion and my fangs tingling, crackling, aching. Then there's a skip,
like a jolted CD player, and a sound like rushing water all through me.

A horrible draining sensation. A deep bruising ache in my arm.
The bloodhunger rasping against my veins, like sandpaper flooding
my circulatory system. Merciful darkness covering my vision, everything in flashes — Sergej's hiss as the needle slid in, Dibs's quiet sobbing, Graves's quick light breathing, the wheelchair rattling as he
twitched, the rising hateful murmur through the assembled nosferat, a
thin silvery rattle as Christophe's chains moved again.

My head fell to the side, my neck turning to rubber. A thin stem
to hold my pumpkin head up. I thought I heard my mother's voice
again — Be brave, sweetheart. Be very brave now.

The blood she'd given me was now sliding into her killer's veins. No oxygen to make it liquid poison for him.

Everything spilled away on that dark rushing water. This wasn't like Christophe's fangs in my wrist and the terrible inward-ripping sensation as something was pulled out of me by the roots.

No. This was worse.

Because it was black, and cold, and I was trying to scream, and I was alone, and nobody would hear me. It was like sitting in an empty house and waiting for Dad to come back, or sitting by Gran's hospital bed while her breathing got shallower and shallower. It was like my mother snuggling me into a hidey-hole in the bottom of a closet, closing me away in the safest place she could, and leaving me in the dark.

I was always being left behind. Like a piece of luggage. Like a toy, set down while a kid runs away to play with something else. Like trash.

Now I was left behind, again, and this time there would be nobody and nothing coming to pick me up.

This was the end of the line.

I heard a sound. I was making it. A chilling, breathless moan. Air escaping past slack lips, a drowning swimmer's final bubbles rising for the surface like silvery fish while the rest . . . sinks.

Fingers against my face. Cold, with the prickle of claws behind them. He scraped at my skin gently, like he enjoyed the feel of it. Something in me roused, knowing I was in terrible danger. It struggled for the surface . . . and couldn't make it.

"Take her away," Sergej said, and giggled.

* * *

No chain cuffed to my wrist. No need for it now. I was as weak as a sick kitten. Dibs held the cup of water to my lips; half of it spilled down my T-shirt. Tears slicked his cheeks. I blinked at him. There was a buzzing in my ears, and everything looked two-dimensional.

The *touch* was weak, too. Contracting, like a slug with salt sprinkled on it. Thin and washed out, the world with most of its color removed, all its solidity evaporated. Just a television show, light played on a flat screen.

"Dru!" Dibs, sobbing now. "Dru, please, wake up. Wake *up*."

I don't think I want to. But I was doing this for him, wasn't I? So I tried to focus through the haze. My mouth wouldn't quite work right.

"Dibsh?" I slurred. Tried again. "Shamuel?"

Because I'd always thought it was kind of funny when Christophe called him *Samuel*. A weird, floaty laugh came out of me, my lips loose and numb. I sounded drunk.

He made a low hurt noise. That snapped me back into some kind of sense.

Buck up, Dru. You're still breathing. Things could be worse.

As "comforting things to think" went, it kind of sucked.

I forced my eyes to open all the way. It wasn't the cell. It was a bedroom. No windows, the blank stone walls faintly sheened with something like greasy sweat. But the bed was a four-poster, done in faded pink, hanging curtains fuzzed with what looked like a century's worth of dust. A small brass lamp on a flimsy black-painted nightstand, its shade a bell of dark pink Tiffany glass, Art Deco and probably worth something. There was also a cut-crystal water pitcher. My left-hand fingers itched a little, and a terrible lassitude filled every inch of me.

A girl I'd hung out with in seventh grade had told me about having mono once. About being so tired she didn't even want to get up to pee. About how her whole body didn't even seem to belong to her. *Just a lump I was hanging around in until a bus came,* was the way she put it.

Sarah. Her name was Sarah Holmes. She had black hair.

I hadn't thought about her in ages. We'd moved on after Dad and I cleared out a roach-spirit infestation and did a little hexbreaking on the side. But now I wanted to see her again and tell her that I understood. And to apologize for promising to be her friend, when I knew I was going to be leaving.

Dibs's face loomed over mine. His eyes were red and inflamed, and his cheeks were chapped under the tearstains. He looked like he'd been crying for a long time.

Christ. Locked up in this room with me almost dead on the bed? No wonder.

"Hi," I croaked. "Don't cry. It's okay." For some reason that set him off again, but I didn't worry about it. I was thinking through mud, each separate thought very slow and stretched out. "Dibs. Kiddo. Calm down."

"I c-c-can't s-s-smell you!" The water glass shook in his hands. "You were s-s-so still, and I—"

"Whooooaaaa." I drew the word out. "Chill, Dibsie. Calm down. Nice and easy." *I am comforting a submissive werwulf.* Wow. For some reason it seemed funny. Horribly, bleakly funny. It would take too much energy to laugh, though. "How . . ." I struggled to find the right question to ask. "How long? Have I been . . . out?"

"Hours," he whispered. "I was scared." Half-defiant, his lower lip pooching a little. There was some grit in Dibs, even if he was sub. He certainly didn't take any crap when it was time to bandage someone up.

"Me too, kid." I tried to move, got pretty much nowhere. But I felt a little sharper now. The *aspect*'s warmth was gone; I never thought I'd miss it. It was *freezing* in here. The cold crept into my fingers and toes in a way that should have alarmed me. "Dibs. My hand. Left hand."

"What?" As usual, once he got something to *do*, he calmed right down. The stutter eased up and the frantic jittering in his muscles settled into an occasional twitch. "Oh, yeah. Blisters and stuff. I b-bandaged it. Looked pretty rough, and not healing r-right. What is it?"

I don't know. A hex so bad it burned me, but it's turning out to be useful. I didn't have the energy to explain. "Poke it."

"What?" He stared at me like I'd lost my mind.

"Poke it. Squeeze it." *Give it a beat and dance to it, just make it hurt.* I brought my attention back with a start. "Make it hurt."

"But—" He set the water glass down. "Dru."

"Make. It. Hurt." I didn't have any patience left, either. "Please."

"Okay." He leaned over me, grabbed my left hand, and squeezed with more than human strength.

A lightning bolt went up my arm, detonated in my shoulder. I yelped, Dibs yelped too and dropped my hand. He was all the way across the room before you could shout Dixie, pressed up against the dark, weeping stone wall. For just a moment the Other shone out through his wide fearful eyes, a flash of orange snarling, and fur rippled under his skin, not quite breaking free.

Even if he was shy and frightened, Dibs was still wulfen. He could kick some serious ass if he was motivated.

The trouble, I guess, was getting him motivated enough to forget he was scared.

The jolt of pain cleared my head. It also made the *touch* ring like a bell, expanding for a brief second before I dropped back into my tired aching body with a click, the exact same sound as Dad chambering a round.

Okay. I propped myself shakily on my elbows. Random curls fell in my face, and I tasted copper. My mouth was dry and aching. My teeth weren't sensitive at all. Well, that was a relief—but there was none of the *aspect,* and the world looked dull. It could've been just the dim pinkish light.

Or maybe I was just seeing with normal eyes now.

If I was, how did people live like this? With shutters over their eyes and cotton wool in their ears? It was worse than being blind.

My arms gave out. I sank back down into the bed. It was choking-soft, and my nose tickled from the dust. But I felt clear. Like I was made of glass, drained and wiped clean. At least I could *think* now.

I licked my lips, wished I hadn't. My dry tongue rasped, and the bloodhunger at the back of my throat was a slow creeping burn. "Door. Locked?"

Dibs eased away from the wall. "Nothing to pick it with, either. I checked. I thought if I c-could g-get you o-out—"

"Calm *down,* Dibs." *I appreciate the thought. Really, I do.* I focused on breathing. In, out, in, out. "Okay. Anything in here that can serve as a weapon? Is the bed breakable?"

"Wood. Not hawthorn. I *could* break it up, maybe make stakes, but they'll just laugh at us before they take off our heads like Pez dispensers." He swallowed hard, his chin lifting. His curls fell back, and for a moment I got a flash of what he'd look like if he ever got older, instead of being teenage all the time.

Pez dispensers? You're gruesome. That's good. "Good point. Can I have some more water?"

I didn't really need it. I just wanted to give him something to do while I poked at the beehive inside my head and figured out something amazing that would get us out of this.

Unfortunately my beehive wasn't producing much beyond a

steady whispered *oh my God we're all gonna die and prolly me first, hooray and oh shit.*

He was halfway across the room before he stopped, his head cocking. I strained my ears, heard nothing but my own pulse. "What is it?" I whispered. "Sucker?"

"N-no." Dibs flushed, and his eyes turned orange. He half-turned and crouched, fluidly, his splayed hands gently touching the stone floor. He didn't quite change, but the Other rippled under his skin and bulked his shoulders, and he exhaled, a growl thrumming out of his narrow chest before he went still and completely quiet, waiting.

Well, great. Then what the hell is *it?* I tried pitching from side to side, but my body wouldn't obey me. A twitch or two was all I could manage. Dust puffed up from the velvet coverlet, and the urge to sneeze tickled me all the way down to my toes.

Great. Just great. I managed to hitch one hip up. I could think and I could send the signals, but they weren't getting through to my arms and legs. It was like swimming in glue. I couldn't hear a damn thing, and the *touch* was dead. It might as well have been dumb meat inside my skull, for all the good it did me. Even squeezing my left hand into a fist, concentrating like hell to make my fingers draw up clumsily, didn't help. The pain just slid up my arm like swamp water, losing its insistent edge.

The door scraped. A key, turning in a rusty lock. How old *was* this room? Did I even want to know? The heavy bed and the lamp reminded me of the Schola Prima, and I suddenly wished I'd never left. Everything I did just made a bigger mess, and now things were as bad as they could get.

I winced inwardly. You're never supposed to even *think* that. Because it's just an invitation for the world, Real or otherwise, to throw something even more incredibly fucked up at you.

The door squealed as it was pushed open. Dibs settled, bracing himself like a cat who sees the mouse but isn't quite ready to spring.

Graves slipped through. I let out a blurt of sound, his eyes a green flash in the dimness, but it was too late.

Dibs leapt.

CHAPTER TWENTY-NINE

They tumbled out into the hall. Normally wulfen growl when they fight, but Dibs was dead silent—and deadly serious. If you've never seen a for real wulfen brawl, rather than just them playing around or shoving for dominance . . . well, it's something. It's a blur of motion, the Other surfacing in both of them, fur and muscle rippling. They move like they're shouldering through tall grass most of the time, compared to a *djamphir*'s quick graceful slink, but the rolling fluid hurtfulness of a serious fight among them is another grace entirely.

A grace that *burns*.

Thuds. A whimper. A scraping, claws against stone.

"I'm trying to *help*." Graves, harshly, a *loup-garou*'s mental dominance pressing down behind the words. "God *damn* you, Dibs, I'm trying to help!"

It didn't sound like Dibs believed him. More scraping, and a low sullen growl that rattled everything in the room.

"If you don't shut up *they'll* come!" Half-frantic, now. "It's day, it's day and *they're* mostly asleep; shut the fuck *up!*"

The growl turned off like a faucet. Two more thuds, shaking the door so that it swung, while I tried to roll the rest of the way over. My left hand was a fist, but the pain wasn't helping. It had turned into a dull ache like sunburn, and that was bad.

That was *very* bad.

"How can I . . ." Dibs, sharper than I'd ever heard him. "Traitor. *Traitor.*"

"Don't make me hurt you." I'd never heard Graves sound so cold. "Fighting *him* off is hard enough without you jumping on me."

A long static-laden silence. Then a short choked sound, another massive thump, and a long dragging noise.

Graves shouldered in through the door. He had my duffel straps in one hand, my *malaika* harness tangling and the wooden swords dragging along with the duffel. One-handed, because he was hauling an unconscious Dibs along in his other fist. He put his head down, his shoulders hulked a little as the change filled him out. His eyes flamed green, and he hauled everything inside, swung the door mostly-to, and turned on one booted heel.

Wearing boots now. Not Converse.

That was good, right? Green eyes was better. My brain tried to process this and vapor-locked.

We stared at each other. I tried to look like I could get up and kick some ass. Probably failed miserably. Because his face changed a little. He turned almost gray under his ethnic coloring, and his eyes slitted as a wave of trembling passed through him. His hands tensed, fingers coming up into claws, and when the fit passed, he was sweating again.

He shook his hair down into his face, a quick nervous movement. "Hi. He'll wake up in a bit."

I managed a nod. "I . . . I can't . . ." Tried once again to get my balky body to do something, *anything.*

"Don't worry." He crossed the room in long swinging strides. "I've got it figured out, Dru." He halted at my bedside, staring down from under the mess of his freshly-dyed hair. "You need blood."

It took a second for the meaning behind the words to hit home. "Graves—"

"Don't." He put one knee on the bed. Dust rose. "Just listen, okay?"

The urge to sneeze tickled my nose again; I held off with an eye-watering effort. He took my silence for agreement, I guess, because he lowered himself gingerly down. The bed creaked a little, and he worked one arm underneath me. He was scorch–hot, feverish through his clothes. His boots against my sock feet; it wasn't really apparent how much taller he was when he was lying down. His arm curled up and I settled against him like a sack of potatoes.

My cheeks were on fire. "Graves," I whispered. *Don't. This isn't safe.*

"Shhh." Like someone would overhear us. "Listen to me."

His trembling came back, and this time it infected me too. I was numb all over, my teeth chattering despite the heat coming off him.

"It's high noon," he finally whispered. "Sun's at its highest. For a little while, I'm free, because *he's* resting. We don't have long. You have to bite me, then we'll get out of here. Then I'm gonna run as fast and as far as I can until I'm sure *he* can't get inside my head again. When I'm sure, when I'm strong enough, I'll find you. You'll go back to the Order. They'll protect you. *Don't* argue with me, Dru. Just do it."

"I can't—"

"You can." He sounded so sure. I couldn't see his face, because my nose was against his shoulder. He didn't smell like *loup-garou* now. Instead it was just a healthy boy-smell, cigarette smoke and whatever harsh soap they gave him here. He kept himself clean no matter what, and now I wondered about that. "You *have* to, Dru. You've taken this asshole on and toasted his cookies before. This ain't no different."

"You don't understand." It was easier to say it with my face in his shoulder. "I *can't* bite you. I know what it's like. It's horrible. And I—"

"You have to. Dibs can't give you what you need to get out of here. He's too sub. Just *do* it, Dru."

How could I explain? I knew what it was like to have a *djamphir* bite you, to have something invisible, the core of what you were, something like your soul, pulled out by the roots, bit by bit. It *hurt.*

There was no way I could do that to Graves. I just couldn't.

Because it made me like the suckers. Like the things Dad would've hunted.

Like the thing that killed him. And my mother. The thing that was sleeping somewhere else in this huge stone pile, with my blood running around in its veins.

Oh, God. "Just get out of here," I managed. "Take Dibs. Just *go.*"

He scooched around a bit, making himself comfortable. His arm tightened, and my nose ended up in his throat. His leg curled over both of mine, and his free hand came up and stroked my tangled hair.

"The only one," he murmured. His chin dipped a little bit. "You know that, Dru? You're the only person who's ever believed in me. You know what that'll do to a guy?"

What? "I—"

"It makes him want to live up to it." A sarcastic, bitter little half-laugh, just like the Goth Boy I used to know. The birdlike one who was a little ugly, sure, until you got to know him and saw what had been under the ugly all along. The *true* beauty.

Sometimes it hides deep, that truth.

Graves made a quick little movement, nestling down. "Only I'm not like you. I was broken before *he* did it. I even just got half-bit. Half-turned, halfass like everything else in my stupid life before I met you. Maybe it's better that way, like Christophe says." He shuddered. "Maybe I'm broke anyway, but at least this way I'm useful."

"Graves. Goddammit." My throat was on fire. The bloodhunger, sensing a pulse very close to my fangs. They didn't crackle or lengthen, but my teeth were sensitive again. No hot-oil feeling from the *aspect* either, but I was suddenly very thirsty. "I can't bite you. It's just . . . I *can't.*"

It wasn't my teeth crackling. It was his wrist. His free hand left my hair, and his arm tightened. His index-finger nail lengthened, sliding free, wicked sharp and tipped with translucence like a cat's claw. "Don't punk out on me, kid." Sarcasm now, but under it the shaking still running through us both as if we were on one of those beds that went earthquake when you dropped a quarter in.

The claw tip scraped delicately against the softest part of his throat. For a moment the cut was white, his wrist held oddly because of the angle, and at the very end of the scratch he dug in a little.

A bright drop of crimson appeared.

CHAPTER THIRTY

The tiny crimson drop was the only thing in the room that didn't look washed-out. It was a rich ruby jewel, and my mouth actually *watered*. Which only made the thirsty worse.

Then the smell of it hit me. Copper, wildness, icy moonlight, and the strawberry-incense tang of *him*. It scraped across the blood-hunger and lit every vein in my body like a tangle of neon.

My fangs slid free, my jaw making little popping, shifting sounds. It hurt, like an overstressed muscle. Each individual tooth rooted in my jaw tingled, exquisitely sensitive.

"Graves," I whispered. With a faint lisp, so I didn't scrape my tongue on the sharp bits. It sounded ridiculous.

"Dru." He slid his free fingers through my hair again and hugged me. My nose mashed against the underside of his jaw, a little bit of stubble roughening up, and my tight-closed lips met the beads of blood. The smell of it crawled through my nose and lit up everything inside my head, like a match flame touching gas fumes. "Just do it. Please. I . . . please, Dru. I want you to."

Oh, God— My head twitched on my weak, aching neck. My lips skinned back from my teeth. I fought it, but my body knew better than I did. It pulled me forward . . . but oh, God.

I tried to be gentle.

My fangs knew just where to press. My tongue lapped once, gathering the trickle from the small cut, and a shiver went through him. His arm tightened under me, his leg tightened over both of mine, and he pulled me into his body like we were raindrops on a window, the moment before they slide together.

My fangs slid in. A burst of sweet, hot perfume filled my mouth, and I drew on it as gently as I could.

Graves's head tipped back. But his arms and legs tensed, twining us together, tighter and tighter. I swallowed. It slid down my throat like silk and exploded in my stomach, and the *touch* came back to roaring life. My fangs drove in deeper, strength flooding my arms and legs again, and he made an odd sound, like all the air had been punched out of him.

It poured into my mouth again, heat and life and light. But with it came a flood of images, swirling through the *touch* and blasting straight into my brain.

. . . *"Stupid little—" The words became a roar, the spilled paint bright blue against the garage floor as the fosterdaddy's slap caught him right on the cheek. Red pain, falling, hitting the side of the car with a dead crack and the pain a red monster, swallowing him whole.*

. . . *crouching on the playground while the bigger kid swings his foot, kick catching right under the ribs, falling and hearing their laughter. The teachers were hurrying to bust it up, but he just hunched and sobbed, because it was too late.*

. . . *sobbing in the middle of the night, hearing the scream as Mom's latest boyfriend took the belt to her, writhing in shame and pain because he was too little, too afraid.* Never, *he swears to himself,* never be helpless again, never never never . . .

. . . *the blue-eyed girl turned in a circle, and his heart was a stone in his chest.* "It's nice," *she said, looking at the posters and the books and the shabby little room he'd managed to cobble together. His hideaway, where he retreated to lick his wounds every day.* "It's cozy." *And just like that, she turned the whole place into a clubhouse, because he wasn't in here alone.*

. . . *she was beautiful, even soaked and shivering, with the gun in her hand. Her eyes blazed, and the grinding in his shoulder from the thing that had bit him was a flaming brand.* "Dru. Don't leave me. Please." *Because she had that look, his mother's look every time she vanished and the social workers came sniffing around. The look that said he was nothing but baggage, and she was better off without him, because he'd make her sink like a rock. So he pulled himself up, as tall as he could.* Don't care what I have to do. "Dru." *Trying not to sound like he was pleading. And when she nodded, the gun pointed at the floor and the tears sliding unnoticed down her cheeks, the relief in him was enough to make the hamburger mess of his shoulder suddenly inconsequential.*

Because for the first time, someone didn't shrug him off. She set her shoulders and nodded. "All right," *she said, and he suddenly understood everything had changed, that he wasn't going to get left behind, that she was going to take him with her. He'd say anything, do whatever he had to—she asked questions, he answered. And finally she nodded again.* "All right, Graves. You and me. Let's go."

And it was enough. More than he'd ever thought he'd get.

I swallowed again. The heat slammed through me, a good cracking-clean hit like a baseball against the sweet spot of a bat. They poured into me, the images, and seeing myself through his eyes was like vanishing. Because he hadn't seen the frizzy-haired, scared-to-death, mousy Dru. No, to him I'd looked like a supernova, flaming and deadly beautiful, an escape from the dead-end world he'd been born into.

And Jesus, I'd known it had to have been bad for him—nobody with a well-adjusted family life lives in a forgotten office in a *mall*, for Chrissake—but I hadn't known *how* bad. He'd never said anything about it. At least, nothing directly. And I hadn't asked because, well, you *don't* ask about shit like that. You just leave everything open in case they want to say something, and you try not to squeeze any raw parts.

When Ash's teeth had ground in his flesh and the change agents worked in with Ash's saliva, Graves had been born again. Dragged out of the dead end and plonked on the highway. He didn't want to look back.

And now I could guess at all the broken places inside him, where Sergej had his claws. Except I had hold of everything else, and I *pulled*, the *touch* flexing as his blood filled my mouth again and he made another harsh grating noise. I wasn't gentle this time, fangs sinking in deeper and my mouth sucking greedily, my arms suddenly around him and the hot sweet taste coating every inch of my mouth and throat and all the way down into my stomach. Summer heat-haze spread out, fighting back the cold swimming weakness.

He might have thrashed, but we were holding each other so tightly it didn't do more than ripple through us both as the blood poured down my throat. I'd lost track of how many times I'd swallowed, and that was dangerous, wasn't it? *Djamphir* never took more than a certain amount, I didn't know why, but—

Wait, that's three, it's always three, why?

Everything else vanished. Red light blinded me, his pulse thudding frantically, a drumbeat my own heart struggled to match. I *pulled* again, something old and slow and black as an oily nighttime river sluggishly waking, rising through layers of sleep, its teeth ivorysharp and champing with a sound like billiard balls hitting each other, bloody foam spattering thin cruel lips.

I swallowed again. Heat and strength poured into me, the *touch* roaring like ocean breakers, the world coming back. My eyes flew open; a tingling flood swept down my skin. Graves's arms solid and real around me. His fingers wrapped in my hair, pulling hard enough to hurt as he pressed my head forward, and for a long moment we were those two raindrops again. Merged together, running down a window as a radio blared something with a driving beat and the wind roared through open windows, life returning in a green spring flood.

I jerked back, trying to free myself from his arms. He didn't ease up, steel running through his muscles, locking down. He was still shaking, a jittering earthquake pouring through him as he made another hoarse dry sound. He was on the edge of the bed, dust rising in swirls, and something inside both of us stretched . . . and *snapped*, an almost-physical sound that blew more dust up. This time the cloud of particles made shapes, long elegant heads with sharp teeth, slim paws, and running fluid lines. I sensed more than saw them, and the old blind thing with its dark clawed fingers squeezing Graves's brain howled in fruitless rage as I shredded at it, scrubbing with a brush made of the way I felt about him.

A bright, hot, *clean* feeling.

Another jet of bright hot life slid down my throat, hit my stomach, and exploded. This time the images were a kaleidoscope, color and motion unreeling under the *touch*, spinning so fast I couldn't process them. They were all *me*, but me seen through his eyes. Me sleeping, me hunched over a lunch tray, me studying a book, me covered in mud and muck and gunk—all shot through with a rose-colored feeling, soft in some places, scary-hard and spiky in others. His heart in his throat and his pulse rising, and one more swallow would give me everything, would break all the walls between us and . . .

I tore away. The bloodhunger snarled, vibrating in my chest with that odd clear-crystal ringing sound, and a hot draft of sticky cinnamon and warm perfume drifted up.

It was like being reborn. The *aspect* smoothed over me, downy wings beating in time with my pulse, and I held Graves, my cheek against his shoulder. The hunger retreated, step by step.

You have control, Dru. Christophe's voice, and why was I hearing *him?* I didn't want to hear him while I was holding my Goth Boy.

Graves shook. For a moment I thought he was crying. But he was laughing, the kind of crazy-sane laughter that erupts when you find out you're not dead after all. His arms had loosened a little, but he was still definitely holding me. He smelled of ashes now, curiously pale, the ghost of incense. Cold, and weak. But his pulse still thundered, and he didn't let go of me.

For a long moment I struggled with the urge to bury my fangs in him again and drain every last drop. To not stop, because it was so *good*. And because I was in my own skin now, separate and oddly bereft.

The laughter shuddered to a stop. He exhaled, hard. Then, a quiet croak. "Do you need more?"

God. No. I want more, that's the problem. I shook my head, clamping my lips shut. Buried my face in his shoulder and fought

239

the hunger, step by step, back into its little box. His fingers slid free of my hair, and he stroked the tangled curls down.

And for just that moment, the darkness behind my eyelids held no danger. But there was no time. I knew, as surely as I knew my own name, that somewhere in the stone warren we were trapped in, Sergej was waking up.

And boy, was he going to be pissed.

CHAPTER THIRTY-ONE

G raves stumbled, the water glass dripping in his hand, and sat down on the bed. Hard.

He wasn't too steady on his feet. And he looked *terrible*—gaunt, ashen, huge circles under his burning-green eyes. My fingers flew, buckling the *malaika* on; I knelt and started digging in the duffel. Ammo, and the spare gun in its holster. Thank God. Plus a pair of canvas shoes, not as good as boots but I grabbed them anyway. I left the cash, the rest of the clothes, and the fake ID; I grabbed a black hoodie and the ammo bag. The lump of fresh strength behind my breastbone scorched, comfortingly. My left hand tingled like it was asleep but waking up.

"Jesus." Graves made it up to his feet, took two staggering steps, and tossed the water in Dibs's slack face.

That did the trick. Dibs sat up with a yelp, scrambled back until he hit the wall, and stared wildly at us.

I zipped the duffel back closed. "Can you get you and Dibs out of here? Is there an exit?"

Graves nodded. "There's one or two. I been prowling around during the day—wait. What are you—"

"Christophe's down there. You two get out. If I can get Christophe free, we'll rendezvous—wait, where are we? What city? Do you know?"

"What did you do?" Dibs braced his shoulders against the wall. He stared at me, his eyes wide and terrified like a little kid's after a nightmare. "Dru?"

"Relax. I'm going to be fine." It was sort of a lie, sure. But it was all I had. "Where are we? Do either of you know?"

"You can't go down there. Someone's always around. Dru—" Graves sat down on the bed again. Or rather, his legs gave out and he just dropped. "You *can't.*"

I strapped the holster on, tested it. Good. Swiped at my hair, found a ponytail elastic in one of the hoodie's pockets. A moment's worth of work gave me a halfass braid-ponytail-thing that would keep my hair back, at least.

My fingers dove into the ammo bag, found a clip, and I popped it in, chambered a round, slid the gun back in the holster and buckled the ammo bag's nylon belt. "I am not leaving anyone behind here." I sounded flat and terribly adult.

Just like Dad.

"Now's our best chance," I continued. "Do you know where the hell we are?"

"Fargo." Dibs shuddered. "North Dakota. We're outside Fargo by about ten miles. Dru, what did you . . . did you drink? From *him?*"

Fargo. They must've put me in a plane to get me up here. For a moment my skin chilled, thinking of being trapped in that metal box again. I was actually *thinking* now, and it was a relief. Back to being my bad old tough-girl self, with a lump of warmth in my stomach sending waves of heat and strength through the rest of me.

I didn't want to think about it. I had all I could do nerving myself up for what I had to do next. I plopped down on the floor and yanked the shoes on.

Graves stripped his hair back from his forehead. It lay lank and dead against his fingers, the dye swallowing light. He was sweating, the ashen tone to his skin more pronounced. He looked absolutely hideous. "I made her. Shut up, Dibs. Look, Dru, *he'll* wake up. Leave Christophe, goddammit. He wouldn't—"

"I wouldn't leave *you* behind." I rose, my body obeying me smoothly now.

How long did I have before the strength in Graves's blood ran out? I wasn't sure. So I had to do this quick.

I ghosted to the door, the *touch* rippling out in concentric rings. Nobody around, but the air was full of the breathlessness right before a thunderstorm. It was beginning to feel almost normal, that sense of crisis approaching. "I won't leave him behind either," I finished, still in that queer flat tone.

"What is it with you and him?" Graves's lip lifted, white teeth showing. Even his gums were pale.

Bloodless.

Don't think about that, Dru. Think about what you got to do next.

I reached up with my right hand. Snapped the *malaika* free. Probably my best bet in a house full of suckers. If the Maharaj showed up, we'd see how good I was with hexing, and a silver-grain round or two might discourage them in a hell of a hurry too.

And if I ran out of ammo, I'd figure something else out.

I glanced down. My left hand was whole now, no trace of the burning. I couldn't see if the blisters were still hanging around, but it felt like they were. Half-healed and tender. It still tingled when I flexed my fingers, but it felt all right.

"Dru. Goddammit." Graves surged to his feet. "What is it with Christophe? Is it that he's *djamphir?*"

I couldn't believe he was even *asking*. "No. It's because he's my friend."

"What am I, then?"

Oh, for the love of . . . "Well, you don't want to be my boyfriend, so I don't know. You tell me. But tell me *after* we meet up. You and Dibs get the hell out of here. There's cash and blank IDs in the duffel; you can get on a train and get back to the Prima. Go there, tell everyone what's going down, and wait for me."

"Wait." Dibs was on his feet now. The bruising up and down his face glared at me; he reeked of worry and ammonia fear, sharp-stinging my freshly-tuned nose. His T-shirt fluttered a little bit, ripped from whatever tango he and Graves had gotten into in the hall. "Dru, you can't—"

My lips skinned back from my teeth now. My jaw crackled as my fangs slipped loose, tender and aching; I could still smell the blood on the air and the dry-fur reek of *nosferat*.

Dibs almost swallowed his tongue. He shrank back against the wall, trembling. Graves stared at me, his face twisting for a second.

Before, I would've called the expression disgust. But the *touch* was still resonating inside my head, the complex stew of his emotions my own for a moment. It wasn't disgust, I realized.

It was pain. Because even when the fangs that made me something dirty, something like Sergej, came out, he still thought I was beautiful. And the pain came from that broken place inside him.

The place where he thought he wasn't worth a damn.

I was across the room before I knew it. I grabbed his shoulder with my left hand, bent down, and pressed my lips on his. He stiffened, but his mouth opened, and I think it was the first time in my life I'd ever kissed like I was a boy. If you know what I mean, great, if you don't, well, I can't explain it any clearer.

Or maybe I can. It was the first time I *took* a kiss instead of accepting one, the first time I didn't think that the person I was kissing might refuse. No, I wanted it. I wanted to feel his mouth, and I did. I *took* it.

And I liked it.

He was breathing heavily by the time I straightened my arm, pushing myself away. I stared down at him, his green eyes opening slowly, heavy-lidded. No shadow of black in them now.

Good.

Make it good, Dru. If it's the last thing he ever hears from you, make it good. Don't get lame at the end. "I love you." The bloodhunger twisted under the words, but I pushed it back. "I've always loved you. Get the hell out of here with Dibs so I don't have to worry about you both. I'll see you at the Prima."

Gran's owl hooted softly. I could sense it circling the room, trembling just on the edge of the visible. I gathered myself, staring into Graves's eyes, and I *moved.*

The air tore and sparkled behind me. It was the first time I ever used the *djamphir* vanish-trick too, going so fast the air collapses behind you with the ripping sound of nasty whispering laughter.

It wasn't that I could do it now that I'd bloomed. It wasn't even that I knew it was a pretty goddamn dramatic exit.

It was that it was so *easy,* with the taste of his blood smoking in my mouth. And it was so easy to think of pushing him back on the bed and greedily getting my fangs in. And drinking until there was nothing left.

There really wasn't anything separating me from the vampires now, was there?

I sure as hell hoped not. Because I was going to need everything I had to get out of here. I wanted to get Christophe free, sure.

But there was a bigger project I had, so to speak.

I wanted to kill the thing that killed my parents. And with a *loup-garou*'s dominance burning in me, his blood whispering in my veins, and the rage beating under my heartbeat, there would never be a better time.

CHAPTER THIRTY-TWO

The owl flew at shoulder height, navigating me up through a stone tunnel, turning right, then up a familiar slope. The last time I'd seen this I'd been in the wheelchair, Graves fighting Sergej's mental pressure and my entire body straining to escape. I was up the slope in a flash, and I hit the doors at the end like a bomb going off. They crashed inward, wood splintering, and the crack they made probably woke up every damn vampire in a hundred-mile radius.

It didn't matter. The huge amphitheater opened under the owl's belly like a flower, and its eyes were mine. Part of me felt the fierce joy of flight, wind rushing through feathers with a low sweet sound, and the other part of me snapped my right-hand *malaika* free and tore through three *nosferat* in a welter of black-spatter blood. They didn't even have time to scream their high chill hunting-cries.

Like this, Anna's voice echoed, her training rising under my skin. I was spinning, soles of my shoes squeaking oddly on the smooth stone, and as the *malaika* sliced through sucker flesh the *nosferat* choked and turned purple, rot exploding through them.

I was going too fast to stop so I didn't, crashing into the table with the transfusion equipment. My shoes touched down, glass shattered, the table splintered as I stamped with incredible force and was airborne. My other foot lightly brushed the arm of Sergej's iron chair, propelling me forward, and I almost hit Christophe's chained body dead-on. Skidding sideways, the owl wheeling and diving, *nosferatu* sleeping in piles or draped over the stone seat-steps beginning to shake themselves awake.

Christophe's head jerked up. His eyes glittered. Under the mask of bruising and blood, his expression was impossible to see. But I thought I caught a flash of it—sheer horror.

It was child's play. Both *malaika* hilts in my left hand now, my right flashed out and the metal of the chains tore with a screech. The lump of heat in my stomach dropped a little, turned into a nova in my belly. I ripped him free as casually as I might rescue a kitten from a yarn-snarl, and he slid bonelessly toward the floor just as the first wave of angry, awake suckers hit the floor and streaked for me, their faces open screams of hate and their hunting-cries rising in shattering crescendo. Fury rose under my skin.

It wasn't my anger. It was Graves's, and in that moment I understood a *lot* about the wulfen.

The Other isn't really something, well, *other*. It's in everyone. Werwulfen can just bring it out. It's why they're all about agreement and consensus. They need to be, with the claws and the teeth and the superstrength and the 220 line right into the heart of the darkness.

I screamed, a high chill cry that tore through the sucker yells like a bullet through glass. The *aspect* flamed, and the *touch* flared out in concentric rings. They started dropping before they even got close enough for me to use the *malaika* on them.

Christophe, behind me. Metal slithered. I could tell without looking he was struggling free of the chains. I was hoping he had enough left in him to run. I skipped forward, giving him enough room to maneuver, but hoping I could still keep him close enough that my shell of toxicity would slow the suckers down. Then they were on me, their faces mottled and their bodies failing them no matter how fast they tried to pile on. The *malaika* flickered, wooden tongues, and Christophe's voice in the practice room shouted.

Left, left, with precision! Straighten your knee! Keep the circles; remember your reach!

I couldn't tell if it was me he was yelling at, or Anna, or my mother. He'd trained all three of us, and even though he hadn't finished with me, I had the benefit of Anna's long years. Hell, I probably had all of Anna that was left in the world.

That was a happy-dappy thought, but I was going too fast to do more than register a flicker of it.

I struck with both blades, my foot flashing out to catch a choking sucker's knee, snapping it with a dry-stick breaking sound as the wooden blades whistled, cleaving air and flesh both. Black ichor spattered, hung in the air, and I drove forward some more, the rage lighting up inside me like a star.

"Dru!" Christophe, shouting. "Dru, God damn you, run!"

Oh, no. I am not finished here. I was through with running. I half-spun, and he was on his feet, shaken free of the chains. He leapt, and the *nosferat* jumping for my back splattered in a wash of rotting foulness. The smell was incredible, titanic, and Christophe's claws flicked as he tore the remaining life out of the thing.

So he was able to fight.

Good.

They came for us, a wave of young-old faces shining with hatred, the females hanging back and the males moving forward. I recognized this from other fights—the females were jumpers; the males would try to distract and overwhelm and the females would drop in to hopefully finish the prey off. They drew closer, closing the ring as Christophe's back met mine and he shoved, both of us sliding out into the middle of the wide-open space. Room to maneuver, and Sergej's iron chair with its black spikes reaching up like frozen fingers.

Get the high ground, Dru. Now it was Dad. *Battle's won with the high ground. Leastways, lots of the time.*

"Christophe?" My ribs heaved, my heartbeat coming fast and light. "We're outside of Fargo, near as I can tell from Dibs. Pick a direction and go. Meet me at the Prima."

He breathed something in Polish that definitely wasn't polite; I could tell just from the tone. "What are you *doing*?"

"Rescuing your half-vampire ass." *What, are you blind?* "Get out of here."

"I'll hold them. You run." He coughed, and the vampires pressed forward. The heat in my belly dilated again. How much had I taken from Graves? Too much? How long would it last? When it ran out, what would I do? Would he and Dibs get out safe? "Do you hear me, *svetocha? Run.* For your life, and for mine—"

"No." The *malaika* whirred gently, cleaving air. "Not this time, Chris. This time, *you* run."

And I flung myself forward.

I figured if I kept moving fast enough, their ring wouldn't be able to close on us. The flaw in that was that Christophe wouldn't be able to take advantage of my little bubble of free air, so to speak, and he looked like hell. But I could just keep them away from him by appearing the bigger threat, right? Which meant I had to get down to some serious business.

I skidded and leapt, crashing into a knot of five males. The *malaika* flickered, whirring like windup toys, and the world opened up inside my head. It was a chorus of the dead, all talking at the same time.

Gran, bandaging my knee and giving me one of her peculiar, all-seeing looks: *You do what you got to. You mind me, now, Dru.*

Dad, holding the other side of the heavy bag while he barked encouragement: *Get in there, girl! Harder, faster! It's you or them; make those sonsabitches sorry they was born!*

Mom's voice, from the shady long-ago time of Before: *My brave girl, I love you. I love you so much.*

Anna, amused and vicious while she examined her crimson-lacquered fingernails: *They're going to try to mass and separate you from Christophe. He's bleeding and weakened. You could even let them have him. It's what he deserves.*

A high painful screech of metal tearing behind me, but I had my hands full. I stamped, left-hand *malaika* cleaving air with a low sweet sound, carving half a male sucker's face off. He was blond and didn't look any older than fourteen, baby-faced, clutching at his throat as he fell like a heap of dirty laundry. Those blond curls reminded me of Dibs shaking in terror, the fang marks in his neck and his tear-chapped cheeks.

The bloodhunger woke in a sheet of flame. It was the same old feeling: I was a girl made of sparkling glass, and inside that glass was a flood of thick red rage. Only now, for the first time, I didn't try to hold back from it.

No. I opened myself up completely, I let it take me.

Black blood flew, stinking and thin. The rage swelled, sweetly painful like scratching at a mosquito bite, not caring that you're shredding the skin, just knowing how *good* it feels. They came like waves, attacking, and I *danced*, feet sliding through a scrim of thin black stinking oil and the *malaika* turned into extensions of my arms. Gran's owl arrowed down, tearing through them, claws crunching and shredding, its wings steel-edged scythes. It looked wicked and predatory now, its golden eyes coins of flame, and I followed.

Christophe yelled something and I spun, my half-braid floating as Graves's blood burned inside me, something rippling under my skin as if I was a wulfen and about to change. It flowed over me like a river, and the *nosferat* scattered. Some were screaming—not their high glassy hunting cries, but lower, still-hateful squeals and shrieks.

Cries of fear. Of pain.

The realization hit me crossways, my stomach turning over with a sick thump. They were *suckers*. They hated, and they killed—

—but they sounded *human*.

The female hit me with a boneshattering jolt. I flew, weightless for an eternal moment, and she was already dying, her claws only scratching weakly instead of digging into my belly.

Crunch. The wall stopped us both, the *aspect* flaring with heat, and she slumped. Her face was twisted, purple, ugly, and still hateful. But maybe once she'd been a child. *Nosferatu* had mothers just like *djamphir* did, unless they were an incomplete kill. Bitten, infected, and turned into this.

Was it the turning that made them hate everything? I'd never thought about it before.

And now was the wrong time to start. Still . . .

Gran's owl circled the auditorium. Christophe skidded to a stop, bare battered feet splashing in the muck. He held something, and I had to blink a couple times before I realized what it was.

One of the spikes from his father's chair, held loosely by the thin end like a baseball bat, the blunt sharp-edged tip of it dripping as sucker blood ran down its length. He glanced up over my head, blue eyes colder than winter sky, and turned.

Broken bodies littered the bowl-shaped expanse. Two suckers left alive, crouching in front of Christophe. Both male, slight and dark, and terribly young-looking even while they snarled, their top and lower canines springing free.

Christophe laughed. A low, terrible sound. "Come, then," he said, very softly. "Come and die."

Silence, broken only by the *drip, drip* of thin liquid from the tip of the barbed spike he held. The suckers glanced at each other, their jaws crackling as they distended further, sharp ivory in the low bloody light.

They broke and ran, vanishing with that nasty laughing sound. Their tiptapping footsteps receded, and Christophe slumped. He let out a long breath, and Gran's owl hooted softly. I could still feel it circling, but when I glanced up there was nothing. Just the directionless red glow, and the smell. The female vampire's body slumped aside; I scrabbled away from it along the wall.

I actually gagged. Nausea twisted my stomach before the *aspect* rose again on a wave of heat, and I smelled cinnamon through the reek. That only made it worse. Christophe backed up toward me, and a thin thread of his apple-pie scent reached me too.

That helped. But still. So many of them. Had I done that?

We. We'd done it. Christophe and me.

Christophe turned on one bare heel. His feet were healing, bruises retreating as the *aspect* crackled over him, heat-lightning. His hair was slicked back, dark under the matted blood, and a muscle in his cheek flicked. A sudden graceful movement and he knelt, his free hand coming down. His fingers met my shoulder, and it was like a spark snapping. I almost twitched.

"Are you hurt?" Level and furious.

I took stock. I was alive. All my appendages. The rage had vanished, like water on hot pavement. The back of my throat was dry and rasping. "N-no." I sounded hoarse, but the thread of silk in my tone wasn't mine.

It was Anna's, and it horrified me. Even my voice wasn't my own anymore. I'd changed. All the broken bodies lying strewn on the floor told me how much. It was like vanishing. Again.

Who am I now?

"Come, then. We have to get you out of here."

My chin set. I pressed back against the wall, and my legs took care of levering me up. His hand fell away. The *aspect* flowed up from my feet, working in, delicious oily warmth. A tremor slid through the center of my bones, but I ignored it. "I'm not leaving. I came down here to rescue you."

"You succeeded admirably." One corner of his mouth lifted a millimeter, but then he reached for me again with his free hand, aiming for my right wrist. I stepped aside, sliding along the wall. Nervously.

Like I didn't want him to touch me.

I swallowed, hard. "Get out of here. Dibs and Graves are heading out, you should take care of them. Don't worry about me. I've got things to do."

"Dru." Calm, quiet, and very cold. "You are coming with me."

I shook my head. Everything I wanted to say boiled up inside me. Hit the wall of what I suspected about him, everything I knew, and how much I doubted everything he'd ever told me.

I'm a plague. Everything I care about gets hurt or dies. I'm here, and I'm going to stay here. I'm not leaving until I kill the thing that killed my parents. "Just go." I couldn't make the words any louder than a whisper, because my throat had closed up. "I want you to *go*. I can't stand to lose you too."

He opened his mouth, probably to argue, but a strange whoosh-ing sound filled the auditorium like water poured into a cup. A spike of diamond pain speared my temples, and Sergej laughed.

"Oh, children." His voice filled the entire vast space as well, and I slumped against the wall. "You make it so *easy*."

CHAPTER THIRTY-THREE

Christophe spun, but Sergej was already moving. I leapt, the world dragging at me with weird clear-plastic fingers, as if superspeed wouldn't even be enough. My right-hand *malaika* flicked, and black blood flew.

I was too slow. He was already past me, my soles slipping in the foul-smelling guck, and Christophe screamed. It was a high despairing cry, with a *djamphir*'s hiss-growl behind it. The crash of the two of them colliding shivered the air into fragments. The entire auditorium rocked, and a sheet of black blood splashed up. They hit the stone wall, and cracks radiated through the sheer, bloodred rock.

Christophe!

Slipping, scrabbling, wishing I had boots or real sneakers instead of these crap flimsy things, needed traction, I wrenched myself the opposite direction and Gran's owl rocketed past me in living color, claws outstretched and wings glinting with sharp-edged metal. In the bloody glow it was a spot of clean white, banking sharply. I threw myself after it just as Sergej turned, blinking through space with the eerie stuttering speed of a badass sucker.

Fast, he's fast, got to slow him down— Something in me stretched, instinctively, and I twisted again, my foot touching down lightly and sending up another spray of that black, thin, sickening fluid. They were just never going to get it clean in here. But I guess cleaning isn't high on a vampire to-do list, really.

Gran's owl arrowed down, and it hit Sergej's head with a crunch much larger than a bird could produce. He went forward, tucking and rolling with jerky, weird precision, as if he was a clockwork instead of flesh and blood.

"Coward!" I yelled, pelting for him. "You *fucking coward!*"

The words stung the air. He rose from the wash of rotting blood on the floor, chunks of decayed flesh clinging to him, his curls tumbled and that black, oily gaze striking like a snake.

I screamed, a hawk-cry of rising effort. There was finally enough air in my lungs—and Gran's owl shot past me, claws out and its golden eyes a streak of brilliance. Hit him square, and it wasn't just me hitting him.

It was the photograph I'd seen just once, the yellow house I found sometimes in my nightmares—the oak tree shading the front porch blasted by some terrible evil, a rag of flesh and bone hanging in its branches; my mother's body hung there like a Christmas ornament. It was the long corridor my father had walked down, toward a slowly opening door that exhaled cold evil—and my father's body standing at the back door of the house in the Dakotas, its blue eyes clouded with the film of death and its fleshless fingers tapping at the glass. It was Gran's house burning and the dark pain in Graves's eyes, the scars I'd seen on Christophe's back and the cold nightmare of the blood drawn out of my veins while Sergej laughed.

There were other things, too. Dibs, flinching and terrified, sobbing. Dylan from the first Schola I'd ever attended, probably dead
because he'd been blown from the inside; August, showing up bloody
and battered in the nick of time. Anna, who had tried to kill me in
her own way, sure, but . . . she didn't deserve what happened to her.

Nobody deserved what this thing had done to them.

Sergej skidded back, one slim iron-hard hand flashing up. He
hit Gran's owl, *hard*, and the impact smashed through me, throwing
me sideways. I went tumbling, splashing through the foulness, and
before I slid to a stop Sergej was on me, his hands around my throat,
and he *squeezed*.

My hands lay encased in cement. The *malaika* suddenly weighed
a ton, and something crackled in my throat. Little black spots danced
at the edges of my vision, and a shrill inner voice screamed at me to
do something, to move—but the lump of heat in my stomach was
fading, and the rage had deserted me.

Because the twisting hate in his face was what I felt. It was the
rage, and it was *mine*, too.

It was how I was like him.

The *aspect* flamed, and he coughed. The purple mottling rose in
his perfect, planed cheeks. But he laughed, a gleeful, hateful sound
that exhaled rot in my face. "Stronger!" he chuckled. "Inoculated
against your poison, little child-bird!" He braced himself, leaning
close, and laughed in my face, rank breath filling the world. "There
will be other *svetocha*. I will walk in the daylight. I will leave your
body for the crows to—"

A meaty *thunk* interrupted. Sergej stiffened, and my *aspect* flared
again. I got my right hand up, braced with *malaika* hilt, and clocked
him a good one across the head.

He pitched to the side, and Christophe's face rose over his shoulder.

Christophe was smeared with even more vampire blood, and the left side of his face looked smashed-wrong. He was oddly twisted, and I realized why—something in him had been crushed. By *something* I mean bones—the entire left side of his ribs was caved in. But he held onto the iron spike grimly and shoved it further into Sergej's back, his lips skinning back from his teeth. In that one moment, he looked more like his father than I'd ever believed possible.

The sharp thin tip of the spike punched out through Sergej's chest. The vampire king writhed, inhaling, the purple mottles sliding up his face with grasping, ugly fingers. He looked *ancient* now, not always-seventeen and too beautiful to be real.

No, this was the face of something old and terrible, something so far removed from human it wasn't even related anymore. The bloody directionless light pulsed, stuttering, and I realized it was coming from *him*.

Oh, Jesus. Nausea grabbed my entire body, a wracking spasm of revulsion. I was on my knees as Sergej scrabbled back. I'd stabbed him with an iron lamp-stand last time, and it had only put him down temporarily.

"No!" Christophe grabbed my arm. "Dru! *NO!*"

He shoved me, with more strength than I would've thought possible. I flew back, my left-hand *malaika* clattering free. *Shit, dropped my sword, junior move, can't do that—* Then I hit the wall, hard enough to stun. Little stars danced in front of my eyes, and I whooped in a breath.

Christophe limped, dragging his left foot. It was a weird, snake-like motion, and Sergej was curling up like a bait worm on a hook. The king of the vampires was making a noise, a queer rattling that scraped against my skin, and the red light deepened. Instead of fresh blood, the light was clotting on every surface, fouling and streaking.

I whooped in another breath, coughed and retched. Still had my right-hand *malaika*. Dragged myself up the wall, the *aspect's* strength a warm glow, but fading now. The voices eased, whispering instead of screaming inside my head, and the *touch* brushed over my skin with feather-soft caresses. It felt . . . clean.

Thank God. But I already felt filthy way down inside, where scrubbing wouldn't reach.

Where the rage came from.

Christophe grabbed the cruel clawed end of the spike jutting up from his father's back. "I warned you," he rasped, and the *aspect* boiled free of him, waves of power visible now in the dull punky glow. "I told you if you touched her, you would die."

He sounded so *calm*.

Sergej said something, the spiked consonants of a foreign language. Ragged, and full of so much fury, so much twisted hate, it turned my stomach all over again.

"Yes," Christophe said. "You are my father. *And I hate you for it.*"

It happened so fast. One moment he was there, holding the iron spike. The next, he jammed the spike all the way through. It hit the stone with a screech, and sparks flew.

But that wasn't the worst. The worst was Sergej twisting, his feet flailing, an animal in a trap. And Christophe on him, the horrid sound of bones grinding as he grabbed his father, wrenched Sergej's head aside, and buried his fangs right where the shoulder met the neck.

The red light flared. Then I was moving, every step taking a hundred years. "Christophe!" I was moving through syrup, through mud, through concrete. *"Christophe! No!"*

Sergej howled. The sound was immense, every key on an ancient bony organ hit at once, wheezing and screaming. It blew my hair back, and the *touch* turned to acid inside my head. The cry cut short on a gurgle that stood a good chance of starring in every nightmare I'd have for the rest of my life, as if I didn't already have so much nightmare material already.

I was on my knees, sliding, and it was a good thing I'd dropped my left-hand blade. Because my fingers curled in Christophe's slicked-back hair, and I yanked his head back.

CHAPTER THIRTY-FOUR

O r at least, I tried to. I got exactly nowhere.

His shoulders hunched. Something ripped as he used his teeth, settling more firmly into his father's neck. Blood sprayed, black and viscous, not thin like the other suckers'. It smoked, and the thought of that oozing down my throat was enough to make me feel even sicker.

I set my feet and yanked again, but it was as if he'd been turned to stone. He gulped, greedily, and the sound forced bile up into my throat. The thought that if I threw up, I'd be throwing up blood— *Graves's* blood, at that—did *not* help.

"Christophe." I swallowed hard. "Christophe, please. Listen to me. You're not him. Don't be *him*. Please. Please, Christophe, *stop*. Stop it. Please. I'm begging you, stop."

Everything paused. I had my fingers in his blood-clotted hair, and a current roared through him and into me. The *touch* flamed into life, and I almost reeled. But I didn't let go of Christophe's head. I couldn't.

"Please," I whispered. "Please, Christophe. Don't do this."

He shuddered, his ribs popping out and mending with horrifying, meaty sounds.

Then Christophe threw his head back and screamed. It was a long, despairing cry, but at least it got him away from his father. Who twitched again, horribly vital, and I could feel him gathering himself. Like a tornado or a thunderstorm approaching.

I brought my right hand up, my knees dripping as I rose too, the perfect angle unreeling inside me. The *malaika* made its low sweet sound, but it was lost in the noise Christophe was making. I might have screamed too, but it was lost in Christophe's cry as well. All the loneliness, all the pain, all the betrayal in the world was in that sound, and the wooden sword whooshed down.

I put everything into it. It wasn't just me. The dead filled me, all of them, whispering and chattering in a vast silence wrapped around me.

This was the way to kill him. Not with hate, not with taking in his blood and everything about him. Instead, it was my mother's hand on the *malaika*'s hilt, and my father's. Even Gran's ancient, liver-spotted hand, her fingers calloused from a lifetime of work and her eyes sharp with take-no-prisoners compassion. It was Graves's hand, too—even though he wasn't dead, it was the hand of the boy he could've been, tight against mine. And Anna's, red nails gleaming, as I felt the tears slicking my cheeks and understood it was for her too. Even though she'd tried to kill me, I wept for the girl she could have been.

The person I would have to try to be, so I didn't turn out like this horrible, twitching thing on the floor.

The blade carved cleanly, and Christophe's cry cut off as if I'd sliced *him*. For a nightmarish moment I thought I had, and it was probably a mercy the dull reddish light failed completely then, snuffed out like a candle flame. The darkness that descended was absolute, the silence a ringing tone.

My knees hit the stone floor with a splashing thump. Another thump brought a hot wad of something up in my throat, because I could imagine Sergej's head hitting the floor. It rolled away like a big granite ball, making more noise than it should, and I dropped my *malaika*.

I was sobbing. Little hitching gasps turned into spasms, racking convulsions, I wrapped my arms around myself and rocked back and forth. The silence was so immense, and the dark was so deep. It was like the needle in my arm and the cold again, and I curled in on myself.

"Dru." A whisper. "Dru."

He reached me in the darkness, and part of me wanted to scrabble back and away. My skin crawled when he touched me, but the rest of me fell into him. Something against my forehead, a soft pressure. His lips. He kissed my forehead, my cheeks, my bloody, tear-streaked, dirty face, everywhere he could reach. I didn't care. The shakes had me now, like a vicious dog shaking a toy, stuffing flying everywhere. Everything inside me was shaking loose, shaking free; there was nothing to hold onto.

Nothing except Christophe, there in the dark.

He held me, murmuring my name, holding me bruising-tight. Kissed my hair, my forehead, again. He couldn't reach the rest of me because I'd buried my face in his neck. We clung together like survivors of some huge natural disaster, and the sobs retreated like an ocean wave.

He was saying something else, over and over again, in between repeating my name.

"Thank you," he would mutter, hoarsely, ragged, into my hair. "*Dziekuje*, Dru, *milna*. Thank you."

Jesus Christ, for *what*? But then he stiffened, and his head came up. I felt the movement in the dark, and I swallowed the last of the sobs, folding my lips over my teeth and pushing them down.

We'd just killed the king of the vampires.

And in the distance, muffled but still distinct, I heard gunfire.

CHAPTER THIRTY-FIVE

He somehow found both my *malaika*. Pressed them into my hands. The wooden hilts were warm and satiny. "Are you hurt? Anywhere?"

I shook my head, realized he probably couldn't see. It was so dark it had actual physical *weight*. I had to cough twice before I could even think about talking. The bile in my throat burned, and the heat in my middle was fading. "N-no. I don't th-think so." Now I was stuttering, just like Dibs. If he felt anything like this, I didn't blame him. "Tired, though."

"Thank God." He grabbed my shoulders, his fingers sinking in, and pulled me forward. This time he was smack-dab on the button, and I don't know why I was surprised. If he could find my *malaika*, he could certainly find my mouth.

There was blood on his lips, but it tasted like spice. An apple pie just pulled from a hot oven, and a desert wind—sand and the windows down, right at dusk, when you're out on those roads that arrow for the horizon and the city is behind you; you're doing eighty and you're not going to stop anytime soon. The *touch*, bruised and aching, shivered as a bolt of feeling went through me—something hot, and scary, and wild. It poured a different kind of strength into me, and when he broke away I actually gasped.

He didn't even pause. "Listen to me. That's probably the Order. We might have to fight our way out to them. Don't worry, the *nosferatu* will be weakened and confused now, with their king dead." The businesslike, mocking tone was back, just like the old Christophe. But under it was a raw edge I wasn't sure I liked.

I'd never heard him sound scared before. And the idea that some of Sergej's blood might have been on his lips—

I didn't want to think about that.

"The aura-dark may hit me. I don't know how much I took before you . . . stopped me." His tone gentled. "Dru?"

"What?" I swayed, he held me upright.

"Thank you. You . . . this is not the time. But I want you to know something."

Oh, God, what now? "Can't it wait until we—"

"No. It can't." He eased up on my shoulders a little, and I suddenly wished I could see his face. "Dru. You make me want to be . . . better. Instead of what I . . . am."

Better? You fought off your father. For me. Again.

And then bit him and drank his blood. But if he hadn't, what might've happened? Would I have been able to . . .

I didn't want to think about that either. There was so much I didn't want to think about, it wasn't even funny.

"You saved me," I whispered. "That's enough."

"Is it?" Now he sounded bitter. "Is it ever going to be enough?"

I swallowed hard. I could still taste him on my lips. And the fading heat of Graves's blood was a stone in my lower belly. "Christophe . . ."

"The *loup-garou*. Graves." Back to the businesslike mockery. "He bled for you, didn't he."

"That's how I could come d-down here and r-rescue—"

"I've bled for you too, Dru."

My feet slid a little in vampire blood, splashing. It still smelled horrific in here, and I wanted some light. I wanted to be outside so bad I was shaking. I wanted to run until I dropped, just to get away. "Christophe, for Christ's sake, can we just please get out of here? This is *not helping!*"

I tried not to sound panicked, and I failed miserably.

But he was just not going to let it go. His hands fell away from my shoulders. "How much is enough, Dru? What do I have to do? Tell me. Now, while we have time."

What the *fuck*? Here we were knee-deep in rotting vampire, gunfire getting closer all the time, God alone knew how we were going to get out of here even if that *was* the Order coming for us, and he wanted to have this discussion with me?

"We need to get out of here." A wave of exhaustion crashed through me, and I swayed. "I don't feel so good. Come on, Christophe. We'll talk later."

"Now is all I have, Dru. It's all I'll ever have." But his fingers curled around my left forearm, gently this time. "But you're right. This way. You can't see, can you."

"No." I stumbled after him. "Christophe, look. It's not a contest. It's not—"

"Dru." Kindly, now. "You're right. I shouldn't have asked. Shut up."

Well, wasn't that a fine how-do-you-do. But I couldn't just be quiet. It was too dark, and if I stopped talking I had the idea that he might just vanish, leaving me down here. Alone. And blind. "How can *you* see?"

He pulled me aside; I sensed something in our way. It was probably a mound of corpses, and I almost lost the battle with my stomach there and then.

A jagged little laugh burst out of him. "It's one advantage Kouroi have over *svetocha*. Even the darkness brings no relief."

He was back to being maddening and cryptic. The relief that flooded me was probably pointless, but it still made me stagger.

He steadied me. "Dru?"

"I'm fine. I just . . . you sound like you. Like normal. It's good." And to top it all off, my eyes welled up again. Two fat tears trickled down my cheeks, sliding through a crust of crap I immediately added to the long and growing list of things I never wanted to think about again. "I like it," I added lamely, trying not to sound like I was having a complete and total meltdown. Not to sound like I was shaking, and crying, and sick, and scared out of my mind, and feeling dirty all the way down to my bones.

Christophe actually paused, down there in the dark. "You . . ." He let out a long, shaky breath. "Once again, *kochana*, you save me from myself." He laughed again, but it was a sound so sharp it could cut. It actually hurt to hear. "Come, this way."

I tried to cry quietly while I followed him. But I don't think I managed.

* * *

I blinked furiously when he pushed a huge heavy door open, the hinges squealing. Even the dim light beyond was scorching, and I let out a little hitching sound of relief. The gunfire was in the opposite direction, but it was moving closer.

And this was actual, honest-to-God *daylight*. Cloud-filtered sunshine falling through small round windows like portholes high up on the stone walls. "Oh, sweet Mary and sonny Jesus," I blurted. It was one of Gran's favorites wouldja-look-at-that expressions, with a heavy dose of boy-am-I-glad.

Christophe glanced at me. We both looked like hell, dipped in seventeen different flavors of gunk and nastiness. But he was almost pristine under it, with the same old air of *I could just step out of all this grime and be perfect again in a heartbeat.* It was hard to believe he'd had his ribs smashed in and the rest of him battered to a pulp.

"Wow. You're okay." I could have smacked myself for Stating The Lamely Obvious once again. The warmth in my stomach stuttered, and I swayed.

Christophe gave a slight, pained nod. "*He* had stolen quite a bit. I managed, it seems, to steal some of it back."

Oh, okay. Great. Fantastic. Wonderful. "You know your way around here?"

"Logic, *svetocha.*" He peered down the hall, blinking as well. "This is the way I was brought in. I marked it in memory. Come."

We set off down the hall, my shoes squishing and Christophe's bare feet leaving black marks. He didn't let go of my arm, and I didn't mind. The touch of his skin on mine, even through the dirt, sent a warm current through me. We stepped out into the sunlight, and I made another relieved little noise. I couldn't help myself.

"Sunlight, and I am not in the aura-dark." Christophe glanced up. "Clouds are breaking. Just in time."

I opened my mouth to ask him just in time for what, but before I could there was a howl and a scrabbling sound. The other end of the corridor had another iron-bound wooden door, and something hit it with incredible force. Gunfire thundered, loud and close, and Christophe pushed me against the wall. My shoulder hit with a bruising jolt, and he was in front of me, his shoulders up and his claws lengthening, the deadly tension in him making the *touch* resound like a brass bell inside my head.

"Dru." Christophe didn't glance back. "Don't worry. If this is *nosferat*, the sunlight will hamper them."

I nodded stupidly, realized once again that he couldn't see me. "We've done the hard part." My voice shook. My tough-girl card was *so* definitely going to get pulled. "This will be easy."

And amazingly, Christophe laughed. The door shivered, splintering. Long cracks popped free of its surface.

When it flew open, I was ready for anything other than what happened.

Ash landed on all fours, and was halfway down the hall before he dug in with his claws, stone shrieking. His eyes danced, he was shirtless, muscle moving under his pale skin. Grass stuck to his hair, and he wore a wide feral grin.

"BANG!" he yelled, and the wulfen flowed in behind him, shifting through changeform and back into boyshape. And there was Nat, skidding to a stop, her sleek hair ruffled and the relief bursting over her beautiful soot-streaked face like a sunrise. Shanks, his head wrapped in a glaring-white bandage, flowed out of changeform and threw his head back, letting out a howl that rattled the thick glass in the porthole windows.

The ruins of the door were still quivering when August stepped through, his blond hair lighting up as the daylight intensified. And there, right behind him, supple quick Hiro appeared, his short black hair lifting up in vital spikes as the *aspect* crested over him and he lifted something to his mouth. It was a comm cell, I realized, and his dark eyes glowed as his lips shaped the words.

She's here. We found her, repeat, we found her, she's alive. Standby for retrieval protocol.

I burst out sobbing and stumbled away from the wall. Nat's arms closed around me, and the rest of the wulfen took up Shanks's howl. It was a joyous sound, high and glassy, uncomfortably like the suckers' hunting-cries.

But this time I welcomed it, even as it raised the hair all over me and pulled at the raw aching places inside my head, still smoking and tender from all that hate and death.

It meant I was safe, and I gave myself up to the shaking and the crying so hard I couldn't speak as they closed around me and started carrying me away.

Chapter Thirty-Six

t was a whirlwind. Across a square of cracked concrete, then out into a cornfield under a cloudy late-spring sky. The young corn was flattened, and I felt a brief burst of regret. It smelled nice and green, and the clouds were breaking. The sunlight, welcome as it was, seemed pale.

There were helicopters, their downdraft battering at even more corn. I was lifted in like a sack of potatoes, then there was Nat and Ash on either side of me and Christophe across, the ground falling away as the bird accelerated. I leaned on Nat, who reeked of smoke and the clean healthy musk of werwulf, her cat-like blue eyes glowing as she put her arm around me and touched my hair, hugging me a little every now and again. I sagged against her and half passed out, not caring. Everything inside me went all gooshy, all the tension and the pain and the struggle running out like water.

I only roused myself once. "Graves? Dibs?" I had to shout over the noise. It took me a couple tries.

Nat leaned close, her breath hot on my ear. "We found 'em. Everyone's okay. Relax!"

And I did. I sagged into her, and across the way, Christophe's eyes glowed. The *aspect* slid over him in a wave, his hair slicking back and his fangs peeking out from under his top lip, but I didn't care.

The heat from Graves's blood was gone. I'd used it all up. That was okay. I'd done what I set out to do.

My eyelids fell down, and I was gratefully, finally gone.

* * *

I heard voices, but it didn't matter. I was numb. I didn't feel like being in charge of anything anymore. I just drifted in a pleasant gray haze.

". . . in shock," someone said. "She's bloomed, we don't have to type her. Get the transfusion kit!"

"But that would—"

"It doesn't matter," Christophe snarled. "This? This is hers. Get the kit, now!"

Sound of movement. It was comfortable where I was, nice and soft, nothing scary. I didn't even mind that I couldn't move. It was just . . . drifting.

It felt good.

"Dru?" Christophe, very close to my ear. "Dru, kochana, little one, hold on. Don't go. Fight it."

Fight what? There wasn't anything around here to fight. I'd taken care of all the important stuff.

Now I could rest.

A sting, on the inside of my arm. It felt familiar, and for a moment I was back in the wheelchair, strapped down, and the darkness was folding around me. Cold and dark, the absence of anything—

"Dru!" Graves, his voice hoarse and cracked. "Dru! Goddammit, don't! Don't!"

"Get him out of here," someone said.

"No." Christophe's voice cut across his. But it was wrong—he sounded breathless, disconnected. Like something was wrong. "Let him call her. She'll listen." A gasp. "Give her everything. As much as she needs, do you hear me?"

"What if it drains you? What if you die?" Dibs, now. I felt a faint flash of interest—so he was okay? And he wasn't stuttering? But there was that thing in my arm, and a burning spreading through me, pins and needles in my fingers and toes.

I didn't like it. I wanted the numbness back.

"I don't care, Samuel." Christophe sighed, a tired sound. "I don't care. Everything, do you hear me? Every drop." The words slurred. "Take . . . as much as . . ."

The gray around me flushed pink. It crept up like the dawn, and the pins and needles swept through me. They hurt, jabbing into flesh that had been drowsily warm just a few minutes ago, and I felt something hard underneath me.

"He almost drained her." Dibs, but not sounding terrified. "By transfusion. Then Graves . . . he made her drink, like he said. She got enough to get her through whatever happened down there, but she's in shock and it's—"

"Reynard!" Another familiar voice. Bruce, with his English accent, the sort-of head of the Order. I mean, technically I was the head, but he took care of everything while I was being trained. I could almost see him, his proud nose and caramel skin, his preppy jeans and starched dress shirts.

Check that. I could see him. The pink haze drew back, shapes looming up like rocks through fog. It was a room, oddly familiar with its sturdy walls and a gurney in the center of its stone-flagged floor, hospital machines standing at attention. The shape on the gurney was so still, and I saw without any real surprise a mop of curling hair and my own face tilted to the side, my mouth slack and everything about my body unfamiliar. I was so still, and so pale even through the pink tint.

I looked just like Sleeping Beauty.

Christophe sat next to the bed. Dibs checked the needle in his arm, and a thin ribbon of crimson slid across the small folding table, up to the hollow of my left arm. Dibs glanced up, worried, and Bruce took two steps into the room. He looked horrified.

The body on the gurney twitched. The pins and needles stabbed through me, rising up my arms and legs. It hurt, and the pink tone deepened. Other colors began to steal in.

On the other side. Graves leaned against a machine measuring a slow, erratic pulse. He had my other hand, and he leaned down, whispering into my ear. I couldn't hear it, but it looked important. I strained to hear, but the other djamphir crowding into the room started murmuring. Hiro was there in his usual high-collared silk shirt, his arms folded, leaning against the wall near the door while his dark gaze focused on Christophe.

"He's determined to kill himself to save her," he said quietly. "Let him, Bruce. He's earned it."

A trio of dark-haired djamphir in white medical coats hovered uncertainly. Ash crouched in the corner, staring straight at the unspace my not-body occupied, his gaze disturbingly direct. He rocked back and forth, his hands flat on the floor, and someone had at least managed to get the grass out of his hair.

"We can't afford to lose either of them." Bruce ran his hands back through his dark hair. It stood up wildly, and that was wrong. He was always so calm. "The Maharaj will only negotiate with her. And it's that Divakarun brat, the one Christophe cultivated."

"Negotiate what?" Hiro sounded interested, but he was watching Christophe.

"They think she might be one of theirs. Or related, or something. I can't even begin to guess." Bruce took another step. "Good God, what a mess."

Christophe slumped in the chair. The bruises were just shadows, but he hadn't cleaned up and a mask of filth still clung to him. Even through the rosy haze I could see his color graying out, and that wasn't good.

He swayed, and Dibs steadied him. The blond wulfen glanced at the machines, hooping and beeping along. "Pulse still erratic. Her respiration's down too. Graves, is she responding? At all?"

The excruciating tingle jolted all the way up my arms, suddenly. The body on the bed twitched again. My head tipped back, almost colliding with Graves's. He jerked back, but his lips kept moving. His bruises were fading too, and his eyes flashed green for a moment. But there were heavy lines scored on his face. He looked older now—eighteen instead of maybe-sixteen-honest, except for the lines slicing down from the outside of his nostrils, bracketing his mouth. That looked a lot older, shocking when compared to the rest of his face.

He leaned in again, and with his free hand, he reached up, smoothing the hair away from my face. I tried to feel his fingers, couldn't.

Dru?

The directionless voice went all through me. It wasn't Gran, or Dad, for once. If I'd been in my body I would've jumped. As it was I jerked again, and the machines started beeping again.

"Pulse is up." Dibs leaned forward, hovering over Christophe. "Just a little more."

"More," Christophe slurred, a long sigh of a word. "More. Every-thing."

Dru. My darling, my brave little girl. *The voice came again, wrap-ping around me with the comfort of a silken blanket.* Now is not your time.

I was suddenly aware of my lips. The body on the bed sighed. Every djamphir *in the room went still.*

"Mommy?" *A child's voice, as if I was five years old and lost in a dream, and a sudden hot flush of embarrassment went through me. The machines went crazy, and Dibs let out a nervous sigh.*

Christophe half-fell sideways. Dibs caught him.

"No more!" *Bruce said, sharply.* "It's killing him!"

"Leave it." *Hiro had Bruce's arm, and the tension between them bloomed a hurtful crimson.* "Can't you see it's what he wants?"

Dru. *My mother's voice again, not sharp, but commanding.* Now isn't your time. Go back.

I struggled. I didn't want to go back into that body on the bed. Here I was free. I could go toward that voice, and something inside me—maybe it was the touch, *but I don't think so—told me that if I did, clear rational light would break over me and this room would fade, and there would be something like flying. That light would enfold me, and they would be there. All of them. All the people I missed, all the people who hadn't come back for me.*

I hesitated for an endless moment. Christophe slumped further, and the rosiness of the scene faded. Now it looked like one of those hand-tinted old-timey photographs, faint blushes of color where the light hit, except for the scarlet ribbon between his arm and mine, loop-ing in complicated swirls. That ribbon glowed with its own light, and Dibs glanced worriedly at my body on the bed, a line between his blond eyebrows.

"I'm taking him off," Dibs announced. "He can't take much more of this."

"Don't." Hiro just said it, flatly, the way he would tell someone not to step in a pile of something foul.

"Hiro—" Bruce objected, surging forward.

The Japanese djamphir pulled him back. "Let him choose the manner of his death, Stirling. It is the least we owe him. He's lucky."

"Lucky?" Dibs actually rounded on them, his eyes sparking orange. "I'm taking him off—"

Christophe's lips peeled back; his gums were bloodless, his fangs shrinking. He was losing his solidity, his outlines fuzzing. Graves's fingers tensed in my hair as the machines went wild, beeping frantically.

And now I could hear what he was saying to that body on the bed. My body.

"Please. Don't go." He kept repeating it, over and over again. "Please, Dru. Please. Don't go. Please."

And I knew that tone, the pleading, the fear that was sitting like a spiked ball in his chest. He'd been left behind too, maybe more than I had.

If I left now, who would pick him up?

My good girl, my mother's voice whispered. Live. Go back, and live.

I smelled her, then. Warm perfume and spice, her hair falling in my face as she picked me up. I was a little girl, nestled in her strong arms, and she was everything good and bright and clean. Every little girl thinks her mother is the most beautiful woman in the world, but mine was.

She really was.

I love you, baby. It faded, that light and the sense of her presence, but I could still feel her arms around me. I love you so much. I am always with you.

The room spun around me, like soapy water sliding down a drain. Whirling, the earth's rotation twisting everything, my unbody compressing as darkness ate the edges of the vision. Static roared in my ears, and I tilted, slid, spun, time stretching as Christophe's eyes opened halfway and he stared as if he could see me too. His arm lay on the small table, the bright red ribbon unfurling from it, but his other hand reached out, toward me. Fingers outstretched, pleading.

Everything accelerated, the machines screaming and Bruce tearing his arm free of Hiro's grasp, Dibs shouting as Christophe slid out of the folding chair and Graves making a sound that cut right through me. It wasn't a cry or a moan or a scream, it was just the faint terrible snap of a heart breaking, snap—

—ped back into my body, flesh closing around me like heavy water dragging a tired swimmer down. I sat straight up, dried blood and dirt a crackglaze on my skin, and screamed. The three white-jacketed *djamphir* descended on me, Graves grabbing my shoulders and holding me down as I thrashed, saying my name over and over again. Ash let out a loud, exuberant yell, and Bruce actually yelled too, more out of surprise than anything else.

CHAPTER THIRTY-SEVEN

A familiar white room, sunshine pouring through the skylights and my mother's books on their familiar stripped-pine bookshelves, the bed white as an angel's wings, the vanity's mirror glowing and the Schola Prima utterly silent in its daytime sleep. I pushed myself up on my elbows, grimacing, but at least the worst of the dirt and dried blood was gone.

I felt warm all over. Hungry, but surprisingly good. And I was, true to form, almost completely unclothed. At least whoever had put me to bed had left me my panties.

I clutched the clean white sheet to my chest. The pounding of my pulse calmed down a little while I breathed, and the shaking came in waves. It was the trembles I used to get after a really bad time with Dad, like when I had to take him to the emergency room to get the big chunk taken out of his calf treated. After all the lies had been told and the doctors had whisked him away, I'd sat in a hard plastic ER chair and shook like this.

It meant everything was over.

After a little while, I got up. My clothes were still in the dresser and the closet; I grabbed a handful and headed for the white-tiled bathroom. My duffel lay inside the door, and my *malaika* were hung on their usual peg next to the vanity.

It was like I'd never left.

The bathroom was just the same—scrubbed clean, full of light, the towels smelling of bleach and fabric softener. I stood under the stinging spray for a long time—that's one good thing about the Schola, the hot water never runs out. My hands looked different when I examined them. Longer, fingers tapered, my palms more cupped. My left palm was still red, faint flowerlike traceries where the blisters had been. It didn't hurt when I squeezed it shut, though.

When I swiped the condensation from the mirror, the face that greeted me was . . . odd. It was pretty much the same as it had been since I'd bloomed. There was the definite heart shape now, my nose proud instead of gawky, my cheekbones higher, everything pared down.

But it was different, because I could see my mother in it. I could see Dad's quirk of disbelief in my eyebrow, and Gran's take-no-guff look when my chin set and my eyes flashed. My hair dripped as I studied myself, seeing them. I touched one cheek, running my fingers over it like I could reach through and touch one of them, or maybe all of them, if I just pushed hard enough.

Someone coughed out in the bedroom. I scrambled to get dressed, and as soon as I was decent I whipped the door open and piled out, scrubbing at my hair with a fresh towel.

Nat set the silver-domed tray down on the small table by the door. Her catlike blue eyes gleamed, every sleek hair in place and her outfit, as usual, perfect. The cream linen jacket hid the gun in its shoulder holster, but it peeped out as she half-turned, looking over her shoulder at me, and her slacks looked freshly ironed. "You're probably all turned around," she greeted me. "I figured you'd be awake soon, it's been twenty—*oof!*"

I threw my arms around her, the towel hitting the floor with a plop. After a moment she hugged me back, so hard my bones creaked. I breathed her in, her strange musky perfume, and my eyes prickled.

I did *not* cry, though. I was done cried out.

"I'm sorry," I blurted into her shoulder. "I was a dick to you, a total *dick.* I'm sorry. I promised if I came back I'd apologize. I'm so sorry, Nat. I—"

"Oh, Jesus, don't be retarded." But she was still hugging me, fiercely. "Because if you do, I'm going to cry, then you'll cry, and we're *all*—"

"*All* gonna cry," I chorused with her, and burst into screamy laughter. She did too, and my heart blew up two sizes just like a balloon. She patted my back, and when we let go of each other she was actually sniffling.

"You had me worried there for a bit, kid." She dabbed delicately under her eyes with her fingertips. "Don't make my mascara run, dammit."

"Sorry." I tried to sound chastened. "Everyone. How is everyone? Christophe, Graves, Shanks, Dibs—*everyone?*"

"Fine. Well, all right. Let's see, Dibs is snarling like he's an alpha, Bobby's highly amused and keeps saying he should've known you'd decapitate the king of the vampires, Benjamin and the crew are beside themselves and polishing their weapons. The Council wants to see you, and your friend Augustine says to tell you he's going to make you some toast, for some reason."

I half-choked on a laugh. It felt good to laugh, but painful, like popping a really righteous zit. "Graves?"

Her face changed a little. The laughter died in my chest.

"He's . . . packing."

"Packing?"

"He's . . . well." She shrugged, spread her hands. "He's going on retreat. That's what we call it."

It was just like being punched in the stomach. And I should know. "*What?*"

Nat's mouth turned down at the corners, uncomfortably. She actually *fidgeted*, shifting her weight. "It's something wulfen do. When they're, um, hurt bad, but not on the outside. Inside. Shanks has kin upstate; they sent word he was welcome to come. He's . . . Dibs won't say what happened. But, well, *he* had him." She took a deep breath, squared her shoulders. "Sergej." The name came out in a long sibilant rush.

And for once, it didn't drive glass shards through my head. "He's dead," I said, numbly. "Or at least, I hope so. Christophe . . ."

"Yeah, Reynard explained. Said Graves put everything on the line, broke free of Sergej's hold long enough to give you . . . what you needed." A flush crept up her cheeks. "And that you took *him* on and cut his head off. Congratulations. But Graves is still . . . hurt. It's different for wulfen, Dru. Sometimes you can get hurt inside, and you need to go away and sort it out."

Every inch of good feeling I'd managed to scrape together ran out like water from a busted glass. "He's leaving?"

Was it possible for her to look any *more* uncomfortable? She actually wouldn't meet my eyes, looking down like the floor was suddenly the most interesting thing in the world.

"Nat." I crossed my arms over my stomach. "Please."

"He might already be gone." She still wouldn't look at me. "He didn't want you to see him, thought it would be easier—"

Oh, no. No. Shit all over *that.* I was past her, suddenly, grabbing for the doorknob. It wasn't locked, so I yanked the door open and ran out into the hall. The *touch* lit up inside my head, and I swear I could taste his blood again, sliding down my throat. Moonlight and that strawberry incense, and something that wasn't an identifiable taste. It was just *him*, my Goth Boy, and I pounded down the corridor, hearing shouts behind me. Nat, and of course Benjamin and the others.

It didn't matter.

I just *ran*.

* * *

Have you ever had that dream where you're running, but you can't move fast enough? Where the entire world is wet concrete, glorping around you, while you're searching for something and knowing you won't ever find it? Heart pounding, stitch grabbing your ribs with clawed fingers, the breath tearing in and out of your lungs while everything around you is suddenly, eerily slow?

But I had the *touch*, and I burst out the front door of the Schola just as the black SUVs were rousing themselves. Two of them, just starting to pull away.

"No!" I yelled, skidding to a stop. "NO!"

The brake lights popped on. They sat there and idled for a few seconds. My hands were fists at my sides, and my cheeks were wet. My hair was probably an unholy mess, and my feet throbbed. Of course—I was only in socks. Goddammit.

"No." I stared at the cars. The *touch* settled, feathers brushing up and down my entire body. "No. Please, no."

The second SUV's engine cut off. The back passenger door opened, and he slid out slowly.

Like an old man.

Black jeans, black T-shirt, boots, no long black coat now. Instead it was a hip-length leather jacket, probably borrowed from Shanks.

My sock feet crunched in gravel. I was off the steps in a heartbeat, and he met me halfway. I grabbed him like he was a lifering, and I realized the yelling was me.

"No, goddammit, you can't *leave*, not just like that, you just *can't*! You *can't* just leave me!"

"Calm *down*," he began, but I ran right over the top of him.

"Calm down? I don't *think* so! What the hell are you thinking? What the *fucking* hell is *wrong* with you? You can't just leave me here and ride off into the sunset, for fuck's sake! What do you think you're—"

"Dru." He tried to untangle himself, but I held on grimly. "Come on. Take a breath. Let me explain."

"I wish you *would*!" I yelled. I grabbed the front of his jacket and actually *shook* him. His hair swung, I shook him so hard. "I wish you goddamn well *would* explain, for once!"

"Dru." Sharp, now. "Shut up."

I did. I held onto his jacket and planted my feet. Stared at the notch of the top of his sternum, where the collarbones met it. Coppery skin on his throat, vulnerable because he'd just shaved. There were two little red marks on his throat, but I didn't want to look at them. They were right over his pulse, and I'd put them there. So I just stared at that notch instead.

Silence. It was a beautiful summer morning, and my heart was on fire and cracking at the same time.

"Is it because I suck blood?" I said, finally. In a very small voice. "Because that's disgusting. I know."

His fingers curled around my shoulders. It was his turn to shake me, twice, my head bobbling a little bit. "No. Dru, dammit, look at me. Look."

I looked up.

His eyes were still green. But there were huge dark circles under them, and his jaw was set. He looked like he was in pain, and his cheeks were hollowed out.

He looked awful.

But the corner of his mouth tilted up slightly, and there was a shadow of the Graves I knew. He let go of me long enough to dig in his coat pocket, and when he pulled out a battered pack of Pall Malls I wasn't surprised.

I let go of him. He lit up, inhaled deeply, and offered me the smoke. I shook my head, my nose wrinkling, and the small smile got a bit larger.

Just a bit.

When I was just about to grab him and start screaming with frustration again, he lowered the cigarette. Twin dragons of smoke curled out of his nostrils. "It's not you." His shoulders hunched. "Cliché. Sorry. I wanted it to be easier on you. Because I . . . there's some things you can't fix, Dru. You're great at fixing things. If anyone could do it, you could. But you can't do this one." A long pause, and he swallowed, hard, his Adam's apple bouncing. "You can't fix me. I'm broke."

"You're not making any sense." The rock in my throat made it hard to talk.

"Sergej." His face twisted for a moment. "He was *inside my head*, Dru. It wasn't the vampires that burned your grandmother's house. It was me."

I just stared at him, my mouth ajar.

"Christophe caught me. I couldn't . . . I couldn't fight *him* off. Not all the way."

"But I . . ." *I fixed that! I cleaned it away!*

I wanted to yell it. But deep down, I knew better.

You can scrub and scrub, but sometimes something doesn't just go away. It . . . it stains you. Like finding your father's ambulatory corpse on your back step, and shooting him over and over because he means to kill you.

He was a zombie, right? He would have killed me.

But he was my *dad*, and I'd done that. I'd *done* it, and something inside me was yanked sideways. There wasn't any going back, and there wasn't a way to feel clean again.

Maybe it was the *touch* telling me this. Frustration swamped me, hot and harsh. "It's *my* fault." My hands twitched. I wanted to grab him again, but I restrained myself. "If I hadn't—"

"*Don't.*" A subvocal thunder slid out of him, a wulfen's warning growl. I froze. "Don't you *dare*. Sometimes shit just *happens*, Dru. It's not your fault. It never was." He tossed the cigarette, a flick of his fingers sending it in a perfect arc. The sunshine beat down on both of us, the dead dyed-black mass of his hair swallowing it.

When he took my shoulders again, it was gentle. He drew me forward and slid his arms around me, and I hugged him. He was too skinny, feverish–hot with a *loup-garou*'s heightened metabolism. A thin sick tremor ran through him, like a high-voltage wire right before it snaps.

"Listen," he said into my hair. "I'm only gonna say this once, so listen good."

I nodded, breathing him in, my face in his chest. Squeezed my eyes shut.

His breath was a warm spot in my wet hair. The breeze swirled around us, full of the green growing of summer and cut grass. "I'm coming back. But I got to fix myself. The wulfen, they'll help. But here's the thing, Dru. I'm not worth you." He took a deep breath, and the way his arms tightened made the protest die in my throat.

"But I'm *gonna* be. I told you before, but you didn't understand. Hell, you might not understand now. But you've got to trust me on this one." His arms tightened. "You have got to let me go. Can you do that?"

It's not fair! I wanted to stamp and scream and hit something. Instead, I swallowed, hard. Had to try twice before the words would come. "Do you promise? To come back?"

"I promise." He sounded sure, at least.

"Do you *swear*?" So I was five years old again. So what?

"I swear. I . . ." He tensed, and I felt him swallow convulsively, too. "I've got to be worth you, Dru. I've got to get strong, so nobody can use me like that again."

"Please." There was nothing else I could say. "Graves. *Please* . . ."

But when he stepped back, I let him go. It tore inside me, way down deep where all the worst hurts settle. He took another step back, the gravel crunching, and when I finally looked back up at him, it was a shock to see.

The tears trickled down his cheeks. His eyes were red-rimmed, but his jaw was set. He opened his mouth, shut it. Opened it again, and what came out shocked me even more.

"I love you. Okay? I promise." Another step back, his green gaze holding mine. "Hey." His throat worked, like he was catching the words halfway and pulling them back. "Dru. What's that short for, anyway?"

I actually *felt* my heart break. It cracked right in half, and a sobbing little laugh that sounded like a cry came out. Got caught at the back of my palate, right where the bloodhunger lived. I forced it down.

"I'll tell you when you come back," I managed. It was all I could say.

I guess it must have been the right thing. Because he turned on one heel and headed back for the open passenger door, head up, stepping like he was walking on quicksand or something that might throw him at any moment.

He grabbed the door. But just before he got in, he looked back over his shoulder, and that soundless flash of communication passed between us.

Once, in Dad's truck in a snowstorm, I'd clung to him. Because we were both wrecked, and when you're wrecked, the only thing you can do is hold onto whatever you can.

Hold on *hard*.

We were still shipwrecked, Graves and me. But that look told me everything. He was still holding on. As hard as he could.

It just wasn't enough.

He ducked down, the door slammed, and the brake lights flashed. There was a pause, but then the SUVs rolled away, bumping up onto the paved drive. Two cars meant guards. He'd probably get wherever he needed to safely.

I stood there and watched as they receded down the Schola's long driveway. The trees arched over, leafdapple shade like water pouring over the cars, and my fingers itched. For the first time in a long time I wanted to draw, and I knew *exactly* what I'd draw. I'd try to capture the way the leaves held the sunlight, the red of the brake lights crimson dots, like fangmarks.

What I couldn't draw was the way my heart finished cracking and fell, and the feeling that took its place in my chest. A kind of emptiness, like a church in the middle of the week, full of murmuring space.

Sometimes you do grow up in an instant. I think that was the first moment I started thinking like an adult.

And I hated it.

CHAPTER THIRTY-EIGHT

Hiro laid a pair of my sneakers on the table right in front of me, his jaw set and his dark gaze level. His face might have been carved from caramel wood, and he winced a little if he moved too quickly.

I didn't want to think about it.

"I don't get it." I sat, numb all over, in the high-backed wooden chair, my arms crossed defensively. "Why do I have to do this?"

"They're envoys," Bruce said again, patiently, his dark eyes worried. He magnanimously refused to note that my face was tear-streaked and I was visibly shaking. "The Maharaj wish to see you—"

"So they can have another crack at hexing me to death? Or poisoning me? I don't *think* so." I pulled more tightly into myself, leaning forward a little. The long mirror-shiny table in the Council room was just the same; the silver samovar glinting against the wall where food was usually arranged looked like an old friend. "Can't *you* just talk to them? Like, you're the one who's really in charge. I'm just a figurehead." *And it's probably a lot safer for everyone that way too. You know what the hell you're doing. Mostly.*

Bruce spread his hands. It was the first time I'd ever seen him in a white button-down that was less than perfectly pressed. His dark hair was messy, and his proud Middle Eastern face was about as close to haggard as a model-attractive *djamphir* could get. "They think you may be . . . one of theirs. Or related, somehow."

"Great." If I hugged myself any harder I was going to crack in half. "I don't give a good goddamn what they—"

"Milady." Hiro, softly and respectfully. But the single word cut through what I'd planned on saying. "Please. Listen."

I wiped at my cheeks with the flat of my right hand. The rock in my throat didn't get any smaller, no matter how many times I tried to force it down. "Fine." I sounded ungracious, to say the least.

"Thank you." He stood, slim and straight, his gray silk high-collared shirt unwrinkled and his eyes, as well, shadowed with exhaustion. It was the first time I'd seen that, either on him *or* on Bruce, and I suddenly wondered where the rest of the Council was. "Milady, you are able to do . . . certain things *svetocha* are not traditionally able to do. We were unsure where these talents came from; the *djinni*-children may believe you have some strain of their blood from your . . . human . . . side." He took a deep breath, half-flinching again like his ribs pained him. "The Maharaj have severe prohibitions against harming a female who can use their particular sorceries. The fact that you were attacked, that you *were* harmed, creates a very large problem for them. A . . . debt, if you will. And that debt is a way we may pressure them into abandoning their former neutrality against, as well as their recent alliance with, the *nosferat*. This is an opportunity. One that is exceedingly rare, one we must press, and one we must ask you to accede to."

I killed Sergej. Isn't that enough? I shook my head. A single curl fell in my face, bounced. "I don't want to talk to them." *Leave me alone. Jesus.*

"You are the only one they will speak to, Milady. Especially since Reynard is . . ." A single shrug. Hiro was economical with his body language. Just one of those things that told you he was older, as *djamphir* go.

Way older.

"Christophe?" A sick thump in the pit of my stomach. I hadn't even *asked* about him. "What's wrong with Christophe?"

"Nothing." Bruce almost twitched. "He's simply resting. But he is unavailable."

I fixed him with a glare. "What's *wrong* with him? Did it . . . did I hurt him? The blood, did it—"

"He's *resting*. He's survived worse." Bruce sighed. It wasn't a Dylan-worthy sigh, but it was close. Dylan had been a world-champion patient-suffering sigh-er. "Milady. Dru. *Please.* A formal alliance with the Maharaj—not just a truce—will save lives. *Djamphir* lives, wulfen lives, and that means human lives as well. I know your *loup-garou* has left—"

It was like a pinch on a fresh bruise. "Don't talk about him." I gingerly uncurled my arms. Reached for my sneakers, suddenly glad it was Hiro who had gone up and gotten them. I didn't feel like I could face Nat right now. "How come the Maharaj think I'm . . ." I let the question trail off. *Two great Houses,* Sergej hissed in my memory, and I shuddered.

Great. *Djamphir* were part sucker, and now they were thinking I was part something else. Where was the human part of me supposed to fit, I wondered?

"Because you killed one of your attackers with his own sorcery."

Bruce grasped the back of a chair—the one just to my left, the one Christophe sometimes sat in at Council meetings. When he wasn't up pacing the room like a caged animal. "And later, something about a smokedog, a *kuttee*, sent to track you. I do not know the whole, Dru. They will not speak unless it is to you. You are our hope."

I never asked for this. It was too late, though. This was what I had.

Everything inside me shifted sideways another little bit and settled unexpectedly. I wasn't used to the whirling sensation fetching up against something, but it did. It held fast, like catching your jeans on a stubborn nail.

I killed Sergej. Yeah, Christophe helped . . . but I was the one that did it.

But it wasn't just that. I'd bled to buy Dibs and Christophe some more time. I'd done the right thing. It was what Dad might've called "findin' out where ya iron's at" and Gran would have just nodded with the particular line to her mouth that meant she was pleased.

I had done that. The nail I fetched up against was knowing, without a doubt, that I'd done them proud.

The Council room was silent and breathless, no windows, just the door to the antechamber with its couches and fireplace. I always thought *djamphir* would want some light and air, until I figured out that it was too easy to take a shot or send a sucker through some plate glass.

My fingers fumbled with the laces. I could almost feel Hiro staring at me. My hair fell down, curtaining my face. I couldn't hide forever, though, and when I had my shoes tied I looked up. "Sergej." The name didn't burn now. It was just a word. "He thought that, too. That I was maybe one of them, I think."

They exchanged a Significant Look. Bruce's shoulders hunched a little. "Hiro and I will be there." He sounded, of all things, defensive. "There is nothing to fear. You won't see Augustine, but he will be there too. There will be others, in Shadow. You're safe now."

"Until there is another to take Sergej's place," Hiro murmured.

I froze, staring at him. Well, it had to be too good to be true, didn't it? That was the way adulthood rolled. I was beginning to get the idea.

"Yes," he continued, pitiless. "There are always more, Milady. We have barely managed to hold them back. Now, with the *nosferat* confused and the Maharaj perhaps willing to come to an accord . . . we could do much more. You are young, and it is not right to ask, but we are asking." He put his hands together, as if he was about to make one of those funny little bows of his. "We would even beg you, *sveto-cha*. Help us."

My head dropped forward. I stared at my hands. My fingernails were bitten down, just like my mother's. I smelled cinnamon, a thread of warm perfume drifting up from my skin, and I wondered if they smelled it too. The *touch* brushed inside my head, soft feathers. "Where's the rest of the Council? Alton and Ezra?"

Bruce let out a short, pained breath. "Alton was in Houston. Ezra was coordinating in Atlanta. Neither of them have reported in."

"That's not good." My fingers tightened. My hands turned into fists, knotting up in my lap, an ache sliding up my bones and settling in my shoulders.

"There's still hope. Dru—" Bruce, pleading, and all of a sudden I couldn't stand it anymore.

"I'll do it. I'll talk to them." I didn't recognize my own voice, that new, flat, grown-up tone. "If it's that important, I'll do it."

There really wasn't any choice. If—*when* Graves came back, I was going to have something to show for all this. And all of them—

the dead who had struck through me to end Sergej—pretty much demanded that I step up, and keep stepping up, for as long as I could.

For as long as I had to.

So what if my heart was cracking? I looked up, scrubbing at my cheeks again, and blinked. Took a deep breath, then put my palms flat on the table and pushed myself upright. Rolled my shoulders back and settled them, and I didn't have to even look at Bruce to see the relief written on his face. Hiro dipped forward—one of those little bows of his, and it was a wonder how he could look so damn *respectful* while he was doing it. Respectful, but completely aware of his own kickassery at the same time.

I couldn't help myself. Every time he did that, I bowed back. When in Rome, right? And he smiled each time, too, a patient grave smile. I suddenly realized why it was familiar—because Gran had smiled that way sometimes too, when I'd done something that must have reminded her of Dad.

And there was another new thing: it didn't hurt to think of them. Well, at least not as much. The ache was still there, but it just . . . it was different. Less sharp. I'd done what I set out to do, right?

Some part of me must've thought that would fix everything. Things just don't get fixed, though. Things get broken, and sometimes they stay that way.

You just have to glue them together and hope it holds.

"Fine," I said again. "All right. Let's get it over with."

CHAPTER THIRTY-NINE

After all that, the Maharaj were pretty much anticlimactic. It was in the huge, glass-roofed room I'd been in once before, when Christophe was on Trial and Anna had emptied an assault rifle at me. This time I sat in the high-backed, red-hung chair on the dais, and the shadows around the edges of the room were full of the staticky sense of *something watching* that told me there were not just one or two *djamphir* doing the little "don't look here" trick they're so fond of.

The sleek seal-headed Maharaj boy who had poisoned me actually got down on his knees; the other two—dark-eyed, proud-nosed, both with the same gold earring and the same scent of spice and dry burning sand—swept me bows that were right off an old pirate movie.

Leander—and yes, I remembered his name; he'd *poisoned* me, you don't forget that—begged my forgiveness in between a long string of foreign words. He even called me "Rajkumari Faulk," and I twitched like I'd been stuck with a pin.

Because "Faulk" was Gran's maiden name.

Bruce had warned me, so I let Leander get all the way to the end before accepting with a nod that was supposed to be queenly but was probably just scared stiff instead. At that point Hiro moved forward, and they eyed him the way cobras might eye a mongoose. There was some diplomatic blather, a schedule set up for further talks, and the "provisional agreement" was that the *djinni*-children and the Order were allies against the *nosferat* and other things.

I just had to sit there, gripping the chair arms, braced for anything that might occur. Anything other than what actually happened.

The Maharaj bowed twice more at me, backed away about ten feet, and bowed again. Then a *djamphir* teacher I recognized materialized out of thin air with the familiar sound of nasty chattering laughter and escorted them out of the room.

I managed to cover up the violent start that gave me. But only just.

And then it was done. Piece of cake.

I was at Christophe's bedside when he woke up that evening, as dusk filled the windows and the Schola began to wake up as well. Benjamin, his dark hair still emo-swooped across his forehead, was right outside the door, standing guard. It was like I'd never left.

Except everything was different.

"Relax," I said as soon as Christophe's eyes opened, pale cold starving blue. "Everything's copacetic. The Council debriefed me and there's another diplomatic thingie scheduled for tomorrow."

He blinked, staring up at me. It was a private infirmary room, windowless and bare except for the bed. Wulfen and *djamphir* both heal pretty quickly. If you're hurt enough to need the infirmary, it's *really* bad. But also, Christophe didn't have a room of his own. He moved around a lot, kept things hidden.

I could see why.

His eyes were very blue. He blinked, once, and it was like a light switch flicking. I could see the thoughts sliding together inside his skull. "The Maharaj."

I nodded. Leaned the chair I'd snagged out in the infirmary proper back on two of its legs, balancing. "We had the first meet this afternoon. Something about me being able to throw hexes; I tangled with a couple of them in Dallas. It's a big deal if they kill a girl who can throw a hex, I guess. They think Gran's family might've been a bastard branch, or something." I swallowed, hard. "Anyway, Bruce and Hiro will do all the talking tomorrow. I just have to sit there and not get kidnapped or murdered. Should be fun."

The covers slid as he pushed himself up on his elbows. At least when he passed out, nobody undressed *him*. He was still dirty, but he looked tons better.

I leaned back in the chair. It squeaked a little. *Don't do that,* Gran would've said. *Fall right on your ass, Dru-girl. You mind me, now.*

"Are you well?" He finished sitting up, gingerly, testing his body's responses.

I shrugged. Who knew what would happen or who would try to kill me next if someone decided I was even more of a freak than I already was? Besides, Gran couldn't be Maharaj. She was a back-woods hexer, and she'd been human all the way.

But would you have known if she wasn't? And how can you do some of the things you can do? Leander sounded pretty sure, and he even knew Gran's maiden name.

I told that little internal nagging voice to shut up and go away, shrugged. "I'll deal." I gave it a beat, decided to add more. "Graves is gone."

Christophe blinked again. That was all the response I got.

Well, great. "He's got some things to work out." It sounded lame. "So do I. So . . ."

"Dru." He slid his feet out of the bed. Still barefoot, his jeans flayed at the knees and stiff with crusted stuff I didn't even want to think about. "You don't have to. You're tired, and—"

I shook my head. My braid bumped my back. I could probably fight another clutch of suckers with my hair done this tight. "I gotta do this while I got the courage, Chris. So just listen, okay?"

He went still, perched on the edge of the bed. He just watched me, his face closed. Shuttered.

Guarded, like he was afraid of what I might say.

I lost my nerve. "You probably want to get cleaned up or something, right?" *Or pee. Because all I want to do when I wake up after almost-dying is find a commode.*

He shook his head a little, a brief economical movement. "It can wait."

Well, dammit, there went that escape. The chair's front legs thudded down. I leaned forward, bracing my elbows on my knees.

"Okay," I began. "You're too old for me. You're scary. It's creepy that you were so all over my mom and now you're all over me. And you . . ." *You watched my father go down that hall,* I wanted to say. But all of a sudden, it didn't seem right. Dad had *shot* him, if the vision was a true-seein and not just a really vivid nightmare. Visions were like that, they twisted together dream and reality, and Gran always warned me not to trust what couldn't be verified.

But still.

I couldn't punk out now. So I licked my lips nervously and plunged ahead. "You were there when my father died. Weren't you."

It wasn't a question.

Christophe actually flinched. "If I could have saved him —"

"You probably would have." I nodded, and he shut up. "Because you owed it to my mom. Right?"

A single nod.

"I couldn't figure out if you wanted me so bad because you thought I could kill Sergej, or if it was me. Something really about me."

That got to him. He flinched again, and I held up a hand. Wonder of wonders, he stayed quiet. But his jaw was clenched so tight he was fixing to shatter his teeth.

My imagination just works too damn well.

I had to continue now. I couldn't just leave it like that. "But every time I've been really in trouble, you've been there. You probably tried to break me out of that Sooper-Sekrit Vampire Hideout all by your lonesome, didn't you? That's how *he* caught you."

Another nod. He watched me like I was a snake getting ready to bite, and I was suddenly so *tired*.

Grown-up shit is *hard*.

"You told Dibs to hook up the transfusion. You didn't care if it killed you. I needed blood, you were going to save me, it was that simple. Right?"

"*Tak*," he breathed, then shook himself. "Yes. That simple. Dru." Soft, like he was pleading.

"Christophe." All the air ran out of me, I had to gasp it back in. "I get that you're interested, okay? But I'm not . . . ready. For anything. With *anyone*. Okay? I don't even know what I'm going to do tomorrow when I wake up." *Besides be grateful if nobody tries to take my head off or shoot me or drain my blood, that is.* "I've got no damn clue at all. So, you can either be okay with that, or I can transfer to another Schola. I've talked to Bruce about it. He'll have kittens, and

Hiro will have penguins, and August will completely throw a fit, but I've made up my mind. It's up to you."

He absorbed this. Time ticked away, and the Schola woke up completely. A faint faraway murmur of voices as *djamphir* got ready—the younger ones for classes, the older students for patrol, the teachers and other older ones for citywide patrol, mission support, or class time.

It was comforting, hearing that murmur. Knowing what it was.

Kind of like I belonged. For once. Like I'd found a place to fit into, a key in a lock.

"Dru." He leaned forward a little, toward me. "Is there . . . a chance? Any chance?"

I thought it over. He deserved an answer.

So did I. I just had to find one I could live with.

"I don't know." I pushed the chair back and stood up. "When I said I wasn't ready, I meant it. Okay? Can you live with that?"

I almost said *can you trust me*, but that . . . it wouldn't have been right. It just wouldn't.

"Yes." No hesitation. "I can wait. Until you know, *kochana*. One way." A slight shrug, his shoulder lifting elegantly, even though he was filthy. "Or the other."

"Really?" *That's . . . um, well.* I hadn't expected that. I'd expected a no. Or some waffling. A little prevarication.

This time he smiled. It was the smile he kept just for me, a soft, private expression. "Really. I know the value of patience, *skowronec-zko moja*. It must be my age."

Must be. "Well." I rubbed my palms on my jeans. "Okay. I'll let you get cleaned up, then. I . . . yeah." Now I was floundering. I backed up a bit, bumping the chair, and he just sat there and looked at me, still smiling. I managed to turn around and head for the door.

Just before I got there, though, he spoke up again.

"Dru." Very soft. "Thank you."

Jesus. I just basically rejected you, right? "For what?"

"For . . . believing. In me."

You know what that will do to a guy? I shook Graves's voice away. "No problem," I said over my shoulder. Found the doorknob with a shaking hand. "No problem at all, Chris. First one's free."

EPILOGUE

I sat on the wide white satin window seat as the last flush of dusk faded from the sky. Nat moved around, tidying everything up with no trouble even though the room was dark. Moving with a wulfen's grace, glancing at me every now and again. Like she was worried.

I didn't blame her. I'd be worried too.

I pulled my knees up and put my arms around them, breathing in the night. Full summer, only it wasn't as close and humid up here as it was down South. I could smell the gardens, and the good scent of grass mowed on a hot day and recovering once soft darkness falls. I read somewhere once that plants only grow at night. I don't know. Seems like they'd need that time for sleeping, too.

Like the rest of the daylight world.

I was thinking. About Graves, and Christophe. About Gran and Dad and Mom, and about *gone* and forever, and about coming back. About promises and shipwrecks and holding on, and how it hurt.

About being human, and what "human" even *meant*.

"You okay?" Nat finally asked. "You wanna be alone, or . . . ?"

A while ago, I would've said *yes*, to save her some trouble. But now, I just told the truth. "No." I put my chin on my knees. "No, I really don't. Have a seat?"

She sank down opposite me. I guess she was searching for something to say. So I searched too. Found it, and plunged ahead before I could lose my nerve.

"So. Did Shanks ask you out yet?"

She laughed. Her eyes glittered blue for a moment. "What?"

My throat was full. "I mean, I've been away. I'm behind on gossip." *Treat me like a normal girl, please. If you can. This grown-up thing sucks.* "Did he?"

And God bless her, but I guess she understood. "Kind of. We got milk shakes. It's a start."

"Guess so." Another long, awkward silence. "Nat . . ."

"It's okay, Dru. Really." She scooched back a little and brought her legs up, crossing them tailor fashion. Settled in, nice and comfortable. "You've just got to decompress. Just take it easy tonight, sleep during the day, and tomorrow night you can go back to your regular round of tutors, sparring, and lunches."

I groaned and she laughed again. A nameless tension I hadn't even noticed eased, and my lungs could expand again. I stared out at the garden below my window. Footsteps passed by in the hall—a *djamphir*'s light tread.

A guard. Probably Benjamin, he kept muttering about not letting me out of his *sight*, dammit, in case I took it into my head to Do Something Else.

I swallowed, hard. "Sergej's dead." It didn't sound real when I said it out loud. "Right?"

"The *nosferat* are still out there. They're just confused and scattered." Nat's tone was sober. "There's other things, too. I wouldn't trust the Maharaj."

Word. "Me neither. They don't seem too warm and cuddly."

She found this funny. At least, she snorted. "But as long as you don't go running off again, things might possibly settle down. I could use some downtime. Haven't been shopping in *ages.*"

I hate shopping. But going out with Nat seemed like a good idea. "That sounds good. We can start at one end of Fifth Avenue and go all the way through. When do you want to do it?"

"Holy *shit!*"

I actually jumped. But when I looked at her, she was grinning broadly.

"Who are you," she continued, "and what have you done with Dru?" The flash of her white wulfen teeth in the faint dusky light should've scared me. It didn't. She was just Nat.

Just my friend.

Oh, nothing. Just went on a several-state odyssey and almost got killed. "Grew her up a little, I hope. Seriously, Nat, when do you want to go shopping? I might even try on some shoes."

"You're a pod person," she announced to the rest of my bedroom, as if there was an audience out there. "You've kidnapped my friend. Sucked her brain out! Not that she had much to begin with, but—"

"Bite me." The laughter didn't hurt, now. I didn't even feel weird saying it. *Bite me.*

Pretty funny, for a part-vampire.

"Ha. You *wish.* Lesbo vamp girl."

"Lesbo?"

"You love me."

"We'd never work, Nat. You're too high maintenance."

We both cracked up, and right then, the darkness was kind.

She was right. Tomorrow was early enough to start worrying about everything else. So I let go of my knees, sat cross-legged like her, and together, Nat and I watched the night roll in.

finis

THE **STRANGE ANGELS** SERIES
BY LILI ST. CROW

STRANGE ANGELS
BETRAYALS
JEALOUSY
DEFIANCE
RECKONING